ALONG TORTUROUS PATHS

**The Amelia Temple Series
Book Three**

by

Vivian Moira Valentine

BLUE FORTUNE ENTERPRISES LLC

Wildflower Press, an imprint of Blue Fortune Enterprises LLC

TABLE OF CONTENTS

To all the artists whose work inspired me,
and to those whom I hopefully inspire one day

"Out-out are all the lights-out all!
        And, over each quivering form,
The curtain, a funeral pall,
        Comes down with the rush of a storm,
While the angels, all pallid and wan,
        Uprising, unveiling, affirm
That the play is the tragedy, 'Man,'
        And its hero, the Conqueror Worm."

                        - Edgar Allen Poe, "The Conqueror Worm"

01

Freedom is a complicated word. People—English-speaking people, that is—use it to mean so many different things. Sometimes they mean that they have the ability to do something, or more specifically, that no one can stop them from doing it. Sometimes they mean instead that no one can *force* them to do something. Other times, it means that they *can* force others to do or not do things as they please. That they are free to exert their will over others. Or should be.

Words are tricky and I don't like them. Thoughts are truth, emotions are truth. Words are just lies all dolled up for Sunday, and most people are bad at lying to me.

At this point in the very busy year of 1954, I had the freedom to sit in a comfortable chair in a well-stocked private library. Unlike most of the people roaming the building's halls, no one was free to tell me where I had to be or when. While the seven people with whom I shared a dormitory had their hours rigorously scheduled, my day was open-ended. There were events I was politely requested to attend. Sometimes I did. Other times I spent my day in the library, morning and night. Well into the night, if I chose. No curfew for me, for the first time in my life. I often took advantage of that, for among its many treasures, this library had a complete collection of my favorite science-fiction magazine, *Imaginary Tales*.

On the other hand, between the hours of five and eight p.m. on select weekends, my roommates were free to leave the mansion's grounds. The world outside the walls was denied to me again, both by the application of certain rules and the ingenious use of a half-magical, half-mathematical language. My current hosts hadn't gone through all that trouble just for me, of course. It was more like the happy side-effect of certain admittedly sensible security measures. The Nova Anima Institute was pioneering novel fields of research, after all. Steps had to be taken to keep accidents contained.

You see how tricky words can be?

I had to admit that as far as dungeons went, the Institute was a step above my previous captor. Both the Institute and the Bureau of Extranormal Investigations had withheld information from me, in addition to outright lying to me. Both felt free to place seemingly arbitrary restrictions on my movements. Both openly treated me as a resource to be exploited. The Institute, however, at least made a show of working with me for mutual benefit, and I didn't have to cook for myself.

Twenty-nine days had passed since I woke up in my dorm room in the Institute's compound. Our investigation into a suspicious hospital had, as my closest friends might have said, gone completely sideways. My friends escaped without significant harm, at least so far as I was aware. So had Dorothy Weathersby, my girlfriend's former associate who'd turned out to be less helpful than we'd hoped.

(My girlfriend, Lucille Sweeney, would likely have described the entire fiasco in more colorful terms. I loved her, but her fondness for vulgarity could be a little trying.)

I hadn't been so lucky. I'd facilitated their escape, but that left me vulnerable to capture by the Institute, the organization sponsoring the hospital's experiments and another branch of the conspiracy we'd been following. The Institute also knew far more about me than I did, apparently. The Director had used that as leverage to secure my cooperation. So far. It wasn't a very fulfilling relationship, but the promise of answers kept me cooperative.

They were going to turn on me the moment it was convenient. I was going to tear the place apart the exact second I ran out of patience. In the meantime, I smiled politely at the Director and his associates, and they spoke of my abilities with the appropriate awe.

Speakers hidden in the corners of the room played a series of soft tones, announcing the hour of one p.m. Throughout the mansion, Institute personnel bustled to their next assigned station. All of them wore mono-color jumpsuits in varying shades of blue. Those in powder blue, the largest and least senior group, reported to various work details. Those in darker shades had all manner of options. Some reported to laboratories to participate or assist in experiments. Others went to classrooms to study the Institute's unique education programs. For three residents of my dormitory, it was a free study period. They headed for the library together. Other than noting their location, I paid little attention to their progress through the building. That is, until the three of them converged around my otherwise empty table.

"Hey, Amelia! Okay if we sit here?"

I hesitated for three seconds, my eyes focused on my magazine. Then I realized I should turn my head in the direction of the person speaking; most people don't have a 360-degree field of vision. The three of them stood on the other side of the round table. Lorraine Matthews, Irene Phillips, and Norman Rogers. Their matching mono-color jumpsuits were baby blue, with black shoulders connected to a V-shape running down the torso. I wore a similar outfit, although mine was a deep purple. As official members of the Institute, the three wore brass pins over the left breast—a stylized Vitruvian Man superimposed over a sunburst, surmounting an intertwined "N" and "A". As a semi-willing guest, I had no such pin. Instead, a badge had been sewn where the pin would have gone, a white circle with a bright red "V" in the middle. Their suits labeled them as "actives": Level 2 members of the Institute, actively involved in its research. Mine marked me as an outsider but somewhat affiliated with the Institute. Officially, I was a "consultant", a hastily invented role with no real meaning or responsibility. I liked that.

Lorraine was short and stout, full of energy and laughter, with a mop of dirty blonde curls. Irene was tall and slender, with long, straight brown hair; a quiet but fierce young woman whose mouth easily curved into a sly smile. Norman was rail-thin and would have been taller than Irene if he ever stood up straight. His mop of red hair, scruffy chin, and habitual slouch were a direct affront to the standards of the day and of the Institute, yet he slid by without more than the occasional easily ignored reprimand.

All three were in their early twenties, like most of the Institute's personnel. They claimed to want young, impressionable minds not burdened by the assumptions and prejudices of the day. I had no doubt they would have recruited even younger if they could have gotten away with it.

Lorraine and Irene were the best of friends, utterly inseparable. They weren't very different from Luci and myself, and at first, I'd mistaken them for a couple. That had almost led to a very uncomfortable conversation. Fortunately, Lorraine hadn't understood what I'd meant at all, while Irene quietly thought it was funny. As it turned out, Lorraine was like Gloria— deeply loving, but utterly uninterested in sex with any gender. Irene had a strong inclination toward men, though idle thoughts suggested that under the right circumstances, she might someday sweep a lucky woman off her feet.

Others typically dismissed Norman as a hanger-on, a perpetual third wheel, and probably with designs on getting into one of the girl's pants. That just went to show they hadn't bothered trying to understand him. The truth was, first, that he was passive and easy-going to a terrible fault. Norman was usually content to follow along with anyone he generally liked, or at least thought was interesting, in order to see what they got up to. It wasn't laziness; he was motivated by a non-specific curiosity and easily amused by human drama. Second, Norman also preferred men—an open secret between the three of them—but was so content with being one of life's observers that the girls despaired of him ever finding love, even if it were safe to do so.

We hadn't *talked* about any of this, of course. Not in 1954. Much to my continual frustration. I'd picked up most of it from stray thoughts and feelings.

We'd all be so much more comfortable if this could be out in the open. Instead, for all its pretenses of pushing the limits of human potential, the Institute was stuck in the mire of "traditional" gender roles. It was amazing they allowed women at all. I suspect they wouldn't have, if their experiments hadn't been so dependent on people with certain rare talents.

All three of my new friends, and the other members of our dorm, displayed varying degrees of psychic talent. So did the overwhelming majority of the Institute's personnel. The Nova Anima Institute wasn't a boarding school or a private college. The personnel may have been college-aged, but they weren't here to study a mixture of sciences and liberal arts on the way to a degree. The Institute presented itself as a research facility, with one purpose: to explore the limits of human psychic potential. To what end? I hadn't figured that out. Yet.

The Institute's motto, proudly displayed above the lobby and the library, gave some hint: *Ad Hominem Perfectionem.* "Toward human perfection".

That mystery, as much as the hints the Director had dropped about my past, was why I stayed here when every part of me ached to rejoin my first friends. Although my new friends couldn't replace Luci and Gloria, they were welcome additions to my life in their own right. And they *were* my friends, I had realized. Up until sixteen days prior, I couldn't shake the feeling that they'd been directed to insinuate themselves into my life in order to monitor me or keep me tractable. That fear had gradually receded, one act of kindness at a time, until now we four fitted together so smoothly that an outside observer might have assumed we'd all gone to primary school together. It was wonderful having more people to talk to. I didn't have to be lonely when Luci and Gloria weren't around.

I hadn't realized until three months ago that I *was* lonely. It was a feeling I was in no hurry to experience ever again.

Irene coughed politely. It occurred to me that thirty-two seconds had passed since they'd asked to sit with me. I quickly applied my warmest smile and gestured to the empty seats.

"Hello, everyone. Of course you can sit with me."

The trio quickly took their seats. To my relief, they thought nothing of the gap between greeting and response. They were accustomed to me "getting lost", as Lorraine put it. I was hardly the only one at the Institute to perceive the world differently from the norm. One was expected to make accommodations.

"That must be a terrific story you're reading if it kept *you* from seeing us coming," Lorraine said.

It took me a second to realize what she meant. I hadn't forgotten about the magazine I was holding, but my mind had wandered away from it. I laughed, trying to cover my embarrassment.

"Yes, actually. There's a particularly good story by K.C. Hunter in this issue. An explorer on another world befriends one of the locals by comparing their respective harvest festivals. There are a lot of interesting details, despite how short the story is, and I like that the real conflict is their mutual fear of unknowingly violating a cultural taboo. Also, if you read between the lines, there's nothing to suggest that either character is actually human. Also now I'm babbling."

That was an unpleasant feeling. I never babbled, not even with Luci. She made me feel *flustered*, certainly, but I was always in control of my mouth. It was happening more often, and always in my new friends' company. I didn't understand why. Fortunately, my new friends wouldn't let me stay embarrassed.

"I can see how that would be engrossing," Irene said.

"I suppose." Norman leaned back in his chair, hands behind his head. "I'm surprised you still have a taste for rockets and ray guns. Geez, isn't the Institute weird enough?"

"The story's not that weird," I said. "K.C. Hunter makes a lot of assumptions about compatibility between biomes that probably aren't very accurate. But I like thinking about people from different worlds finding common ground. It's optimistic. I think we can use a little optimism these days."

"That sounds really cool," Irene said. "Don't tell me any more about it. I'll read it when you're done. We can compare notes."

I smiled shyly. "I'd enjoy that."

"At least you can get your magazine," Lorraine said with a faux-haughty sniff. "I can't get the Institute to subscribe to *Mad*. We're being robbed of culture, our imaginations *stifled* by bland authority."

"You pick up a copy from the newsstand every month." Irene propped her chin on her hand and leaned in with a smirk. "It's a dime."

"It is the *principle* of the thing, Irene. Who is the Director to decide what is fit for our young minds and what is mere low-brow trash?"

"Pretty sure that's his entire job description." Norman fetched a toothpick from his breast pocket and tucked it in his cheek. "Which is why it's our job to flaunt his restrictions whenever possible, man."

A thick textbook sat in front of him. Titled *Animating the Corpus Lucis*, it was one of the key texts of their program. Irene and Lorraine had their own copies, but theirs didn't have November's copy of *Tales From The Crypt* hidden poorly between the pages.

I quirked a skeptical eyebrow. "That's not impacting your studies?"

"Hey, this program is all about expanding our minds, yeah? We're supposed to be charting the course of imagination and stuff. That means exposing the minds to the *possibilities*, man. We can't restrict ourselves to what some grayface wants us to read. That's the *old* way of thinking. We gotta look forward to the now!"

Irene rolled her eyes, but her smile was friendly. "You criticize Amelia for reading about rocket ships when you're spending valuable research time with ghosts and goblins."

"Hey, I don't expect to run into any long-legged beasties or things that go bump in the night, but if I spend enough time here, I might just see a flying saucer."

"How *is* Dr. Traynor's experiment going?" I asked.

Doctor Matthew Traynor was one of the Western world's leading researchers in clairvoyance. Specifically, in what would be known in fifteen years as "remote viewing". Under the Institute's guidance, he had pioneered a discipline he called "psycho-astronomy". The science behind it seemed dodgy at best, but Traynor insisted he had produced results. He claimed to have surveys of Mars' surface that put Antoniadi's observations to shame. There were no Martian canals, he had once told me, but far stranger structures.

His team of young psychics were attempting to map the edges of this solar system. Specifically, the volume of space around a particular stellar object in trans-Neptunian orbit, which the defunct Apollonian Society for Illumination had discovered years before Clyde Tombaugh discovered Pluto. I was leery of any avenue of research that had its roots in the Apollonian Society's meddling, but as the Institute was one of the society's many offspring, I couldn't be surprised.

It must be said, it didn't take much to be a leading researcher in any field the Institute explored. The competition was hardly thick on the ground. On the other hand, I was living proof that it wasn't all hokum and humbugs.

"Dr. Traynor *is* impressed with how quickly we're progressing through his meditation program," Irene said. "We're some of the most promising candidates, if I say so myself."

"Well, I suppose *somebody* has to," said a snotty voice behind her.

My friends turned to see the source of the intrusion. As one, we scowled. Harold Bates and Richard Seyton stood a few meters away, sneering. Harold was tall, broad-shouldered and fair-haired, the sort of blandly handsome young man that newspaper sports sections called "All-American". His accent was unmistakably Boston Brahmin. Richard was shorter and stood in a way that immediately brought to mind a snake about to strike. His thin black hair was perpetually slicked into something my friends referred to as a "duck's bottom" haircut, which he somehow thought was cool. His voice placed him from anywhere in the Mid-Atlantic. Both men were as pleasant as stepping into a cold puddle in only socks.

The terrible twosome was in the same program as my friends, but in another dorm. To encourage a "healthy" sense of competition, the Institute had ensured the technicians in various programs were evenly distributed among the dorms. Supposedly a "friendly" rivalry would encourage them to work harder, in hopes of showing one another up. It worked, up to a point. Harold and Richard embodied that point. Competition brought out the absolute worst in them. It wasn't so important to them that they succeed as it was that others be seen to fail.

I looked at them and immediately thought of Lucas Dowling. Lucas had been the architect of the disastrous experiment that set my involvement in these events in motion, or at least so he believed. He was an arrogant young man too convinced of his own genius to realize how he'd been manipulated. That in no way removed his culpability for the damage he'd caused.

More Lucas Dowlings. Would I ever be rid of them?

"You really don't think Dr. Traynor's going to waste valuable time on the likes of you, do you?" Harold said. "He's only going to get so many chances at this. Only the best will get to take point."

"And that's going to be Howard," said Richard, a born lackey.

"You should request to sit in as an observer, Miss Temple," Howard continued, his tone suddenly cloyingly sweet. "It should be quite an event. The first successful viewing beyond the asteroid belt."

I didn't return his smile. "We'll see, Harold. I expect I'm going to be too busy consulting with the other senior staff. Unless one of my friends is selected, of course. Then I might be able to find some time available."

The smile dropped from his bland face. He turned up his patrician nose in affront. This wasn't a man used to being told "no", especially not by a woman.

"Your loss, Miss Temple," he said, his voice frosty.

He started to go, but a childish impulse flared. His hand darted over Norman's shoulder, too fast for him to object, and flipped open his textbook. Harold snatched up the comic book and let out an ugly laugh.

"Come on, Seyton. Let's leave these amateurs to their *studies*."

He tossed the comic over his shoulder as he sauntered away, snickering, with Richard in tow. Something stirred in the back of my mind, something cold and wet and spiteful. My fingers twitched. I felt a powerful urge to reach into Harold's mind and silence his laughter.

Only momentarily, I assure you.

My passenger didn't make themselves visible in the outside world. They simply uncoiled, like a fungoid cat momentarily stretching before returning to sleep. Very briefly, they tickled the back of my mind.

You're sure? There are all sorts of ways you could punish his insolence. Without doing much permanent damage.

"No," I said aloud. "He's not worth it."

"I agree," Norman said, chipper. He scooped his magazine off the floor, theatrically dusting it off while paying no heed to his retreating would-be rivals. "He'll be sorry when the Nephilim unfold from infraspace and make me king of the Fifth World."

Irene smirked. "Were you supposed to say that part out loud?"

"Don't worry. When the Shining Ones descend, you three will be my queens."

I wasn't entirely certain how serious Norman was. He somehow managed to be deadpan even within his own mind. Irene and Lorraine burst into laughter. After a moment I joined them. Norman's face creased into a wide grin.

"Well, until that glorious day comes, we have lessons to master." Irene gently plucked the comic from Norman's hand and slid it under her own open textbook. "I don't know about you, but I have no intention of letting Harold Bates claim any credit for the discovery of a lifetime."

The three shared a laugh and bent over their textbooks. I admired their dedication, even if I felt a measure of trepidation at their work. This wasn't like Lucas Dowling's disastrous experiment—they were meant to be looking out, not dragging something in. I couldn't shake the feeling that something was going to go terribly wrong with Traynor's big experiment. Possibly it was because I was consulting on a completely different program. I wouldn't be there to help if anything went wrong.

I couldn't see the future, not the way I can see the past. Now, long after the fact, I can't shake the feeling that someone else could.

The Institute's third floor was a maze of hallways, but it had a coherent layout. Ten labs clustered in the middle, forming a rough horseshoe around an opulent lounge on the building's south face. A mix of offices and storage rooms sat on either side.

In my first two weeks "consulting" with the Institute, I spent most of my time in Lab 303. It was the personal workspace of Dr. Vincent Stewart, one of the Institute's seven "noetic savants", its highest level below the Director. Stewart claimed to be North America's leading expert in telepathy. I was skeptical when the Director first introduced us, but he quickly demonstrated that he was indeed capable of communicating by thought alone. It wasn't the same way I spoke into other minds, and certainly not how I read them, but it was genuinely impressive.

Stewart was a slight, pleasant man with a swiftly receding hairline; he joked that it was a consequence of his psychic powers. That caused no end of distress among his technicians. Stewart had painstakingly assembled a team of actives, all of whom had demonstrated a talent toward telepathy. So he hoped, at least. His testing methods weren't the most comprehensive—he'd relied primarily on Zener cards and sealed envelope tests. It fit his outlook.

He wasn't one for precise measurements and line graphs. His desire was to nurture connections between others. He once referred to quantifying psychic power as akin to dissecting a frog—few were interested and the frog dies.

Yes, I eventually learned that he was mangling a quote about explaining jokes.

I liked Stewart. He was pleasant to deal with and grateful for my help. At this point, he was the only savant willing to accept my assistance. I had been very helpful. Over half of the Institute's technicians were "proto-noetics" or "prots". These folks were willing to believe in the paranormal phenomenon the Institute dealt in but hadn't yet demonstrated any true psychic talent. Dressed in powder-blue jumpsuits, they spent their days performing most of the labor an organization this size required to function. Periodically, the savants would sift through them, trying to identify what sort of talents they possessed, if any.

That's where I came in. When I began working with Stewart, I quickly discovered that my unusual perspective made me far better at detecting genuine psychic activity. I could see the activity in the deep structures of their brains, the unique nerve clusters that facilitated psychic communication. In the first week, I had helped him nearly double his team, from five telepaths to nine. I'd also identified another dozen who displayed little facility with telepathy but an inclination toward other skills. None of them had been advanced to the ranks of "noetically active" yet—the other savants didn't appear to need more technicians—but I was sure it was just a matter of time.

Thus, six powder-blue proto-noetic technicians joined us in Lab 303 that morning. Stewart and nine actives sat on cushions in a triangle formation, with him in the center. He created a psychic link with one of his actives and passed along a phrase and the name of a teammate. They would then follow suit, transmitting the phrase down the formation one link at a time until someone dropped the signal. Currently three phrases were bouncing around the room, all lines from his favorite Walt Whitman poems.

Every so often, Stewart would link with one of the prots lined up against the wall, challenging them to join the relay. I monitored their brain activity, seeing how well they did at receiving and establishing links. Reception was one hundred percent, of course. Stewart was very skilled at his own program. Transmission was far less successful. For the first hour, the prots established a link twenty-five percent of the time, but never succeeded in passing a coherent message. For half of them, I thought it was inexperience; this was a new skill they were building. For two others, it seemed likely their talents didn't lie in telepathy. As for the last, I wasn't certain what had brought Vernon Calloway to these halls, but it certainly wasn't his psychic potential.

"Darn it," he said after dropping his third attempted link in a row. "I can't get this!"

"Focus." I knelt beside him, cocking my head to signal that I was examining his brain closely. The structures were present, but barely used. "It's a skill. It takes time to build."

"I don't know, Miss Temple." Vernon's accent marked him, as Norman once said, as from out in the high corn. "I really don't think I can get this."

I patted his shoulder in what I hoped was a sympathetic way. He wasn't the only one trying to build a skill. "Keep trying, Vernon. Feel for the minds around you and reach out. If you must, pick whichever you sense best instead of the one Dr. Stewart assigned."

Stewart's team included two of my other dormmates, Rob Packard and Paul Dempsey. Rob was slender and fair-haired with a permanent grin, as if the world was a joke only he was in on. Paul was dark-haired and husky, with a serious face that belied his quiet warmth. I wasn't nearly as close to them as I was to Lorraine, Irene, and Norman, but then neither was almost anyone. This caused problems during this exercise. They were adept at building connections between one another; they were far less skilled at linking with anyone else. Thus far, two of Vernon's three failures had been attempts at connecting to them.

I was about to send Stewart a request to transmit another phrase to Vernon when he jerked his head up, out of his trance. He turned toward the door. My attention followed him. My stomach tightened. We were about to have company.

"Drop connections, everyone." Stewart rose smoothly out of his lotus position. "Let's take a tight five."

A trio of men, tall and pale with close-cropped blonde hair, entered the room. They wore crisp, bright white Institute jumpsuits. They were all identical—not relatives with a close resemblance, not triplets, but utterly physically identical. Every element of their too-symmetrical bodies matched one another, and they moved in eerie synchronicity. Despite their appearance, I knew they couldn't be human. The fluid that flowed through their veins was not blood but a thick, milk-white substance, and whatever scaffolding held up their carbon-copy bodies wasn't bone. Most disorienting of all, their minds were a hollow echo. I could sense no surface thoughts as I could with my human companions, no emotions or sense of individuality. Their responses to stimuli reflected back on each other, forming an endless susurrus flowing through the caverns of their minds.

Dozens more of them were scattered throughout the Institute grounds, performing whatever tasks the senior researchers assigned them. The technicians appreciated them to a degree, as they relieved them of most tedious laboratory work, but they were still unnerving. Most of the Institute's rank and file knew little about them, except that the Institute considered them valuable resources and didn't permit the technicians to interfere with their work. An unknown active had once dubbed them "myrmidons", and the name stuck.

Myrmidons were never found in fewer numbers than in pairs, and more often in groups of four to six. They never spoke, but they understood and followed verbal instructions. Thus, I was unsurprised when the lead myrmidon (to the extent that there was such a thing) said not a word as it approached and offered me a sealed envelope. The three didn't wait for a response. The moment the envelope was in my hand, the myrmidons spun on their heels and departed, the one on the left pivoting to the lead.

Stewart's team stared at me. I ignored most of them—their glances were furtive, over shoulders and behind hands. My dormmates, on the other hand, eagerly leaned in, staring at the white envelope with unmistakable curiosity.

"Well?" Rob said. "Aren't you going to open it?"

I couldn't help smirking. I fanned myself with the envelope, drawing out the moment. "Why? I already know what's inside."

"How?" Paul asked.

Because seeing inside a sealed envelope was as easy for me as it was to see their teammates seated around the room. I hadn't told my newfound friends about the fullness of my abilities, though. They knew I had talents, just as they did, but not their extent. It would raise too many questions I wasn't ready to answer. Fortunately, my correspondent had provided an easy explanation.

"Because he signed it."

I flipped the envelope over and showed them the seal embossed on the other side. It was an art deco figure of the titan Prometheus, holding a torch overhead. A larger version of that image adorned the wall in the Director's office, worked in bronze. I believe he considered it a metaphor for his own work.

"It's from the Director," I said. "I'm guessing it's a summons disguised as a friendly invitation."

Rob whistled, impressed. "You sure do spend a lot of time with the boss."

"Miss Temple is a consultant," Stewart said, smoothly slipping up behind his technician. "With whom do you think she is consulting?"

"Indeed," I said. "My apologies, Dr. Stewart, but it appears I have an appointment to keep. I'll have to bow out of the rest of this session."

"It's of no worry." Steward waved a magnanimous hand at me. "Thanks to your methods, you remain with us in spirit. Back to places, everyone! We resume in two minutes."

The actives groaned but returned to their seats in the pyramid. I gave them a friendly smile before heading out the door. It wouldn't do to keep the Director waiting.

As one might expect, the Director's office was huge—larger than any of the labs. It needed that space to fit a full wet bar, a felt-topped card table, small library with leather reading chairs, and the vulgar massive executive desk that dominated the space. If one were the sort to be overawed by the trappings of wealth and patriarchy, the office signaled its occupant as a man of power.

He raised his glass as I entered. "Miss Temple. Thank you for accepting my invitation."

Two high-backed leather chairs sat in front of the desk, far enough to make most guests feel insignificant. I sat, folding one leg primly over the other. "I wasn't aware it was an *invitation*, Mr. Director. It seemed more like a summons."

He smiled, showing blindingly white teeth. The Director took care to stand out among his subordinates. Where everyone else wore mono-colored jumpsuits with black accents, his uniform was reversed: a crisp black suit with white shoulders and V-shape. He was slightly under four and a half feet tall, with dark hair and a neatly trimmed beard. As ever when I saw him, he had a gin and tonic in one hand.

"Please, Amelia. You're a valued colleague, not a subordinate. On what authority would I summon you? And it's Octavian. Or Dr. Pretorius, if you insist on formality."

"I do, in fact, insist on formality with people I don't know well. Unfortunately, we both know that Dr. Pretorius isn't your name. Or anyone's name, for that matter."

I didn't know why he chose to name himself after a mad scientist from a Frankenstein movie. Like most members of the conspiracy, he had a weakness for theatrics. He also enclosed his mind in a shell of psychic interference. I didn't think the primary purpose was to block my ability to read his thoughts, any more than the Institute's barrier was intended to hamper my movements. It was merely a convenient side effect.

I suppose it was somewhat hypocritical of me to refuse to address him by his chosen name, given that no one had named me "Amelia". The difference, to me, was a matter of purpose. "Amelia Temple" is my identity, a declaration to the world of who I am. "Doctor Octavian Pretorius" was a persona this man adopted, a costume he wore for reasons I did not completely trust.

I sighed, a touch theatrically. "I suppose it's possible Octavian *is* your given name. With that in mind, we'll have to be on a first name basis… Octavian."

"Splendid, Amelia!" Octavian flashed his too-intense smile. I didn't need to read his thoughts to tell that he took this as a small victory. "Would you like a drink?"

He gestured to the wet bar to my right. It was, as Octavian never tired of saying, fully stocked with all manner of beverages, but I didn't feel inclined to test that. A soft drink would be refreshing enough; through Luci, I'd discovered I had a sweet tooth. I was going to get a cavity, if I wasn't careful. If that was even possible for me.

"A Coke would be fine. You'll recall that I'm still seventeen."

"Mm." Octavian nodded knowingly, then gave me a wink that I felt was entirely inappropriate. "Only for another week and a half, I believe? We'll have to arrange a celebration."

It was true. My eighteenth birthday was swiftly approaching. I, of course, hadn't told anyone my birth date. The Director loved that sort of thing—dropping hints as to what he knew of my origins without giving me any real answers.

I smiled insincerely as Octavian handed me my glass. I locked eyes with him over the glass as I drank. A light that I thought I recognized as humor danced in his.

"I'm serious, Amelia. A young lady only turns eighteen once in her life."

"Yes, that is how time generally works."

"You have to let us do something to commemorate the occasion."

"Hmm. Let me think." I leaned back in my chair, adopting a pose of contemplation. "Why, perhaps you could finally share the information you've been withholding from me."

Octavian's smile dropped. He didn't scowl at me, but he did shift uncomfortably in his seat. I wasn't sure if it was guilt over what he was keeping from me or his discomfort at being directly challenged. Probably the latter.

The Director claimed to know who my mother was. Not only that, but where she was now. That, more than anything else, was how he'd finagled my initial cooperation.

"I'm not *withholding* anything from you, Amelia." He took a big gulp of his drink. "We had an arrangement. Information in exchange for your assistance."

"I believe I've held up my end of that deal."

"You have, certainly. Vincent has nothing but good things to say. His progress has improved by leaps and bounds since he began consulting with you."

That was certainly true. Prior to my unwilling recruitment, Dr. Stewart's telepathic research program had been largely theoretical. The man had a tremendous psychic talent, but his position as a teacher was owed more to a surfeit of confidence than the ability to nurture that talent in others. I had helped improve his methods for testing telepathic potential, which is to say, I had helped him actually develop one. His accuracy had improved greatly in just two weeks. I wasn't sure I was doing the right thing by helping him, but a dozen prots were certainly happier after having lifetimes of uncanny feelings validated.

"And, of course, our monitoring team tells me you've stopped making unauthorized multidimensional movements," Octavian continued. "That is certainly appreciated."

I had stopped testing the wards surrounding the compound after I'd agreed to become a consultant and once I thought I'd measured them enough. I didn't think I was fooling him, but an unspoken agreement to let it slide helped our relationship. I nodded over my Coke, smiling in what I hoped was a winsome fashion.

"I don't want to provoke another response from your security detail," I said. "I didn't much enjoy the last one."

I tucked my free hand behind my back to hide the way it suddenly clenched. I could feel the myrmidons' milk-white fluids oozing between my fingers. I suppressed a shudder.

"You needn't worry about that. I assure you, the trouble at the hospital will be the last." Octavian took no note of my distress. He downed his drink and got up to mix another. "I don't consider you to be a risk. Not anymore. You're a valuable colleague."

I was certain he was about to say "asset" initially, but with his mental shielding I couldn't prove it.

"With all that in mind, I believe very soon we could see clear to bringing you in more fully to the organization." He smiled over his drink, as if he was offering me a great prize. "Once that's done, there should be no issue sharing more… *sensitive* information."

"*We* could?" I quirked an eyebrow. "I thought you were the ringmaster of this psychic circus, Octavian."

"No man is an island." He swirled his drink thoughtfully. "Oh, I have a wide range of latitude here, but I too am accountable to others. Investors, interested parties, and the like."

I'd suspected as much, although I couldn't prove it. Wherever the Institute's records were, it was a secure location my senses couldn't yet discern. No poking about like Luci.

"Such as the Chambers Foundation?" I asked innocently.

"I'm really not at liberty to say." Octavian grinned. "But your recent involvement has raised some concerns. Fortunately, I've been able to pour oil on those troubled waters."

"I'm ever so grateful."

"There's no need for sarcasm. You have to understand how significant you are. You have the potential to knock over several game boards without even trying. I'm trying to demonstrate that your presence isn't simply benign but actively beneficial."

I rolled my eyes. The Institute wasn't that different from the Bureau. I was still being treated like a resource rather than a person, but with more comfort. Recognizing my annoyance, Octavian raised his hands to mollify me.

"Things are tense now," he said. "It's not only your presence. We're very close to seeing results on our most important project. Once Traynor shows results, I'll have more room to maneuver. You'll see. I just need a little more time."

I shook my head in disbelief, but what else could I do? I had even less leverage.

"We'll see, Octavian. We'll see."

03

"Count back from thirty. At zero, run Preparatory Sequence Alpha."

Silently, Irene, Lorraine, and Norman began counting in time with the metronome ticking away in the background. Even without it, their individual counts would have been almost completely in sync. They had a great deal of practice by now.

At zero, they opened their minds to one another. Human minds work differently from mine. They require active effort to establish a psychic connection. The Institute had developed various methods of preparing the mind to receive such a connection. My help had vastly improved those methods.

Every afternoon, the three reported to a small lab on the third floor with six other Institute technicians. This was Matthew Traynor's personal workspace. It was divided into two rooms. The largest was a classroom space, where his technicians studied noetic theory. They sat in groups of three, divided by dorm assignment, and went over the techniques Traynor had designed to direct their psychic talents. The nine members of Traynor's team had all been designated "noetically active", the Institute's second level of mastery, and wore baby-blue jumpsuits to match. The Institute believed they had identified their psychic talents and trained them well enough to begin utilizing them.

In the smaller room, they worked to prove the Institute right.

Three narrow, padded surfaces dominated the small room, more like stationary gurneys than actual beds. My friends laid back in their stations, each wearing a net covered with electrodes on their heads. The gurneys were oriented along the axes of a triangle, with their heads together at the center.

Banks of complex equipment lined three of the four walls, all electrodes, magnetic tape and vacuum tubes. Traynor sat a desk in the corner next to a bank of printer readouts, wearing a navy-blue jumpsuit. Needles drew line graphs along the technicians' individual feeds, reading brain activity and other indicators as they ran through the program. Traynor's thoughts were closed to me; like all the Institute's Level Fours, his mind was hidden behind a mirror-smooth shield. My perception slid smoothly off his defenses whenever my senses passed across him. Nonetheless, the way the corners of his mouth kept twisting upward suggested he was pleased with what he saw.

It took two minutes to run Pre-Seq Alpha. Traynor counted them carefully on his pocket watch, an ornate piece of gold and crystal that kept accurate time in three different time zones, one of which wasn't terrestrial. When two minutes had passed, he double-checked the readouts. He gave the printers a curt nod and issued the next direction.

"Count back from thirty. At zero, run Preparatory Sequence Beta."

The actives began counting down again. At zero, they reached out to the mind on their right. As Traynor had taught her, Irene pictured herself lying on her station in a blank white room. Soft light pulsed gently from the six surfaces in time with the metronome, giving the cognitive space a heartbeat. She felt Norman's mind drifting near her, his psychic presence a smooth, deep current. Her presence slipped easily into his, and he appeared in her mindspace to her right. At the same time, she felt a tentative touch akin to a warm sunbeam. She welcomed Lorraine's familiar presence, but their connection wasn't very strong. Lorraine appeared on her left, but her psychic image flickered like a television screen with a poor signal. Irene felt a deep twinge of sympathetic disappointment. This was the best Lorraine had done in two weeks.

Traynor certainly noticed. He frowned at Lorraine's readings, jotting down notes in a secret shorthand. His expression brightened when he moved to Norman and Irene's measurements—the graphs showed their connections to their respective partners were high. I could have told him that myself, if he'd simply been willing to let me sit in. Psychic pulses flowed counterclockwise around the room, weak but smooth. The pulses carried no information. They simply connected the three minds in a circuit.

He clicked open the pocket watch again, waiting for the second hand to tick up to twelve before issuing the next instruction. "Count back from thirty. At zero, run Preparatory Sequence Gamma."

The actives turned to the teammate on their left, seeking to stabilize their existing connections. Irene followed the sunbeam to Lorraine's mind. Her best friend was easy to find, readily welcoming Irene into her sunny presence. Her psychic image in Irene's cognition snapped into coherence. Norman's image didn't grow in strength, as the connection she had established with him was already stable. Nonetheless, she felt his presence flow into hers, reinforcing their psychic bond. Together, the three could maintain this small network nearly indefinitely, easily balancing their respective power with one another.

That was Traynor's intent. He nodded and mumbled banal observations as he watched their graphs rise. When the sync ratings indicated they'd finished running the third sequence, he instructed them to hold the network steady until he directed otherwise. He jotted down more notes; Irene was performing excellently, and Norman was setting a personal record. The team's readings remained high as he wrote up a preliminary report on this test. My three friends harmonized well with each other, validating his current approach. It would remain to be seen whether that proficiency would translate well to the more advanced program his experiments required, but that would be determined soon enough.

After twenty minutes of observation, Traynor instructed the three to begin teardown. On his mark, they withdrew their psychic connections in reverse order. Lorraine fell out of Irene's mindscape, unable to maintain the connection on her own, while Norman's presence dimmed. When she was alone in her mind again, Irene dismissed the mindscape entirely. She opened her eyes, staring up at the plain, white-tiled ceiling.

"Well done. You all appear to have mastered the basic techniques." Traynor glanced at Lorraine's graph and frowned. "At least, to the best of your individual abilities."

"I hope so." Norman hopped out of his station and put his hands to his lower back, stretching until the vertebrae popped. "We've been doing it enough, man."

"Repetition is reinforcement, Rogers." Traynor gave him a cross look, but his tone suggested amusement. "It's certainly paid off in your case."

It had been paying off for Irene as well, but Traynor had no words of encouragement for her. She hadn't expected any yet still frowned at him as he led the three into the study room.

The other two groups perked up immediately when the door opened. Their attention wasn't focused on their fellow actives, but on the paper Traynor pinned to the corkboard next to the door. It showed the group's Integrated Psionic Sync rating, a scale Traynor had invented to theoretically measure their ability to harmonize their psychic abilities. It was his primary means of demonstrating his program's success, as well as motivating his actives. Traynor believed wholeheartedly in the Institute's policy of improvement via competition.

Reports from Friday were posted across the board's bottom half. Today's reports went on top. The others clustered around to compare my friends' scores with the previous team's. It was Harold and Richard's, of course.

"Group Two, you can resume studying," Traynor said. "Group Three, to the testing chamber."

Group Three—Edward, Patricia, and Albert—lingered just long enough to read their fellows' scores. Eddie whistled appreciatively. Group Two had come in at eighty-one on a hundred-point scale; in contrast, Group One had posted sixty-six. Both scores were a five-point increase over Friday's test. The report broke down their individual contributions—Norman scored thirty-one, Irene thirty, and Lorraine twenty. Group one had a similar breakdown, although Norman and Irene both outscored all of them. The actives of Group Three gave them respectful looks before filing into the testing chamber.

Group One—Harold, Richard, and George—hung around the board. Norman turned to find Harold standing directly behind him, reading the report over his shoulder with a sour look on his patrician face. Norman shrugged nonchalantly and gave Harold a half-smile before returning to his table. Irene smirked at Harold and Richard as she followed them. It turned into a genuine smile when she passed George, who really didn't deserve to be lumped in with his partners. A much more friendly rival, he gave them a polite golf clap, inspiring Irene to perform a flourishing curtsy.

Lorraine ducked her head, trying to slip into her seat without drawing any attention. She didn't feel she had much to be proud of. Her score was comparable to Richard's, who also hung around the program's bottom half. Luckily, she wasn't the focus of Harold's ire.

"Your luck can't hold forever, you know," Harold said, a touch too loudly.

"It's not luck, Harry." Irene smiled sweetly. "We're just better at this than you."

"Don't make me laugh." Harold tossed a scoff over his shoulder as he returned to his own table. "Rogers is clearly carrying you two *girls*."

The claim was so on-the-face ridiculous that Norman broke his carefully constructed cool. He stared incredulously at Harold, as if he'd spontaneously turned purple and grown a second head. Irene just rolled her eyes, refusing to rise to Harold's chauvinism, while Lorraine gave him an ugly look. Richard snickered at their irritation, while George flushed with embarrassment.

"You're being absurd, Harold. You and Irene have been trading off high scores for weeks." George laughed. "Heck, she's outscored you for the past three tests."

"Shut up, Georgie." Richard scowled, puffing himself up as if he might throw a punch. "No one *asked* you."

"It's fine, Seyton." Harold waved a gracious hand. "Not everyone understands the *intricacies* of psychic harmonics."

"*Oh?*" Irene leaned forward, propping her elbows on the table and her chin on her folded hands. "*Do* tell."

Harold deliberately ignored her, directing his words to George. "Irene's supposedly high sync rating is easily explained if you know anything about the female mindset. Women are inherently drawn to masculine power. Granted, Rogers is hardly what I'd call *masculine*."

"Cheers, man!" Norman said brightly, feet on the table.

"But I suppose she doesn't have much choice. Rogers is clearly carrying his team, based on their *connection*."

Irene and Norman looked at each other, faces blank. Then they burst into laughter. "Are you *really* implying that we're *dating*?" Irene said between laughs.

Harold drew himself up, offended to realize he'd somehow become the butt of his own joke. "I can't imagine any other reason."

"Of *course* you can't."

Irene fixed her eyes on him. Psychic energy passed across the room. His mind wasn't open to her, which only made it worse. Her presence slammed against the walls of his mind, putting incredible pressure on his psyche. Veins bulged at his temples and beads of sweat broke out across his brow. His face turned beet red. He let out a harsh snort of effort, trying to steady himself. Then he fell backwards, clutching his head as a spike of pain drove through it. He landed heavily on his backside. Irene stood and glared down at him, ignoring his whimpers of pain and Richard's outraged shouting.

"Let's make this clear for the last time, Harold." Contempt was written across her face in billboard letters. "This isn't Daddy's yacht club in *Bah*-ston. I will never be impressed by you, your supposed masculinity, *or* your last name. All that matters here is how good you are."

She knelt down and whispered in his ear. "And I'll always be better."

Irene stood and turned her back on Harold, returning to her seat. "The doctor's going to choose pilot candidates next week. I'm looking forward to being picked over you."

From the floor, Harold glared at her through tears of pain and shame. "We'll see about that. We'll just see."

04

"That arrogant piece of crap!"

Irene stormed into the common room, Lorraine and Norman hot on her heals. Lorraine flinched at the sudden outburst. Irene had held her poise all the way from Lab 306 to our dorm, not making small talk but otherwise appearing undisturbed. She dropped the mask—practically threw it across the room—the second she banged open the door.

I was sitting in a corner reading when they came in, having decided I wanted company. Three of our other dormmates—Rob, Paul, and Polly Grayson—were gathered at the round central table playing Scrabble. They formed a trio as inseparable as the others, one that hadn't quite opened up to me. Polly was pretty and curvy, two traits she used to hide her quick wit. The three didn't look up at Irene's shout, but I dropped my book and jumped to my feet, asking her what was the matter.

Lorraine glanced warily at Irene. "Harold Bates is being his usual self. He said some pretty ugly things to Irene after our test."

"He can't handle that she's better than him." Norman shrugged. "Just keep showing him up, Reeny. The doc'll see how good you are."

Irene gave him a skeptical look but didn't say what she was thinking.

Instead, she fell into the empty chair between Paul and Polly. Turning in her seat and leaning against the table, she threw an arm across her eyes.

"I've been working my tail off to sync up with you two," she said. "It's not easy. I deserve to be recognized for my work, not have it chalked up to some schoolgirl crush on *Norman* of all people."

Norman smiled amiably, ducking his head in faux humility. Paul stared at Irene in mock surprise, eyes wide.

"You have a schoolgirl crush on Norman?" he asked breathlessly.

"I knew it!" Rob said. "What did I say, Polly? I said, 'Watch out for Irene and Norman, we'll catch them necking in the closet'."

Irene lowered her eyelids, looking cooly at Rob through her lashes. She picked up his tray and flung the tiles over her shoulder. I ducked as the little wooden squares flew past me, clattering in the far corner. Rob didn't change expressions.

"According to the rules, I get to pick new tiles."

"I don't think that's true," Polly said.

Rob ignored her, picking up the bag and rummaging through the remaining tiles.

"You definitely don't get to look," she added.

"I do, it's in the rules." Rob pulled out a fistful of squares. "It's not my fault I'm the only one who's read them."

Paul grabbed his wrist playfully. "You have twenty tiles there, you fink."

"*Read* the *rules*, Paul!"

Irene couldn't help but laugh and shake her head at their antics. Polly leaned over and gave her a quick hug as her anger evaporated. Irene patted her arm and leaned her head on Polly's shoulder for a moment.

"No, I do *not* have any sort of romantic feelings for Norman," she said. "No offense, sweat pea, but you're not my type."

Norman crossed his hands over his heart and moaned loudly, slowly collapsing to the floor as if stricken. More laughter echoed around the room. I smiled politely and stared at them, trying to puzzle out why this was supposed to be funny.

"What *is* your type, Irene?" I asked, mostly to say *something*.

"I've been wondering that myself," said Rob, who was no more interested in women than Norman. "You certainly seem immune to *my* charms."

Irene smiled warmly. "A lonely widow who hasn't seen a man in years would be immune to your charms, Rob."

"I'll have you know the Widow Douglas dropped off a casserole *every* Saturday night for two years," Rob said haughtily.

"Was she courting you or did she not trust you to feed yourself?"

"It can be both!"

Everyone laughed again. Everyone but Lorraine. She held back, trying to smile despite her concerns. I went to her and put a very awkward arm around her. The top of her head barely came up to my shoulder.

"Are you okay, Lorraine?" I asked a touch more loudly than necessary, as if I couldn't read the insecurities written across the forefront of her mind. "Did Harold say something unkind to you, too?"

Lorraine looked at me shyly. She tried to shrink in on herself, not wanting to draw attention to her problems. I wouldn't let her; I'd spent too much time trapped in my own head—metaphorically speaking—to let her do the same. I nodded to Irene, who immediately sprang from her seat and grabbed Lorraine's hand.

"Oh, darlin'!" she said, ire immediately forgotten in favor of comfort. "I'm so sorry, I didn't even think!"

"It's okay," Lorraine whispered. She smiled and blinked back tears.

"All right, someone needs to clue in the rest of us, because I'm starting to get worried." Polly's smile was wide but brittle.

"Don't be embarrassed," I said softly into Lorraine's ear. I gave her a little *nudge*, enough to tamp down her insecurities. "We're all friends here."

Irene squeezed her hand, nodded emphatically in agreement. Lorraine's smile vanished as she took a deep breath. She held it for a moment, calming the tremors in her limbs. Then she allowed herself to speak.

"Irene and Norman are doing great." Her voice was low and soft. Paul and Rob had to lean forward to hear her. "Me, not so much. I haven't gotten any better in weeks."

A glittering tear ran down her cheek. Lorraine leaned her head against my shoulder. I put my hand on the back of her head, petting her hair in what I hoped was a comforting gesture. It didn't help. The dam broke, and Lorraine started to cry.

"I'm really worried I'm going to be cut from the program," she wailed.

"Oh, honey!" Irene put both arms around Lorraine, squeezing her tightly. "Traynor's not going to drop you! We won't let him."

"You're still doing better than half the other guys," Norman said. "Have you seen Richard's scores? He's awful."

"*There's* someone being carried by his teammate," Irene said knowingly.

That pulled a small laugh from Lorraine. "Can you imagine if he wasn't on a team with Harold?"

"He'd practically be a blank," Norman said.

Another laugh rippled around the room. I smiled uncomfortably and forced an awkward chuckle. Among the Institute's junior personnel, "blank" was an unflattering bit of slang for people without psychic training. Officially, the Institute discouraged it—the preferred term was "pre-noetic"—but as such things did, it stuck. I didn't like the implication, but these were my new friends.

"Listen, why are we worrying about this?" Paul waved at me. "Don't we have an expert right here? I bet Amelia would love to help you."

"Yeah!" Rob stood, leaning forward and hanging his arms low in what I assumed was a passable Ed Sullivan impression. "We have something really special for you right here in this studio tonight. None other than the Great Consultant herself, Miss Amelia Temple!"

He held one hand out to me and wiggled his eyebrows dramatically. Paul and Polly applauded wildly. Irene caved and joined in, while Norman shook his head and grinned. Lorraine brushed the tears from her face and looked at me hopefully.

"Of course I'll help you, Lorraine." I smiled. "We all will."

Rob and Paul had good reason to be confident in my ability. They were part of Dr. Vincent Stewart's team, researching telepathy. So far, Stewart was the only member of the senior staff who'd been willing to consult with me. As a result, his research had expanded by leaps and bounds. With my help, his actives had advanced beyond a light empathic connection to genuine telepathic communication. Stewart's advances had helped the rest of the Institute, if indirectly.

It was an open secret that Traynor had been cribbing from Stewart's notes. In theory, the Institute was a collaborative environment, the senior staff working together for the advancement of the human species. Or at least, certain parts of it. It hadn't escaped my attention that everyone, from the Director on down to the most recently inducted proto-noetic, was white. The men behind the organization recognized with some reluctance that restricting their inductees to only men was needlessly confining but hadn't made the leap to desegregation. Their ideals fell so short in practice.

Likewise, despite preaching the virtues of collaboration, the Institute was a viciously competitive environment. Stealing his colleagues' work might have had serious consequences for Traynor if not for one fact: he was getting results. The Director's favor was fickle, but right now it rested on Traynor. Stewart's revenge would have to wait. In fact, it would never come.

On the other hand, that meant that even though Traynor wouldn't accept my help, I was familiar with his work. The same methods I'd used to help Rob and Paul would be efficacious for Lorraine. I took a seat on the floor and gestured for everyone to join me.

"I know this isn't quite how Dr. Traynor does things," I said, "but it will work better with everyone's participation."

At Irene's urging, Lorraine sat quietly across from me. Irene and Norman sat on either side of her. Rob sat between Irene and me, Paul on the other side of Norman, completing the circle. Polly held back, unsure.

"Looks like it'll be unbalanced if I join in," she said.

That wasn't the only reason. I could see, hiding in the recesses of her mind, a reluctance to join a psychic network. That came from her mentor, Dr. Ravenna Adler, the Institute's expert in astral travel. I suspected, and would know for certain later, that Adler had discouraged her team from permitting such connections for reasons of her own. I didn't want to push the matter. Adler wasn't the most influential of the senior staff, but my brief interactions with her warned me against making her an enemy.

"It's up to you," I said. "I know a viable configuration for six or seven participants, but if you can't join…"

The others looked at Polly expectantly. Her resolve wavered, but her obedience to Adler outweighed her loyalty to her friends. For now. If Rob had asked, she'd probably have given in, but he just looked at her, somewhat confused. She laughed nervously, gave us all a small wave, and backed through the door, bumping her shoulder on the jamb as she went.

"I wish I could. Really, I do!" she said through the closing door. "I'm due at Dr. Adler's lab soon, though!"

That much was true, for certain values of "soon". But it wasn't my business. I had more than enough people to help Lorraine. I smiled sweetly and waved to the closed door.

"That was a little odd," Irene said.

"Dr. Adler's not like the others," Rob said. "She's *tough*, and her team keeps weird hours. Polly is usually out when we're sleeping."

"We don't want to interfere," I said. "Besides, the six of us are more than enough. Everyone, relax and clear your minds. Focus on my presence."

Dutifully, the others closed their eyes and linked hands. As they had been trained, Irene, Lorraine, and Norman began counting back from thirty before running Pre-Seq Alpha. Rob and Paul visualized a circle rotating in blank space, Dr. Stewart's preferred meditation exercise. For my own part, I fell into my own mind, forming a mindscape around me. My jumpsuit tessellated away, replaced with a sensible A-line dress. Out of consideration for the Institute's color scheme, I left it dark violet.

Normally when I went inside my mind, I pictured my old dorm room at the Bureau campus. That would raise questions I didn't want to answer. As far as my new friends were aware, I was an expert the Institute had brought in from across the country. More to the point, after a few weeks of living at the Institute, I'd come to realize how bare and lonely my old living quarters were. I preferred now to leave them behind. I hadn't known I was lonely until four months ago. That revelation was only bearable thanks to my friends.

I'd intended to create a cognitive version of the Institute's library. It was familiar to everyone as a gathering place and as a site of collaboration. Instead, I found myself conjuring a memory of the Lane Diner, owned by my friend Gloria's family. The small diner was perhaps the only place I'd ever felt at home. Gloria, Luci, and I had spent so many happy afternoons there, giving me my first taste of a normal life. Its gleaming surfaces, shiny chrome appliances, and bright neon lights spread out around me, smoothly resolving into place. Without thinking, I hopped onto my usual stool and leaned an elbow on the counter. The diner was empty, but I could hear the echo of a memory of forks and knives clinking against plates, of snatches of conversations, of Andre bustling in the kitchen. A pang of sadness clenched my chest when I looked at the empty space behind the counter where Gloria should be. I imagined her leaning across it, a warm smile on her friendly face, and then she was there.

It *wasn't* Gloria, of course. Just a simulacrum, a figment of my imagination. I could animate her, even imbue her with pieces of memory, but it wouldn't be the real her. Only a version of her that existed in my head.

I knew I had to get off this train of thought before the bell rang and an imaginary Luci walked through the door. It was hard enough looking at a facsimile of Gloria. I couldn't bear seeing a puppet of my girlfriend. I hadn't seen either of them in over a month—not since the incident at St. Audaeus Hospital. Though I enjoyed my new friends' company, I missed those two terribly. I didn't want them to hurt the way I did, but I also hoped that they missed me a bit. It would be nice to be missed.

Enough. I was there to help Lorraine, not wallow in my sadness. With a silent apology, I dismissed Gloria's image. I stilled the rest of the mindscape, silencing the echoes. An aura of comfort and friendship still hung over the cognitive space, which made it a perfect environment for Lorraine's training, but I'd insulated it from the depths of my mind. Privacy was a concept I'd come to late in life, but it was becoming increasingly important.

Mostly insulated. The diner floor shivered, like the surface of a still pond rippling in the wake of a fish almost breaching. Something cold and damp slowly churned beneath me—within me. My passenger was making themself known again.

"Not now." My tone was friendly, or so I hoped. "I haven't come to talk."

Previously, I'd been annoyed at best when speaking with the Watcher Within. We'd developed a better relationship since the incident at the hospital. We weren't friends, exactly—I still didn't trust them—but we were trying to work together. Make the best of a situation unwelcome to both of us.

I put out a hand. The floor puckered, like a drop of water falling into a pond in reverse, and a small tendril of murky liquid spiraled up to touch my palm.

"We're going to have some company. I'd prefer it if you stayed out of sight."

A tremor of irritation flowed up the ooze. My passenger didn't like the idea of sharing space with more minds. Too bad. I shook my head.

"You're a guest here too, remember? After a fashion." I cocked my head to one side, putting my other hand to my hip. "You're just going to have to accept the inconvenience."

The tendril's spiral briefly reversed, a liquid shrug. The Watcher radiated reluctant acquiescence. I was in charge, after all, and they recognized that they *were* quite a bit to explain. The tendril flowed back into the floor. The sensation of cold damp retreated as the Watcher Within returned to their lurking place somewhere in my brain.

"Thank you," I said kindly. Then I reached out for Lorraine.

To Irene and Norman, Lorraine's psychic presence felt like a ray of sunshine in the early afternoon—warm, comforting, and friendly. I didn't perceive minds in quite the same way. Where they sensed a resonance that mixed their interpretation of the other person with the other's own sense of self, I saw actual surface thoughts. I saw *all* their surface thoughts, spread out in an arc before me. Lorraine was anxious but desperate to hide it. Irene was at once confident and doubtful. Norman was as relaxed inside his head as he appeared to be outside it. Rob was excited to show off his skills to his friends, while Paul was nervous about connecting his mind to someone who wasn't Rob.

I could have gone deeper if I focused on one of them, but there was no need. They deserved their privacy as much as I did. I could bridge the gap between myself and any one of them without more than skimming the surface.

The first time I'd done this, it was in a panic. I'd been far less gentle. The Watcher had breached my mind, was trying to take over my nervous system. Instinctively, I'd lunged for Luci and Gloria, grabbing hold of their consciousnesses as if I was drowning and they were life preservers. I hadn't merged our minds, but I'd formed a much deeper connection than was necessary. I'd since practiced with them both, learned a defter touch. As easily as opening an unlocked door, I connected Lorraine to my mindscape.

She appeared in the booth closest to the door. Unlike me, she was still wearing her baby-blue Institute jumpsuit. Her eyes widened in surprise, her pretty mouth forming a red-lined O.

"Oh, my!"

"Welcome to my mindscape," I said.

"That was so easy!" She stared at the simulacrum in wonder. "Normally it takes at least a half hour of practice and Dr. Traynor's exercises."

I smiled. "My abilities work a little differently from yours."

Lorraine slid out of the booth, wandering down the length of the cognitive diner. She'd never seen such a detailed mental space. Traynor's methods didn't exactly call for interesting scenery; he wanted them looking *outside* their own heads, not building worlds within them. That made a certain amount of sense, but it didn't appear to be working well for Lorraine.

She ran a hand over a booth's red leather seat, marveling at the tactile feedback. "What is this place?"

"The best dining spot in Chatham Hills," I said, a trifle too proudly. "My best friend's family owns it. It's somewhere I feel comfortable. At home."

"Chatham Hills? That's practically next door."

I filed that tidbit away for later. I hadn't thought the Institute had taken me far. Now I had confirmation. "Maybe we'll stop by for a blue plate special sometime soon. My treat!"

I slid into the booth she'd appeared in and invited her to join me. She sat down across from me. I took her hand.

"Let's get started. Steady yourself. Center your mind. Feel the space around you. Then reach out to Irene."

Lorraine nodded, a trifle nervous, and closed her eyes. The color bleached out of the space around her as her mindscape merged slightly with mine. She executed Traynor's program, one sequence at a time. The sequences were a series of mental exercises that focused the deep structures in her brain that controlled her psychic talent. I watched her mind closely as she ran through the steps, seeing the way her thoughts lit up those parts of her brain. I noted the errors she made, particularly the ones that had hardened into habit through repetition. Without drawing attention to what I was doing, I touched her mind and helped a bit, *nudging* her thoughts into place where appropriate. It was like a trainer correcting an athlete's stance during practice.

I saw an immediate improvement. Lorraine felt it too. When she reached out to Irene, her psychic touch wasn't shaky or tentative. She firmly extended her presence into Irene's, mingling them as their one tic signatures harmonized. In no time at all, Irene popped into the booth next to me, her psychic image as strong and steady as she appeared in the material world.

Lorraine's face shone with pride and surprise. "I did it!"

I reached across the table to grab her hands, giving them a proud squeeze. She beamed at me while Irene ran Pre-Seq Gamma, strengthening her end of the connection. Though it was best practices according to Traynor's program, there was practically no need. For the first time, Lorraine could hold up the psychic connection on her own.

"Good job, dear!" I said. "Now, let's grab Norman."

05

Most of the events of my time at the Institute, I didn't witness at the time they happened. I only saw the things for which I was directly present. I pieced the rest of this together long after the fact, by looking back in time or reading the memories of the survivors. While I tried to hide it, the barrier around the manor did more than keep me imprisoned. It interfered with my perception, much as the Apollonian Society's abandoned headquarters did. Looking outside of myself was like looking through radio static. I spent most of my time there experiencing something between a constant headache and the feeling that I hadn't had enough sleep. I was distracted, and consequently a great many things I should have expected took me by surprise.

I don't like surprises.

The Institute's spaces were designed in gleaming Streamline Moderne, a choice that made the place look at once vaguely futuristic and slightly old-fashioned. Ravenna Adler defied that convention. The two spaces reserved for her research were relentlessly baroque. Entering Traynor's lab was like boarding a spaceship; entering Adler's was like stepping into a witch's study.

Adler kept her lab dim, favoring candles over electric lights. She claimed the electromagnetic radiation would disrupt her work; I suspect it was mainly for the ambience. In place of lab tables and banks of electronic equipment, a large crystal sphere dominated the room. It was a meter and a half in diameter, set atop a pedestal of brass and dark wood. A flat band of silver encircled it. To my eyes, the band glittered with the strange yet familiar light of a seal, the symbols etched on the inside. The flashes of weird light inside the sphere were visible to everyone, though a dark violet mist obscured their source, even to me.

A half-dozen ornate chaise lounges upholstered in dark red were arranged in a wide circle around the sphere. Five members of Adler's team lay on the lounges, their blue jumpsuits incongruous against the decor. A small table sat beside each chaise. They held notebooks and fountain pens to record her actives' findings, as well as porcelain cups that held mostly tea. The five women—Adler had deliberately selected for sex over specific psychic talent, something her colleagues had been more than willing to accommodate— lay insensate. Their bodies were here, but their minds were elsewhere. Adler was the Institute's expert on the astral realms; her actives were exploring astral space under the guidance of her sole noetic specialist. The nature of her research was not dissimilar to Traynor's, but her methods could not have been more different. They clearly hadn't seen the value of collaboration.

Adler stood before the sphere, pondering the entity within it as she half-listened to her sixth active. Her jumpsuit was navy blue, marking her as a "noetic savant", the fourth level of the Institute's hierarchy. Polly, normally bright and bubbly, stood a few feet behind her mentor, nervously twisting her fingers together. She'd asked to speak with Adler privately; this hadn't been what she expected.

"Lorraine's aces, Dr. Adler, really she is." Polly only stumbled over her words a little bit. "I don't want you to think she's not. Just because she's struggling…"

"The Institute is a demanding taskmaster." Adler didn't look at Polly. Her tone was difficult to judge. "Many potentials have struggled under its demands."

"Yeah. Yes, ma'am."

"Not you, of course. You're doing well under my instruction."

Polly blushed and looked down at her feet. "Thank you, ma'am."

"Unfortunately, I can't do what you're asking, Polly." Adler drew her hand away from the sphere. A ribbon of violet-ish light followed, crackling in the air. "Or rather, what you're trying to work yourself up to asking."

Polly jerked her head up, brown eyes wide. "I—I was looking for advice, doctor."

Adler looked over her shoulder with an expression of unmistakable skepticism. "Come now, Polly. Simper at the boys and play the airhead for them if you must. Not here. I know how clever you are."

She twisted her hand, releasing the ribbon of energy. "You can't poach another savant's active. Me least of all." She rolled her eyes thoughtfully. "Maybe not least of all. Jeffrey would have an even harder time. Still, it would become a fight, and not one I'd necessarily win. You girls might not have noticed, but I'm not the most influential researcher here."

Polly started to say something, a bit of empty flattery, but seeing Adler's expression, thought better of it. Instead, she folded her arms over her stomach and turned away, head down. She took a couple of steps away from Adler, moving through the line of lounges. Adler watched her, expression unreadable, at least to me.

"I'm worried, doctor," she finally said. "So is she. Lorraine's afraid she's going to be dropped like Brad was."

Something flickered across Adler's face. Regret? Pain? Fear? I couldn't say.

"We haven't heard from him since he left," Polly continued. "They dropped him out of the Institute entirely. We didn't get a chance to say goodbye." Her voice dropped. "I really like Lorraine. She's nice, even when she doesn't want anything from you."

Adler watched her for a moment, seeing the way Polly' shoulders shook. Then she came up behind her, placing a gentle hand on her back.

"Don't worry, dear. What happened with Bradley Finch and the others was a special case and unlikely to be repeated. Dr. Voss was under a great deal of pressure to produce results." She looked away and added under her breath, "And Matthew became the favorite anyway."

Polly looked plaintively over her shoulder, her fear obvious even to me. "How do you *know*, Dr. Adler?"

Adler caught Polly's chin between tender fingers and stroked her jaw with her thumb. She moved her other hand up to Polly's shoulder, massaging it slowly. "Because you aren't going to let her fall. She's your friend. You and the rest of your dorm are going to lift her up. That's the whole point of mixing you all together."

Polly flushed guiltily. "The others *are* helping, actually. Amelia had everyone build a network to help her practice. I didn't join. You said we shouldn't."

Adler pursed her lips. "You can't be that concerned for your friend if you're not willing to break the rules for her. Even mine."

Polly' mouth fell open. Adler laughed, a quick rifle-crack of amusement. She tapped Polly beneath the chin, closing her mouth for her, and let go of her shoulder.

"Never you mind, dear. That reminds me. I need you to deliver a message for me. I think it's time Miss Temple and I had a chat."

There were, for reasons Mark Pressler couldn't quite understand, no passenger elevators anywhere in the Institute. Two freight elevators facilitated movement of supplies and large equipment to the sub-basements, but their use was highly restricted. Instead, a handful of stairwells allowed passage from one level to the next; none spanned more than two floors. The upper floors were something of a maze, and the sub-basements were worse. With the Institute's tendency to assign lab spaces across multiple floors instead of concentrating personnel in specified areas, performing basic assignments could become something of a journey.

The Institute had a reason for its complicated layout. Like the massive barrier that covered the grounds, it was a defense measure. In theory, an incursion on one level would find it difficult to spread to others, giving the security team time to mount a response. In practice, this would turn out to be less than effective.

Mark, the eighth member of our dorm, cradled a wooden milk crate in his arms. A red and white checked cloth covered it, hanging down to obscure the now-faded markings that read "Nelson's Dairy". Inside, small glass jars clinked with every step. Whatever was inside them writhed wetly.

He tried to look nonchalant as he made his way up from the second sub-basement to his mentor's lab on the third floor. He didn't want to explain what he was carrying or if, perhaps, he ought to use a more secure method of transport. He had one major advantage in that regard. He wore the cerulean blue jumpsuit of a "spec"—a noetic specialist, the third level of the Institute's system. Prots and actives alike were conditioned to defer to them. The handful of specs acted as the savants' right hands, assisting in their experiments and directing the actives in their tasks. In theory, they had developed their psychic abilities to such a degree that they were adept at a particular talent; hence, the name. Mark did have a specialty, and a rare one. He was a biometric, able to read biological functions the way I read minds, only not nearly as well. He held out hope that he might eventually develop that ability into direct manipulation of biological processes; thankfully, no one had figured out a reliable method for that. For now, his position was owed less to his psychic ability and more to his willingness to facilitate the moral lapses of his mentor, Dr. Jeffrey West.

West was the first of the Institute's senior staff I'd met upon my unwilling arrival at the Institute. That would have given me a terrible impression of the organization—even more so than basically being kidnapped—if not for the fact that the Director openly hated him. West was their expert in "esoteric biology", a field I suspected he had largely pioneered himself. I'd gathered from my interactions with his colleagues that he represented the Institute's old direction, the sort of research St. Audaeus Hospital had secretly been pursuing. The current director was trying to move away from that sort of butchery, but West hung on like a tick, pursuing his own horrible work.

Accordingly, Mark was unsurprised to find the lab empty, at least of other people. He was West's only technician. The main room was full of equipment, primarily six long glass and metal tanks. Rubber tubes and hoses ran from equipment in the ceiling down to dark shapes floating in thick, orange fluid. Three smaller rooms adjoined the main space. Mark worked regularly in two of them, which held more glass tanks, these upright and cylindrical. The third, on the south wall, was West's private lab space. Mark had never been allowed inside.

A double row of smaller tanks hung on the short east wall. They were a foot tall, roughly rhomboid in shape, and each full of more orange fluid. Eight of them held small bundles of weird matter; the last four had recently been emptied and refilled. Ready to receive the new samples.

Mark set the milk crate down on the long counter against the south wall and withdrew the sample jars. He lined them up carefully, checking their contents one by one to ensure they were viable. He gathered up a selection of tools—glass pipettes, an Erlenmeyer flask, forceps, and a syringe—and laid them out neatly on a metal tray. Then he retrieved several chemical compounds from a cabinet in the corner—organic compounds, enzymes, three brightly colored and uncategorizable fluids, and three vials of what was certainly someone's blood. He added each compound carefully to the flask, taking careful notes on the mixture in a notebook he carried in his thigh pocket. This was the thirteenth such mixture; he was sure this time he'd gotten it right.

Once the mixture was finished, he set it to the side and unmounted the four empty tanks from the wall. He dumped the contents of his sample jars into the tanks, three per container, and sealed them. Then he drew the chemical mixture into the syringe. The tanks had injection ports installed near the top; he injected a careful measure of the mixture into each one. He remounted them, hoping the new mix was indeed up to the task. He could feel the weird matter doing *something* in the orange fluid, but it was like trying to read a passage in an unfamiliar language. Hopefully it was growing; hopefully this was what would cause the weird matter to thrive in the weird fluid. The stuff in these tanks was key to West's main experiment, and Mark was sure they were close to a breakthrough.

He didn't want it turning out the same as West's *last* main experiment.

The small rooms on the north side held four cylindrical tanks, each with an attached bank of monitoring equipment. Three of the tanks were empty, their former inhabitants long-since disposed of. A person floated in the fourth tank, submerged in the ever-present orange fluid. Mark wasn't ready to dismiss the body as "remains" yet. The monitors indicated vital signs, but the man—what used to be a man—had been unresponsive for weeks.

Mark placed a palm against the glass, staring into the man's unresponsive eyes. He was naked except for restraints and monitor cuffs. The changes worked on his body were easy to see. Weird flesh grew across a third of his body, pale and rubbery, like nothing seen on any terrestrial creature Mark recognized. His left hand was growing vestigial digits. Additional new eyes grew within puckering sockets on the right side of his head and chest. The way his elongated right leg and left arm hung suggested his bones were being absorbed into the new flesh.

Part of Mark wished the subject could speak, could tell him what his transformed body experienced. The rest of him remembered how he had screamed. How he had screamed until they figured out how to shut his altered brain off.

"A shame, isn't it?" said a smooth voice behind him. "Poor Bradley couldn't handle the strain."

He didn't startle. He'd become used to West's sudden appearances. The doctor didn't tolerate skittishness. He needed a spec with calm nerves and a strong stomach. That was Mark. He swallowed, settling himself. When he spoke, his voice was strong and calm.

"None of them could. Not everyone is fit to embrace the future, sir. You taught me that."

"Indeed." West sounded as if he was in good humor, which was surprising considering his recent struggles with the Director. "Mister Finch couldn't meet the requirements for Voss' program. We shouldn't be surprised he couldn't meet mine, either. I really should talk to Octavian about our recruitment standards."

Mark smiled weakly. "If you do that, where will we find subjects for human trials?"

He was joking—mostly—but West missed the humor. "We're weeks away from that, I'm afraid. Maybe months. Recovering from the disaster at St. Audaeus is going to consume all our resources for the foreseeable future. I can't believe the Director saw fit to invite the creature responsible into our facility. It's a disaster waiting to happen."

That took Mark aback. West had been singing an entirely different tune when I first arrived. His opinion must have changed when he realized he wasn't going to be allowed to dissect me.

"Amel- Miss Temple seems harmless enough, so far."

West gave him a sharp look. Then a thought must have occurred, for he rolled his eyes and softened his expression. "Temple's been assigned to your dorm."

"That's correct." Mark's eyes shifted back and forth, as if he was walking on uncertain ice.

The doctor shook his head, considering the matter. "That could be useful. We can keep an eye on her. Just don't let her get too close, of course."

"Of course not," Mark said, a bit too enthusiastically. "The incident at the hospital wasn't *all* bad, sir. It opened an all-new resource for us."

He followed West into the main lab and gestured at the double-row of small tanks. The alien matter inside writhed and wriggled in the orange fluid.

West stroked his chin thoughtfully. "True enough. How goes cultivation?"

"I think we almost have the nutrient mix correct now. I wasn't prepared for how different the samples were from the West Formula."

West ran a finger over the closest cultivation tank, staring into the orange fluid. "Science is a matter of learning from our mistakes, Mark," he said, his tone magnanimous.

"We made quite a few." Mark gestured to the four tanks on the left side. The fluid within was dull and cloudy, more brown than orange, the cultured tissue piled limply at the bottoms. "Specimens 11A through D are a total loss at this point, but I'd like to continue observing necrosis."

"I'll consider it. And the others?"

Mark turned to the second batch of four in the middle. The fluid was murky, but the tissue within was growing—in each tank, a fist-size knot of blue-green polyps, writhing and wriggling like eyeless eels.

"12A through D aren't thriving, exactly, but they've shown the most stable vitality so far. I think they'll make it. It's too soon to say about Batch 13—I just started culturing them moments ago—but I have high hopes."

The small clumps of alien matter bubbled quietly at the bottom of their tanks. The blobs were the size of marbles and already starting to elongate. West pondered them, tapping the side of the nearest tank.

"Good, good," he said. "Keep up your observations. We have a budget meeting in two days, and I'll want evidence to bring. Depending on the outcome, we may be able to move into production soon."

"That will be a nice Christmas gift."

West cocked his head with a frown. "I thought better of you than common superstition, Mark."

Mark flushed and glanced at his feet. "Just an expression, sir."

West nodded, as if he wasn't really hearing. He turned to look in the direction of the smaller lab. "With that in mind, I think the previous experiment has run its course, don't you? Time to dispose of young Bradley."

"Are you sure that's necessary?" Mark said quickly. "Tissue conversion continues at a steady pace. I think we should continue observation."

"Direct human implantation of Subject 27 tissue was a failure in four out of four subjects, Mark. This is a dead end."

"With respect, sir, *physical* implantation has been a resounding success. The complications were all psychological."

West made a skeptical noise, but didn't disagree.

"We can still learn something here," Mark said. "Wasn't penicillin discovered by accident?"

The doctor tilted his head and stroked his chin. After a few moments' thought, he nodded grudgingly. "I suppose that's a fair point. Well, let it never be said that I'm not indulgent. We'll keep Bradley's remains for observation a little longer. So long as it doesn't interfere with our actual work."

"Of course, sir. Thank you."

West clapped Mark on the shoulder, then went into his private lab. Mark let out a sigh of relief when the door closed. He had the greatest respect for his mentor; he also had the greatest fear of West's caprices. There was something about the way West looked at the world that worried him; as if they were all raw materials, Mark included. He looked over his shoulder at his former roommate, floating insensate in his tube. Mark's face creased apologetically. Then he set to cleaning.

O6

I mentioned two reasons I stayed at the Institute: my desire to find out what exactly this branch of the conspiracy was up to, and my need to learn about my past. There was a third. He waited in a hospital room in the second sub-basement.

Ralph Connor had been Lucas Dowling's assistant in his half-baked attempt to summon an ultraterrestrial from the fifth-dimensional segment of space-time we knew as "the aether". That experiment had been a partial success. The being downloaded into local realspace and immediately set to building themself a new temporary body, with Lucas and Ralph intended to be among the initial building blocks. In the end, Lucas had absconded into parts unknown, Ralph had been rendered comatose, and Gloria had trapped the aetheric entity in a spare section of my brain. It was that or allow them to effectively eat Chatham Hills. The situation was hardly ideal, but we'd had little to work with at the time.

The Chambers Foundation, the mad science conspiracy that had sponsored Lucas' experiment, had arranged to have Ralph moved to St. Audaeus Hospital in Regina. We had inadvertently precipitated another crisis when we'd tried to rescue him. Now both of us were effectively prisoners of the

Nova Anima Institute, although my accommodations were considerably more comfortable.

On top of that, the entity trapped inside me had begun manifesting themself *as* Lucas Dowling, which after six weeks hadn't become any less disconcerting.

"We think he looks good," the Watcher-As-Lucas said.

I gave them a sharp look. "Don't you start."

Ralph lay in a hospital bed, covered only where leather restraints and rubber tubing crossed his body. Exotic organic matter threaded through his skin, muscles, and internal organs, tendrils and polyps of blue-green fungoid life. It was the same sort of matter the Watcher Above had used to build themself a body, converting human tissue into that weird flesh. They'd infected Ralph and Lucas with it after spraying them with spore-filled ichor. Such fluid leaked from rents in Ralph's skin where tendrils of Watcher matter had torn through, grasping at the empty air like so many alien anemones. Or they would, had Ralph not been locked behind a stasis seal.

It had been inscribed on the floor beneath his bed, freezing him in a single point between moments. The seal was a circle composed of dozens of smaller interlocking symbols, connected by myriad straight and curving lines. It looked like nothing so much as a diagram of clockworks composed in calligraphy. As Gloria described it, that was sort of how the seals worked, directing energy through the design in a precise pattern that altered local physics. I had to take her word for it. No matter how well she explained it, no matter how hard I studied the symbols and the way they interacted, I couldn't understand how Prospero's Keys actually worked.

I recognized a handful of Keys. Here was the Daimon Key, which described ultraterrestrial beings such as the Watchers Above and myself; I didn't want to think about that. There was the Adamite Key, which described humans. Several smaller Keys connected them into a single element. Deduction said that somehow, this set of Keys defined whatever Ralph had become, so that the seal affected only him. I couldn't possibly say how.

I did understand that a seal required energy. I could see the matrix with my unique senses, the way the energy flowed around the defined space to carve out a void in time. Some seals relied on internal energy reserves that required periodic replenishment. Others drew on continuous power sources. For those, Gloria favored candles; they were cheap, easy to transport and easy to snuff if necessary. That was too old-fashioned for the Institute. This seal drew power from a set of electrodes standing on either side of Ralph's bed. Electrical cables connected them to a dedicated generator in another room, ensuring Ralph stayed frozen even in the event of a facility-wide blackout.

I could free him as easily as severing the cables or, less destructively, by throwing the switch on the wall. I wanted to. I wanted to see if Ralph's normal consciousness would resume, now that he'd been freed from the influence of the hospital's ultraterrestrial warden.

I didn't dare. Not yet. It was cruel, but at least the seal was holding the Watcher infection at bay. The weird flesh had spread rapidly through his body in the first weeks after the Dowling Experiment. We'd tried to save him. Unfortunately, our attempt to excise the infection had gone badly. The conspirators had imprisoned another entity in the bowels of the hospital and charged it with keeping their test subjects quiescent. That being, the Gaze That Chains, had interfered with our rescue attempt. The infection had gone wild. Ralph might be able to wake up, but who knew how much pain he'd be in? The infection might have irrevocably altered his body if it didn't just kill him. Would the person who woke up still be Ralph?

No. Much as I hated it, much as it felt like a betrayal, it was better to keep him in stasis. It gave me time to figure out how to help him, or to smuggle Luci and Gloria inside.

Not that I wanted Luci to see Ralph like this. She felt fiercely protective of him, even more so than she did of me. Holding vigil over him was my way of keeping her close in my long absence. I couldn't be with the girl I loved, but I could protect the boy she thought of as a little brother.

Not that I was doing a good job of it. Stasis seal or not, the infection wasn't entirely unchanging.

"Look at this," I said.

I reached into the field, touching one of the tendrils. The energy matrix crackled around me, but the seal had been designed very specifically. It couldn't affect an entity such as me. Even if it could, I'd discovered over the past several weeks that time meant something very different for me.

The tendril's tip had been neatly lopped off. Ralph's body was covered in small incisions, dozens of them, thankfully only on the Watcher-infected flesh. I had no way of telling how old they were—the stasis seal kept them all at an identical state of freshness—nor if they'd been made simultaneously or over a period of weeks. Worse, the seal confounded my ability to look up and down the flow of time. Within the bounds of the seal, it was always "now".

"Taking samples?" the Watcher-As-Lucas asked.

I scowled. "More like harvesting."

I glanced at the Watcher, gauging their reaction. They were standing outside the range of the seal, on the steel stairs that lead to the upper floor of the split-level chamber. Conceptually, at least. They had taken to projecting a simulacrum into my sensorium whenever one of us wanted to talk. It was more convenient than taking a time-out to visit my mindscape, although sometimes more disconcerting.

I'd done the same to Gloria once. I'd have to apologize to her if I ever saw her again.

The Watcher Within had altered their presentation significantly since they first manifested the Lucas persona. Initially, they had appeared as Lucas in the early stage of infection—boils and tumors of Watcher matter growing across the right side of their body, pale skin split and weeping ichor where the growths erupted, their right eye bulging from its socket, all swollen with alien fluid. Now they didn't appear as late-stage infection, at least according to the memories they'd shared. It was more like a marriage of Lucas' form and the Watcher's temporary body. The Watcher-As-Lucas' skin was rubbery, the blue-green of Watcher matter entirely replacing Lucas' previous pallid complexion. Beneath their clothes—a modified version of the consultant's jumpsuit I wore—I could see bulges that spoke of growths, but more regular and without tearing the skin. Their limbs had elongated, moving more like tentacles than single-jointed arms, and they had six long, slender fingers on each hand. Their right eye still bulged three times the size of the left, but the flesh around their socket was healthy, not tortured by sudden growth.

I chose to take this as a sign that they had been trying to regard humans as a life form worthy of respect. Perhaps instead they were simply trying to make themself more comfortable in this persona.

When they spoke, their voice lacked Lucas Dowling's habitual sneer. I chalked that up more to our slowly improving relationship than any internal change in perspective. Still, it was a welcome relief.

I gestured to Ralph. "This isn't uncomfortable for you?"

The Watcher-As-Lucas descended the stairs slowly, hands in their pockets. They circled the edge of the seal, head cocked to one side. They regarded Ralph's body as one might a cleverly sculpted topiary.

"It's odd," they said. "We haven't observed one of our… *subjects* in this stage in… we find it's hard to say. It's difficult to reckon linear time from our perspective. Certainly not since our first couple of spawnings." They glanced at me, wary of my response. "We didn't care."

I nodded slowly. It was irksome to hear, but another lecture on the rights of humans wouldn't help things. "And now you do?"

The Watcher paused, searching for the correct words. Or perhaps the ones that wouldn't offend me.

"No."

I crossed my arms and quirked an eyebrow. The Watcher-As-Lucas raised an open palm in supplication, which wasn't necessary. I wasn't angry. I *was* disappointed, but not surprised. Not wanting to scare them off or browbeat them into submission, I invited discussion.

"We are unconcerned with the flesh. Particularly this flesh. It is…" They looked away, searching for an appropriate comparison. "Like a discarded dress that never fit right."

"You're comparing my friend to old clothes."

"Ralph Connor is not your friend. You care for him barely more than we do. You only feel that you should because he is important to your companion."

I drew my mouth into a tight line, my spine stiffening. I took a step away from Ralph and turned my back to the Watcher, as if that mattered.

"I'm not pleased that you think you understand me so well."

In fact, it was irritating having someone read me as well as I read others. I *wasn't* going to apologize to Agent Walsh if I ever saw him again, but I did feel a momentary pang of sympathy.

"Don't blame *us*." The Watcher put a hand to their chest, mock-offended. "*We* didn't ask to be locked up in your ridiculous meat brain."

"And if I let you out, will you eat the entire Institute?"

"Of course not. No more than half. We would let you pick the half you liked least."

I glared over my shoulder. "That isn't funny."

"We're trying to be reasonable, Amelia. We require significant mass to support our presence on this plane, even if we don't intend to spawn."

I sighed, but it was true. I'd certainly taken the measure of their psychic presence when I had grappled with it. It wasn't as vast as they liked to suggest, but once embodied, it would make significant demands of the flesh.

I had promised to free them from their mental prison, provided they agreed to coexist with Earth's autocthonic life. It wasn't right, locking them in a cage. I hated being a warden and a prison at once. It was a betrayal of myself. I could have returned them to the aether, if it weren't for the Institute's barrier, but I didn't think that was a good idea yet. Not until they learned to respect non-Watcher lifeforms. Otherwise, we'd end up back where we started.

"So, we'll need to find a source of organic mass. *Non-human* mass."

"If you insist," the Watcher said, failing to not sound bored. "Although that raises the question of *when*."

"Don't get ahead of yourself. I'll need to find a suitable place for you. Somewhere *out of the way*. I don't want people stumbling across you."

"You make it sound like we're unfit for polite company."

"I think you fit right in with the sort of people who run the Chambers Foundation. That's what worries me."

"We are unsure whether to take offense at that."

"Besides, I can't do it alone. I don't think I can take down the binding seal on my own. I'll need Gloria's help to release you, which means I have to convince her it's a good idea." I put my hands on my hips and looked them over. "I'm not even certain *I* think it's a good idea."

"Now we *do* take offense." The Watcher circled the edge of the seal like a shark, teeth bared. "Haven't we been loyal? Haven't we been helpful?"

"I've repeatedly had to remind you that humans are *people*. As recently as moments ago, in fact."

The Watcher-As-Lucas scoffed. "You have to admit it sounds implausible."

"You're trying my patience."

The Watcher didn't respond right away, though a small wave of fear rippled through their cognitive body. They retreated to a corner of the room, sitting silently. Once again, they considered their response carefully. By the aura of conflicting emotions radiating off them, I could tell they were having difficulty.

Horrifying as it was, it was difficult to blame them entirely for their perspective. The Watchers Above were psychic beings, the remnants of an ancient civilization that had abandoned the material world entirely to escape the collapse of their home world's environment. A collapse they had almost certainly precipitated through rapacious and thoughtless exploitation based on their current behavior. To support their existence on the aether and continue propagating their species, they periodically descended on fresh, living worlds in the material, devouring the biomass until the planet's environment collapsed, just as their home world had. They were cosmic locusts, a cancer in the form of a civilization. It could only work if they denied that any other form of life mattered.

Somehow, the Watchers believed I was a key part of this process. I didn't understand why, and an early part of establishing an accord with the Watcher Within had been declaring that topic off limits to discussion.

The Watcher Within was not part of the first generation to abandon their lost homeworld. They had been spawned on another world generations later, one murdered by a cosmic accident. They had been made to believe that the Watchers' consumption of others was right and proper, that other life was simply a resource to be exploited.

And yet. They insisted that they were a record of the extinct species indigenous to the world that spawned them. Each Watcher was a gestalt entity, a nation. This one claimed to carry the memories, histories, even engrams of the lost Utsoggthua. Even the face they wore to interact with me was born of the original Lucas Dowling's active mind-state, copied during their brief moment of communion. In their own way, they did recognize other beings as having some significance.

I had to believe they could learn to value them as equals.

If only because I wasn't sure what to do with them if they couldn't.

07

"You asked to speak with me?"

This early in the morning, Dr. Adler was alone in her office. She stood in front of a large piece of abstract art, a print of interlocking geometric shapes that hung next to her door. Her mass of dark curly hair fell down her back like a waterfall. She turned when I opened the door, giving me a half-smile. I waved an envelope at her. It was scented with her perfume and addressed to me.

"Good morning, Miss Temple," she said. "I thought it was high time we finally spoke."

"'Miss Temple'? That's oddly formal for this place."

"We don't all play Octavian's power games." Her eyes twinkled, suggesting she might play games of her own.

"I'm surprised." I joined her at the print. What I had taken for abstract art was a diagram. The interlocking shapes were labeled in a language I didn't recognize. "Most of the savants aren't interested in me. I had figured you as one of them."

"Oh, I assure you." She leaned in close and gave me a lopsided grin that sent a flush to my cheeks. "I'm *very* interested in you. It's just that Vincent hasn't been willing to share you."

I looked away, willing my face to cool down. I hadn't expected Dr. Adler to be so… well, never mind what she was. "Dr. Stewart has been very grateful for my assistance."

"I can see why." Her voice was low and throaty. "Your help has advanced his work by leaps and bounds. Sadly, not enough to propel him ahead of Matthew, but it's not your fault he was so behind. I didn't ask you here to talk about that, though."

She put a hand on my lower arm, almost at my wrist. A tiny electric jolt leapt up my arm. Without thinking, I moved closer. She lowered her eyelids, looking up at me through her lashes.

"Do you drink tea?"

Much like her lab, Adler's office was ornate and cozy in a way that was completely incongruous with the rest of the Institute. She didn't have a large, authoritarian desk dominating the space. Instead, an antique writing desk stood in one corner. A slim reclining chair sat in the second, and two high-backed chairs upholstered in red occupied the third. A small round table between them held a small tea service. A glass-faced cabinet filled with oddments stood against the wall between the desk and tea corner. The room felt more like a witch's sanctum than a scientist's study; I wouldn't have been surprised to see a cauldron bubbling ominously in the middle of the room.

"You're a very unusual woman, Dr. Adler."

She winked and ran her fingers up my arm. "I could say the same to you. And it's Ravenna, please."

I felt something in my stomach that I told myself was absolutely not butterflies. "Then I suppose I ought to be Amelia."

"Good." Dr. Adler—Ravenna—sat in one of the chairs in the corner and pressed a button on the wall. A distant bell rang. "How are you finding your time here, Amelia?"

I took the other seat, crossing my legs primly and putting my hands on my knee. "I'm not sure yet. I feel valued. That's a nice change. How much do you know about me?"

Ravenna cocked her head, as if choosing her words with care. Just before she spoke, there was a knock at the door. A prot opened it, standing awkwardly in the doorway in her powder-blue jumpsuit. Ravenna held out the silver teapot, not looking at the young woman who went to fill it. Then she smoothly changed the subject. I didn't notice at the time. Her eyes and lips were too distracting; she must have been counting on that.

"My girl Polly has been worried about your roommate. Lorraine, yes?"

"It's more that Lorraine has been worried, and she's a bit contagious." I explained about her stagnation relative to Irene and Norman. "I've started working with her, though. Despite Dr. Traynor's objections. I think she's showing improvement."

Ravenna shook her head, tight curls bouncing. "Matthew. All of them, in fact. So proud. So territorial. Always jealous of their own positions. They don't know how to cooperate. Not like we do."

"We?"

She smiled brightly. "Women, of course."

Something about that seemed incorrect, but Ravenna recognizing me as a woman filled me with a sudden flush of warmth that overrode my doubt. On top of that, I very much enjoyed the way Ravenna smiled at me. I didn't want her to stop.

"Are *you* asking for my cooperation, then?" I asked.

"In a manner of speaking," she said. "I truly don't need your help with my experiments—although unlike the others, I won't hesitate to ask for it, should that change. What I'm looking for is more personal. A friend. A colleague."

"A voice to argue in your favor at meetings?"

"And vice versa, of course. Assuming you ever decide to *attend* one. If you think this place is about pure science, I'm afraid you're going to be disappointed. It's as cutthroat as any conventional university, or a city council for that matter. Unfortunately, the lines here were drawn some time ago."

"Cutting you out?"

Her smile disappeared. "Octavian may be willing to recognize that women have potential, but not the same as a man. As a result, my work isn't taken as seriously. My girls aren't taken as seriously. The men won't work together, but they will unite long enough to freeze me out. You, though… your presence alone disrupts things. You're powerful, you're knowledgeable, yet you have no formal training or prior allegiances *and* you're a woman. They don't know how to deal with you."

I frowned and held my chin in my hand, considering this. "What is it you're proposing, exactly?"

"That we help each other. You can't be here just to sit back and observe. You must have goals. So do I. You do me a favor, I do one for you."

She leaned forward, putting a hand on my knee. My breath caught in my throat. The skin of my hand tingled where hers touched it. My brain spun, trying to come up with a response. It didn't have one. What to say about all this? What sort of help was she really asking for?

Another knock at the door broke the spell. The prot returned with the steaming teapot. Ravenna favored her with the briefest smile before dismissing her.

"So, how do you take your tea?"

I hesitated, still trying to catch up to what was going on. I ended up picking a number at random. "Three sugars, please?"

She dropped three cubes into my cup and passed it to me. The tea smelled delicious, the warm aroma of tea mixed with hints of orange and sweet spice. I dipped the bag, letting the leaves infuse the hot water with flavor and giving me something to focus on other than the absence of Ravenna's touch. It didn't work. She kept pulling my attention back to her—her long, slender fingers, the quiet amusement in her dark eyes, the thick curls of her black hair. I cast about for something else to concentrate on. My attention slid across the diagram on the wall, and I turned to face it.

"That's an interesting design," I said, trying to keep a conversational tone.

"My life's work, or part of it." Ravenna's pride was unmistakable and unashamed. "It's an abstract representation of the astral realms we've explored."

"Your team here?"

She made a non-committal noise. "Between you and I, I'm not that fond of the design. It's too mechanical, and the astral is anything but. It's something of a compromise for my colleagues' sake. Something that matches their biases."

"I like it, actually."

I blew lightly on my tea, sending tiny ripples across the surface, and took a sip. It was good, and I told Ravenna so. She bowed her head.

"One thing about your diagram," I said, setting the cup down. "It's a bit difficult to read. I don't think I'm familiar with the language."

"No? It's Enochian."

I raised my eyebrows, inviting explanation.

"An esoteric language introduced by John Dee, a mystic in the court of Queen Elizabeth. The first one, that is."

I nodded wisely. "So there was more than one?"

Ravenna sipped her tea politely, eyes sliding to her right. "Goodness. You *are* sheltered, aren't you?"

That stung, especially coming from such a worldly woman. My knowledge of the world outside Regina and Chatham Hills was limited, yes, but I didn't need that thrown in my face. I sat back in my chair. Ravenna's face immediately became apologetic. She set her cup down and offered me her hand.

"I meant nothing by that, dear. The British crown is barely relevant, after all. I'm more surprised that you're unfamiliar with Enochian. Dee claimed it was the language of angels."

The flattery was so obvious that even I picked up on it. I allowed myself to be mollified. It wasn't *that* harsh of a criticism. I took Ravenna's hand and gave her a sly look.

"I'm from Texas, actually."

"So I've heard."

That hung between us ominously. I kept my eyes on hers as I took another sip of tea. She held my gaze while opening a package of tea cookies. I accepted the one she offered, but didn't take a bite.

"Do you really know why I'm here?" I asked.

I let the ambiguity whirl around us. She inclined her head conspiratorially, as if acknowledging without addressing it. "I know why you think you're here."

"Well, *that's* mysterious and presumptuous."

She bowed with a flourish, inviting me to speak. I took a bite and rolled my eyes to the ceiling as if I was pondering it.

"Octavian claims to have information about my origins. He'll share it with me if I help the Institute achieve its vaguely defined goals."

"Mmhmm. I take it he didn't provide a time frame for rendering payment?"

I sighed. "No. I'm not in much position to bargain."

"Does this strike you as a fair deal?"

"It's valuable information," I admitted, "and what he's asked in return hasn't exactly been onerous."

"But...?"

"But..." I locked eyes with her. "What is the Institute doing with my friend?"

Ravenna reared back in surprise, but the corners of her mouth twitched upward. "That's not the question I was expecting."

"It's the most important one I can think of at the moment," I said. "You're holding him in a lab, and as far as I can tell, no one's doing anything to help him. *Why?*"

"*I'm* not doing anything to Mr. Connor, Amelia."

I tilted my head and scowled. "The organization to which you belong *is*, Dr. Adler."

"Now that was unkind, Amelia." Her tone was light, but she put a hand to her breast as if stung.

"What happened to Ralph was unkind." I was no longer in the mood for games. I jumped to my feet, fists clenched. "What the hospital did to him was *unkind*. What your Institute is doing to him is *unkind*. Don't play coy now. The Institute is treating him like an experiment. Or a resource."

Ravenna's face was inscrutable, more so than most. She weathered my outburst easily, sipping her tea while she waited for the anger to drain from my face. When I returned to my seat, she set her cup down and leaned forward. Her chin rested on her folded hands.

"All right, Amelia. No more games for now. Just explanations. What do you know about the Institute's origins?"

"You're aligned with the Chambers Foundation, which is an offshoot of the Apollonian Society for Illumination. Most likely the Institute is as well."

She nodded gravely. "Do you know what the Apollonian Society wanted?"

"The same thing wealthy and powerful men always want. More wealth and more power. They saw the vastness and complexity of the wider universe and looked for ways to exploit it."

Ravenna nodded again, this time with satisfaction. "Good, that saves me time explaining. From what I've gathered, the Apollonian Society's downfall was precipitated by a disagreement on *how*. One faction believed they could reach the aetheric realms themselves, physically. Another believed it was better to draw those resources down to Earth. At the end, a third faction arose—those who became convinced the risk outweighed the reward."

"That's surprisingly sensible, for the Apollonian Society."

"Apparently, even the very foolish can only stomach so many experiments leaving mass fatalities before they reconsider the cost."

I put my hand to my chin, turning this over in my head. A thought that had lurked in the back of my mind for months was beginning to become a revelation. When I spoke it aloud, my voice was small.

"…believed they could reach the aether themselves… is that why I exist?"

Ravenna said nothing for a long time. The silence between us twisted like a living thing, growing larger by the second. Her thoughts lurked behind the mirror of her defenses. My own churned, a storm of fear and confusion. I wanted to scream at her, demand that she tell me what she knew, what she believed. Instead I sat in my chair and shook, somehow too upset to cry.

"It doesn't matter what other people want from you," Ravenna said at last. "All that matters is what *you* want. Why are you *really* here, Amelia?"

My hand flew to my head, fingers digging runnels through my hair. "I *told* you, I'm here because—"

Ravenna darted forward, catching my other arm just above the elbow. Her nose brushed against mine, sending an electric spark up my spine. I held my breath, her perfume dancing in my nose.

"You're here because for the first time in your life, you're surrounded by people who respect and value your special abilities. You're here because the Institute is encouraging you to be *you*. You could have found a way to escape by now, no matter what barriers Octavian put up. You could have found a way into his files, no matter his security. You're still here because on some level you *want* to be."

Her words rang in my ears. My mouth hung open, unable to speak. I sat there, my face not even inches from hers, while the world spun around me. I'd never been allowed to make my own choices before. Was she right? Was this something I had chosen?

Ravenna smiled softly, making a slight sympathetic noise. She placed a gentle finger against my jaw, making slight circles on my bare skin. I breathed her in, unable to think.

"It's all right," she said, her voice low and soothing. "It's a hard thing, becoming an adult."

My heart thumped in my chest, craving her approval. Goosebumps ran up my arms and legs. I could control those reactions, if I wanted to, but something about Ravenna kept catching me off guard. I took a deep breath and tried to center myself. My heartbeat slowed, my skin settled. A current of cold swirled in my mind.

Assistance/consultation query.

Not now, thank you, I thought.

A handful of memories floated up like bubbles from the depths of a swamp. The Watcher Within offered memories of interpersonal relationships from a half-dozen remembered civilizations. Most were fragments of courting rituals, which was ridiculous. I had a girlfriend. Luci meant everything to me and I missed her terribly. Having tea with an intriguing and attractive woman didn't change that. It didn't mean *anything*. And it was highly unlikely Ravenna loved women as Luci and I did. The Watcher clearly still didn't understand people.

My distraction must have shown on my face. Ravenna titled her head to the side, brow furrowed slightly. "Is everything okay?"

My eyes flew open. "Fine. Just fine. I was thinking, that's all. The Institute—which side of the argument did it spring from?"

The question caught her off-guard. Ravenna let go of my arm and sat back in her seat, crossing one leg over the other. She swirled her tea, a tendril of steam rising from the still-hot surface. I thought I might have caught a hint of disappointment in her eyes, but probably that was wrong.

"Both, actually," she said. "The Institute's founders came to recognize that Maxwell Thorpe's argument held validity. You know the name?"

I nodded, frowning. He was the one ultimately responsible for the disastrous experiment that left Ralph in his current condition.

"Thorpe had always argued that the human body and mind couldn't survive in the aether, or in other extreme environments outside this Goldilocks world that spawned us. The men who founded the Institute then leapt to what they believed was the next logical step. If humans couldn't survive out there, why, they would *make* a human who could."

"That's what they were doing in the hospital?"

"More or less. The Chambers Foundation has always kept many different plates spinning at once. That, if anything, was the lesson they learned from the Apollonian Society's fall. Don't rely on one plan."

"Or one organization."

"That's right. I don't know about your friend, Amelia. I honestly don't. If you'll take a guess, then I suspect he's become involved with Jeffrey West's experiments."

"But Octavian hates West. I'm still not sure why."

"Because West is a typical eugenicist, and for all of Octavian's many and glaring faults, he recognizes that way lies horrors." Ravenna took on a far-away expression, as if an awful memory had suddenly burst open. She shook her head sharply, dismissing it. "Also, West once suggested he could 'fix'

Octavian's 'height issue', which went over about as well as you might expect."

"Unbelievable. Then how would he have gotten hold of Ralph?"

"Because Octavian answers to the Institute's board of directors, his connection to the Chambers Foundations. Some of them are committed to the Institute's original goals, and West has been good at currying their favor."

I shook my head, disgusted. "You obviously don't approve. I can hear it in your voice. Why are you still involved with them?"

"As Canada Bill Jones once said, 'I know it's crooked, but it's the only game in town.'" She stood abruptly. "Let's take a walk."

Ravenna bustled out of her office. It took me a second to register what she was doing and follow. She led me through the maze of third-floor hallways to her lab, clustered in the middle with the others. It was empty, thanks to her unusual research hours. She gestured to the crystal sphere, asking what I thought of it.

I stood stock still, hands behind my back, and examined it thoroughly. There was something inside it, I was certain of that now. I couldn't make out what it was, which frustrated me. I wasn't certain if that was due to the seal wrapped around the sphere, its makeup, or some property of its inhabitant.

"It's a containment device of some sort," I said at last. "Beyond that, I can't say."

Ravenna nodded, her smirk suggesting satisfaction. "How familiar are you with the astral realms?"

"My… my very dear friend was attacked by an astral creature not long ago." I wasn't sure whether it was safe to properly describe my relationship with Luci. "A *zedu hath baagu.*"

She cocked her head, confused. "I'm sorry?"

Now who wasn't familiar with an esoteric language? "A dream eater. It scoured her mind of what happened at the hospital."

"Ah! I know what you mean now. Awful little things. I've had to take steps to protect my girls from such creatures."

She made a significant gesture at the sphere and said something—a word or set of words, not pure vocalization. Something in Enochian, I suspect. A series of rings blinked open on the sphere's surface, drawn in violet-ish light. Mist spilled forward from the central ring, followed by a bright glow. Inside the crystal sphere, a creature sang back. Its song resonated with my nervous system, but not unpleasantly. A warm sense of calm blossomed inside me, starting from the base of my skull and spreading through me.

The being emerged from the mist. They undulated through space like a ribbon of violet-ish light. Beams like tendrils or whiskers hung from the end I presumed was their head. They hummed as they floated, the sound occasionally rising to a high chime. The creature flowed around Ravenna's outstretched arm, then wrapped around her shoulders. Their luminescence pulsed gently. I could swear they were purring.

"What are they?" I asked.

"My girls' pet. They call her Archie for some reason I can't fathom. I found her three years ago in a realm of light and water, and we formed a contract. I believe she's a sort of eidolon, like an idea of protection. Certainly she guards my girls during their explorations."

Ravenna stroked the astral creature's head. She trilled, chimes ringing psychically. Ravenna cooed at the creature, then gave me a serious look.

"West represents the Institute's old methods. He believes he can hybridize the human body, probably his own eventually. The other men are dedicated to its new direction, cultivating psychic talents, but it's the same old thing—conquer the aether and beyond.

"I'm trying to do something different. I believe we can work with beings from beyond, not dominate or be dominated by them. Evolve not physically or mentally, but *socially*. I'm not alone, but I am alone *here*. I could use some help."

She offered me her free hand.

"Will you help me, Amelia?"

I stared at her outstretched hand. I'd like to say I took time to consider her offer, but in truth it wasn't a difficult decision. Certainly, I'd had my fill of being controlled. I needed peers, not handlers. More to the point, I felt a kindship between her goals and my attempts to rehabilitate the Watcher.

Perhaps she might be able to help with that as well.

I smiled and took her hand.

08

etween infrequently sitting in on Stewart's meditation sessions, late afternoon training in the dorm, and late-night talks with Ravenna, my daily schedule was full. I enjoyed finally being busy—it was like the weeks I'd spent teaching the indoctrination program for new agents at the Bureau, only more useful. Unfortunately, it also kept me distracted even more than the Institute's barrier. In retrospect, I might have concluded that was the goal, had the Institute not been so disorganized.

Between my guidance and our friends' assistance, Lorraine showed sharp improvement in just a few days. She was never going to be a virtuoso, but she was becoming more confident in her psychic abilities. More importantly, she was no longer afraid of being removed from the program. When the final sync test came, she went in with confidence.

The other teams noticed her change in demeanor as soon as my friends entered the lab. Eddie, Patricia, and Albert looked up from their studies and smiled to see her come in at the head of her team. A happy Lorraine was a force of her own. It was difficult not to smile in the light of her cheerful face. Nonetheless, Harold and Richard still managed.

"It's about time you deigned to join us." Harold frowned haughtily over the book Richard held for him. "It's not as if we have an important test today."

"We're right on time, Harry." Norman sat in his usual chair and stretched out, feet on the table, hands behind his head.

George looked pained. "I hate to back up Harold here, but the three of you *are* about five minutes late."

"That's practically on time for Norman." Irene slid into her own seat.

Richard banged his hand on the table, glaring at George. "What do you mean, you hate to back up Harold? You're supposed to be on *our* side."

"Shut up, Richie," George said, bored.

Richard fumed. Before he could formulate a comeback, Traynor emerged from the testing chamber. He glared around the room, stern expression relaxing when his eyes settled on my friends.

"It's about time. Group One to the synchronization stations. The rest of you, review your sequences. This is the *final* synchronization test. Today's outcome will determine who takes the lead in the Object C Observation."

Norman sketched a sloppy salute, but didn't pick up his book. Lorraine and Irene cracked theirs, while Group Three returned to their studies. Harold, Richard, and George rose from their seats and filed to the door, the Boston brahmin in the lead as always. George gave everyone a friendly wave. Harold ignored the others, patrician nose in the air. Richard threw a smug look over his shoulder.

"Don't feel bad when the doc posts the results," he said to no one in particular.

"Feel bad about what, Richie?" Irene smiled sweetly, still looking at her book. "Your performance up to now has been underwhelming."

"I expect that's what most of his dates say, too," Patricia added.

Richard's smirk disappeared, turning into a snarl. "You uppity little—"

"*Seyton*," Traynor snapped. "A little professionalism, please. The same to you, Miss Philips, Miss Dorn."

Richard rolled his eyes, but only after he'd turned so that Traynor couldn't see him. He stomped through the door, oblivious to Irene's tongue sticking out at him. The others laughed merrily, then returned to reading.

After an hour, Group One returned to the study room. Traynor posted their results on the corkboard and called Group Two to the testing chamber. Harold and Richard passed them with smirks on their faces. My friends glanced briefly at the posted scores. They weren't anything to crow about; Harold and Eddie had improved by a point each, while Richard had dropped by five. Norman nodded enthusiastically and gave them two thumbs up. Richard's face collapsed into a scowl.

Inside the testing chamber, my friends climbed into their stations and made themselves ready. In previous weeks, Lorraine had approached her station with a sense of creeping dread. This time, she smiled enthusiastically at her partners, giving Irene a quick side hug before hopping onto her station. If Traynor noticed her change in demeanor, he gave no sign of it, but Irene and Norman relaxed.

As soon as the three had strapped themselves in, Traynor restarted the metronome and gave the instruction to run the first pre-seq. The three opened their minds to one another and fell into the desired trance state. This time, Irene and Lorraine deviated from Traynor's program. Rather than imagine themselves in his blank white void, they crafted individual mindscapes the way I did. Irene's station materialized in the heart of a beautiful garden, surrounded by slender trees festooned with hanging vines and tall, beautiful flowers. Birds chirped in the background in time to the metronome. Lorraine found herself in a room that could only be described as *pink*—a boudoir bedecked in gauzy pastel pink canopies and draperies. It was a fairy-tale version of her childhood bedroom, a place she felt utterly comfortable.

When Traynor gave the instruction to run the next sequence, Lorraine reached out for Irene's mind. Irene's psychic presence was a storm wrapped in a shell of easy calm. Before, Lorraine's attempts to reach her had been halting, fumbling, the sequence run in fits and starts as doubt deadened her abilities. Now, secure in a place of comfort, she found Irene's mind easily. A wall in her mindscape melted away, replaced by a wooden arch wrapped in pastel pink ribbons. It opened onto Irene's garden. For the first time, Irene's psychic image was clear and strong without her intent buttressing the connection.

At the same time, she felt the cool current of Norman's psychic presence mixing with hers. A corner on the other side of her mindscape bleached of color as his psychic image manifested. He was still following Traynor's program, but there was no friction between the two methods. The network they formed was strong and stable.

Traynor's eyebrows shot up as the readings came out. His mind was unreadable, but the way his heart sped up was unmistakable. His stern mouth curled up into a smile. It was working. His program was finally working.

When the test was finished, Traynor didn't try to hide his exhilaration. He clapped Norman on the shoulder and took Irene and Lorraine each by the hand before bustling them out of the testing chamber. He slapped the test report on the corkboard with an uncharacteristically giddy flourish.

"Excellent show today. Excellent!" he said. "You've all improved dramatically. Especially you, Miss Matthews. I told you, focus and dedication were what you needed. I trust you'll all appreciate Sunday's announcement."

The other actives clustered around the corkboard, staring at the results. As he said, all three members of Group Two had improved—Norman by two points, Irene by five and Lorraine by a whopping ten. Not only had they set a new record, Irene had outscored Norman.

"I believe I know who will be leading the Object C Observation," Traynor said. "We're almost ready for the big event."

As almost an afterthought, he told Group Three to hurry into the testing chamber.

The Institute's auditorium was on the manor's east end. It was a vaulted space, roughly hemispherical with a domed ceiling that stretched halfway up the second floor. Tall, narrow windows filled the curving outer wall, with rectangular panels of white, blue, and yellow glass. A circular window depicting a stylized eye sat at the top where the roof began to curve. It overlooked a tall stage. Two large gongs stood on either end. A semicircular row of seven tall thrones dominated it; the savants were already seated. An eighth chair, taller than the others, sat behind them. It stood empty, waiting for the Director's entrance.

The doors opened promptly at 6:30 am. Unlike the rest of the manor, this room lacked artificial lighting. The Institute's junior members, all one hundred of them, filed two by two into a space lit only by the gray pre-dawn. Two columns of wooden pews sat on either side of the auditorium. The procession broke off by dorm assignment, each to its own pew.

I was already waiting, standing in a corner at the back of the room. The Institute hadn't figured out where I fit in to its ceremonies. I normally solved the problem by not attending Sunday services. This, however, was a special occasion, and one I felt I couldn't miss.

My friends were seated in the third pew on the left-hand side. Irene sat between Lorraine and Norman. I could feel her tension even from where I stood. I wished I could put an awkward arm around her shoulder and reassure her; even I knew I was bad at offering comfort.

When the last prot took their seat, two specs stood and mounted the stairs to the stage. They took position in front of the gongs. At a mental signal from Stewart, they each spread a hand in front of their gong and released a psychic pulse. Deep, bone-rattling tones rang across the auditorium. The doors opened again, and Director Octavian Pretorius entered.

Pretorius. I still feel ridiculous saying it.

The Director strode up the aisle. As he passed a pew, the technicians stood. A wave of respect followed him up to the stage. He climbed the steps, then turned and raised his hands. The technicians did not break into applause. Instead, as one they intoned a mangled portion of a foreign mantra. *"Ommmmmmmm."*

The effect was the same. I didn't need to read Octavian's mind or his expression to tell how he felt. A hundred pliable young minds offering him adulation? How else would he feel?

After a minute, Stewart sent another mental signal. The two actives rang the gongs again. The technicians sat as one. Octavian nodded paternally, then turned and went to his throne, standing in front of it as he addressed the Institute.

"My friends! We are gathered on a most auspicious day. You came to this bastion of learning for many reasons. Some of you were lost. You sought purpose and direction. Some of you had experienced things you could not explain. You needed reassurance and education. Some of you already knew the truth. You needed fellowship.

"Whatever the reason, you came here, and here you found yourselves. You had many reasons, but you have one purpose. *Our* purpose. That which will someday become the purpose of the entire world—the perfection of the human mind and spirit."

Behind him, the sun began to rise. The early morning rays streamed through the colored glass, painting the stage in blue and gold. Octavian raised his arms, outlined in morning light.

"We are the New Anima Institute! We are creating a New Man! Through dedication, study, and experimentation, we will purge the imperfections from our minds and spirits. We will unlock the power bound within you, unleash your true potential. Someday, *you* will stride across frontiers as yet undreamt of. You will solve mysteries as yet unformulated. You will steal fire from the heavens themselves and bring it to the masses. You will herald a new age of man, one free of material shackles.

"These are not empty promises! Oh, no. Some of you have already taken steps along the path to perfection. Today, we will recognize three who have come a stage closer to perfection."

Octavian took his throne. Traynor rose, moving to center stage. He raised his hand, and four more specs stood and slid out of the pews, Mark Pressler among them. A table sat off to the left side. It held three neatly folded cerulean blue jumpsuits and a bowl filled with orange fluid. Mark and two specs each picked up a jumpsuit and moved to stage right. The fourth took the bowl and stood just behind Traynor.

The sun rose higher in the sky. Patches of color stretched out to cover the audience. The golden orb hung just behind Traynor's head like a halo. The technicians focused their eyes on him, leaning forward, eager to hear the names of those to be elevated.

"Over the past few months, I have guided nine of your peers along the path to perfection." Traynor's voice rang across the auditorium. The congregants hung off his words. "All have made great strides under my guidance, but three in particular have achieved a remarkable degree of spiritual evolution. Their third eyes are now open. Their spirits are ready to shake off the shackles of mere gravity. They are noetic specialists!"

The technicians intoned the mantra again, louder. It reverberated through the space, bouncing back to enfold them. Many shook in their seats, unable to contain their ecstasy. Traynor stretched out his hand, as if he would pluck the chosen from their seats himself.

"Edward Simpson!" he said. "Step forward and be recognized!"

Grinning, Eddie leapt to his feet, shaking his dormmates' hands as he squeezed past them into the aisle. He walked up the aisle and steps as solemnly as he could, but the skip in his step was obvious to everyone. He stopped in front of Traynor, who dipped his thumb into the outstretched bowl. He traced the shape of an eye onto Eddie's forehead in that strange fluid, then told him to disrobe. Eddie did at once, without hesitation or shame, stripping off his baby-blue jumpsuit and standing before the Institute in just a flimsy white undershirt and shorts. One of the specs handed him his new jumpsuit. The intoned mantra grew louder as Eddie clambered into it. He turned and cased his peers, face flushed with pride, before moving to the left side of the stage. The mantra dropped off, the technicians anticipating the next name.

"Norman Rogers!" Traynor said. "Step forward and be recognized."

Norman stood as my friends patted him on the back and shoulders. Before he slid into the aisle, he glanced back and gave Irene an apologetic look. She smiled, tight-lipped, then nodded toward the stage. He obeyed, sauntering up the aisle and taking the stage. Traynor anointed his forehead, and Mark gave him his new jumpsuit.

Tension filled the air. There was one name left to be called. Despite the human tendency toward gossip, the Institute had always kept the names of the elevated a closely guarded secret until the ceremonies; only the Director and the savants mentoring them knew who had been chosen. Even so, there were only so many actives, and their progress was a regular topic of discussion in the common rooms. The next name should have been obvious to anyone in the know.

"Harold Bates!" Traynor said. "Step forward and be recognized."

I always underestimate human biases.

Harold stood, smirking as if the outcome was inevitable. Still, the other actives in his dorm didn't congratulate him the way Norman and Eddie's had. Except for Richard, they simply nodded respectfully as he passed. The intoned mantra was disrupted. The other actives in Traynor's team stared at Harold and one another in confusion. Some snuck glances at Irene. She glared daggers at Harold's back while he mounted the steps.

Across the room, I locked eyes with Ravenna. Her expression was unreadable. She shook her head once, almost imperceptibly, then flicked her gaze back to the ceremony.

Traynor anointed Harold's forehead. A spec from another dorm handed Harold his new jumpsuit. He shrugged into it, then turned to smirk at what were once his peers. He joined Norman and Eddie stage left, shoving his way between them to stand in the middle. Just then, the sun crept into the highest window, sending the sign of the eye across the technicians.

Traynor raised his hands again. "Behold, these who have been elevated! They will serve as your guideposts on the path to perfection!"

The technicians rose as one, humming loudly. The newly elevated specs beamed down at them. Even Norman was affected by the outpouring of respect; it would have taken a stronger will than his to avoid being swayed by the adulation of a hundred people.

Irene stood silently among her peers, head bowed, shoulders shaking. Lorraine slipped her hand into Irene's, squeezing it. They couldn't join in the chant. Not while Harold Bates claimed the honor that should have been Irene's.

"Ah, Miss Temple!" The Director raised his glass. "You've finally chosen to join us!"

The Institute's staff lounge was large and opulently appointed, a college student's idea of a gentleman's club, or perhaps the rooms in a casino reserved for the highest rollers. Here again, the Institute abandoned the gleaming whites and chromes of Streamline Moderne for rich wood paneling and wall-to-wall red and black carpet. Plush leather chairs were strewn among dart boards, pool tables, and a felt-topped card table. A granite-topped hardwood bar dominated one side of the room, tended by a tired-looking prot.

I've spent a lot of time in prisons over the decades—don't interrupt, dear, I don't have the patience for your objections—and the accommodations have seldom been pleasant. The Bureau has certainly never cared about my comfort. The fragment of the star god *Shomo-Elnak* tried to trap me in a reflection of my greatest trauma. And then there was my unplanned stay in the village of Harmony… but I'm getting ahead of myself. We'll keep this in order, one moment after the last. Mostly.

My point is, as far as prisons went, the Nova Anima Institute wasn't that bad. I probably would have enjoyed my time there if I'd been invited instead of press-ganged. Before it all went to Hell, I mean.

The Director of the Nova Anima Institute was holding court amid a semi-circle of leather chairs. Four savants joined him, all doctors in esoteric fields. Matthew Traynor and Vincent Stewart were accompanied by Charles Voss, the Institute's other expert in clairvoyance, and Kenneth Pike, the resident master of multidimensional geometry. Voss was nearly as wide as he was tall, his red-faced ebullience belying the way he chafed at being the firm number two in his field. Pike was tall and emaciated, the result of a strict fasting schedule intended to enhance his finely tuned psychic senses. That, combined with a carefully designed regimen of hallucinogens, left Pike continually somewhat distracted, as if he was always focused on something just out of sight. I would have sympathized if I'd ever detected whatever he was looking at.

Off the Director's greeting, Voss raised his martini in my direction. Stewart followed suit, adding a gentle, inebriated psychic pulse. Traynor merely gave me a cold nod, while Pike momentarily pulled his attention away from a phantom in the ceiling to direct a slight wave to a point over my shoulder.

I debated whether to sit or stand. Sitting with the savants would imply a degree of collegial camaraderie I didn't feel for them, regardless of whatever Ravenna implied. On the other hand, standing outside the ring of chairs would probably be seen as deliberately rude and stand-offish, even though I personally would feel more comfortable that way. I compromised by leaning against an open chair on the end. Possibly I'd come off as a mysterious outsider. I thought I might like that.

I tossed my hair the way I'd seen Luci do, although the result wasn't nearly as glamorous. "You're clearly in a celebratory mood, Mr. Director."

Octavian favored me with another of his too-intense smiles. He held his ever-present gin and tonic higher. A burnished steel statue stood behind his chair, looming over his shoulder. It was an art deco rendition of a vaguely feminine figure, with three arms upraised. It brought to mind "The Genius of Wisdom", a statue carved out of an unidentified blue-gray stone that stood on the Chatham Hills Public Library's front lawn. That had been a gift from the Chambers Foundation; this was an uncomfortable reminder of the Institute's connections to the conspiracy.

"Why shouldn't I be celebratory? It isn't every day we elevate *three* of our technicians to the higher levels. That's progress. *Measurable* progress. Just the sort of thing we need!"

He wiped his free hand across his brow. Despite his cheery demeanor, it was clear the stress was getting to him. He might have been the undisputed master within the Institute's walls, but his unseen patrons had him by the throat.

It was the wrong time to confront him, but I was going to do it anyway.

"Are you certain you've selected the right people, Octavian?"

Octavian frowned and glanced at Traynor. The other man drew himself up, affronted.

"Of course we have," Traynor said. "It was my decision. I know my technicians. I selected the three best. They're going to be integral to my psycho-astronomy experiment."

"The three best? Irene Phillips has been regularly demonstrating a superior sync rating than two of the men you advanced today."

Traynor's face went beet-red. "First of all, the results of my experiments are proprietary information! You have no business prying into my records."

Stewart gave him a meaningful look but didn't say anything.

"I don't need to pry, Dr. Traynor. I'm very good friends with a third of your team. I know how well they've all been doing."

He snorted, offended, and turned to Octavian. "Dorm room gossip. Your 'consultant' is questioning my methods based on disgruntled prattle."

Octavian looked at me, apologetic. "Amelia, I understand your loyalty to your friends, but I have to trust my savants' judgement. There's more to recognizing a noetic specialist than a score in this or that rating. If your friend is as skilled as you say, I'm sure her awareness will mature very soon."

I was about to challenge him when a sour look crossed the Director's face. Another man had walked in, flanked by a pair of myrmidons. It was Doctor West. Voss and Traynor each let out an exasperated sigh, while Stewart looked uncomfortable. Pike rolled his eyes knowingly at nothing. Even with my difficulty reading facial expressions and body language, I could tell West was incensed at not being invited to this informal meeting.

"Something I can help you with, Jeffrey?" Octavian asked, a touch louder than necessary.

West hesitated before speaking, prompting an exaggerated eye roll from the Director. Octavian downed his entire drink and leapt from the chair, waving to the prot behind the bar for another. He pulled himself onto a stool and gruffly demanded West get on with it already.

The other savants took that as a cue to scatter throughout the room, not wanting to be in the middle of this. Voss and Traynor took a sudden interest in a game of darts, while Stewart became fascinated by a painting hanging next to the bar. Pike settled into a chair in the far corner, mumbling indistinctly at whatever imaginary entity had captured his attention. I stayed where I was, unmistakably interested in their exchange.

"I was looking over the budget allocations for the next quarter, Dr. Pretorius." West stumbled over his words, having difficulty meeting Octavian's eyes. "I couldn't help but notice that *my* department's budget is rather *low*."

"The budget was allocated in accordance with the Institute's priorities for the next year, Jeffrey." Octavian turned his back to West and took a big gulp of his drink. "I do recall you were at the planning meeting."

"Yes, and all of my inputs were clearly ignored." Bright red spots rose on West's cheeks. He flapped the papers at the Director. "The materials required for my work are expensive. This doesn't match our production costs!"

"Perhaps you should try to spend *my* money more wisely."

"I won't apologize for the cost of progress. I'm working with a variety of exotic materials that aren't easy to come by. Furthermore, I have to divert materials from research to production if I'm going to replace the assets lost during…"

West trailed off, staring at me. I stared back, trying to hide the way my flesh crawled. I knew exactly what he meant. He intended to replace the myrmidons lost at the hospital on Hallowe'en. The ones I'd destroyed so my friends could escape.

I folded my hands behind me, wringing my fingers together. I could feel the myrmidons' thick internal fluids again, hear their unusual skeletons cracking as I broke their bodies. They never cried, never shouted. Not even when I tore them apart.

The men took no notice of my distress, of course.

"The budget is the budget and you're going to have to work within it, Jeffrey. That's all there is to it. Do you think I'm independently wealthy?" Octavian paused, then smiled widely and, I was sure, completely insincerely. "Because I am. Nonetheless, you get what you get. If you have to delay your horrible project by a few months because you want to brew up another dozen of your little toys, ghastly things that they are, I'm afraid that's your problem. Not mine. Make up your mind and stop wasting my time."

West stared at him, aghast. "The delays will be closer to a year than a few months!"

"Oh well."

"My project is *crucial* to the Institute's goals!"

"*Matthew's* project is crucial to the Institute's goals," Octavian said nastily. He waved his drink in Traynor's direction, spilling quite a bit on the carpet. He didn't notice, and no one said anything. "*Charles'* project is crucial to the Institute's goals. *Vincent's* project is crucial to the Institute's goals. *Kenneth...*" He trailed off, watching Pike chuckling at something that probably wasn't there. "Kenneth provides useful infrastructure. *Your* work is a weird little side project held over from the previous administration, and I only let you keep it running out of a morbid sense of curiosity. Frankly, I'm starting to wonder if it's worth even that."

West's jaw tightened. I could hear his teeth grinding from halfway across the room. His hand curled into a fist, and for a moment I thought he was going to strike Octavian. I wasn't alone in that. Traynor and Voss turned and moved toward Octavian, trying and failing to do it casually. Stewart stepped in front of me, I suppose to protect me, even though he was a full head shorter than me. The myrmidons took a step away from West, hands dropping to the shock prods in their holsters. Unlike the humans, their attention was focused entirely on Octavian.

The Director, for his part, simply stared coolly at Dr. West. He swirled his drink, ice cubes clinking quietly against the glass. Then he took a measured sip.

West grabbed the tip of his collar, rubbing it between finger and thumb. He didn't deflate or back down. I believe he deliberately chose to de-escalate. The words he wanted to spit at Octavian hung in his throat, but he swallowed them. He tried to force a smile, the corners of his mouth twitching arrhythmically. Fingers shaking, he spun on his heel and stalked out of the lounge, the myrmidons falling into step behind him.

Octavian watched them go with an unreadable expression. Then he turned to the rest of us and shrugged. "Some people can't take criticism."

I turned to face the door, choosing my next words carefully. "It looked like he had something else to say."

"Probably his 'I'll show you all' speech." Traynor chuckled.

"I'm sure he's still rehearsing it," Voss said.

The two shared an ugly laugh. Octavian didn't join in. He also stared at the door, taking another long pull of his drink, his third since I arrived.

Traynor took no note of Octavian's suddenly changed mood. He signaled to the prot for a fresh drink, then looked over his shoulder at me. "Sure we can't tempt you with something alcoholic? I certainly can't imagine dealing with Jeffrey West without a hard drink."

"No, thank you."

I took another sip of my Coke and glanced around the room. With West gone, the mood in the lounge shifted. Traynor, Voss, and Stewart settled in their chairs. Traynor fished a cigar and matches out of his pocket, while Voss opened a silver cigarette case. He selected one for himself, hand-rolled in black paper, and passed another to Octavian. Voss cut his eyes to me as Traynor lit his cigar, puffing out black smoke.

"You don't mind, Miss Temple?" he asked, suddenly self-conscious.

"Adler always minds," Traynor growled, more to himself than anyone else.

I did too; in fact, I minded quite a bit. The smell is deeply unpleasant, and while I don't think my body is vulnerable to carcinogens, I didn't enjoy watching others put themselves at risk. The room's atmosphere was tense, however, even with West's departure. I could have left, but I had to admit a sudden curiosity.

"Is it wise to antagonize him like that?" I asked the room but directed my gaze at Octavian.

"That's a good question." Stewart laughed. "Jeff might write another pointed memo."

Voss rolled his eyes. "What does it matter if he feels slighted? His ghoulish 'work' is a waste of time and money."

"The drones are useful," Traynor admitted.

"To you. I don't find much need for them." Voss sniffed. "Frankly, anything they can do, the prots can handle. It would be good for them. Idle hands and all."

Octavian grunted. "I'd eliminate his position entirely if I could. The man has no *concept.*"

Interesting. I widened my eyes and nodded, trying to copy Luci's "enraptured ingenue" act. I slid into Pike's now-vacant seat, leaning close to Octavian.

"What do you mean?" I pitched my voice higher than normal, trying to sound younger.

"West is obsessed with the *physical.*" Voss' distaste was unmistakable.

"That was the Institute's original focus, you know," Traynor said. "Directed evolution. Reshaping the human form into something that could survive... well, anything, really."

"A preposterous notion." Octavian rolled his eyes and tipped his drink into his mouth. "They've had decades now, actual decades, and what to show for it? Landfills full of mutated monkeys and metric tons of inedible crabs. West has allies in the Foundation, though, so I'm forced to humor him. *And* his dilettante colleagues at the hospitals. I've cut his funding to the bone, though. No sense throwing good money after bad."

I nodded, catching the inadvertent plural. *Hospitals*. Luci and Gloria would want to know about that.

Octavian took no notice of the slip. Instead, he tapped his temple with one finger. "No. The physical is simply an accident of matter. *You* understand that. It's the *mind*, the *soul* that we must perfect."

He finished off his drink and leapt from his chair. He turned slowly, arms spread wide as if taking in the cosmos. "Look at the dangers we face outside this terrestrial soap bubble. An airless void, high levels of radiation, an absence of gravity. And those are only the horrors we know about! Just imagine what conditions could exist in the subtler spheres. How could we ever prepare the fragile human body to weather them?"

"It does sound dubious," I said carefully.

I felt a slight psychic whisper behind me. The Watcher-As-Lucas was now sitting on top of my chair, figment legs hanging down over my left shoulder. They leaned forward, elbows on their knees, hands clasped.

"Interesting," they said, conversationally. "That's what our predecessors thought."

Mentally, I waved at them to shush. No need to make this conversation more complicated than it had to be. On the list of things I didn't want to explain to the Institute, my passenger was at the top. Fortunately, most of the men took no notice. Octavian was too drunk, and his audience was more concerned about that. Pike glanced momentarily at the Watcher and simply nodded.

"The NACA has ideas for space travel, you know." He leaned forward conspiratorially. "I've seen some of them. Years away. *Years*."

Traynor looked suddenly like he'd swallowed a frog. He coughed, waving away cigar smoke. "Dr. Pretorius, are you sure we should—"

"Their solutions are entirely mechanical. Mechanical, if you can believe it! Rockets and big planes! Real whiz-bang stuff!"

Traynor's admonishment finally caught up to Octavian's drink-addled thoughts. He tipped me a wink and tried to tap the side of his nose. "All hush-hush, of course. Can't let the Reds find out."

He waved his empty glass at nothing. "Another preposterous notion. What, are the laws of physics suddenly different in Russia? Do the Soviets lack scientists? What even *is* a nation-state against the infinite?"

Voss' round face went pale. "Doctor, we've been warned about that kind of talk."

"Oh, go soak your head, Charles." Octavian let out a deep guffaw. "Who's going to report me? I assure you, Miss Temple has even less loyalty to the idea of a nation than I do!"

I shrugged. I couldn't argue with that. The neglect with which the Bureau had raised me certainly hadn't inspired any loyalty to the government it represented. My handlers hadn't bothered trying to instill a sense of patriotism, either; the benefit of not being seen as a person.

Octavian stumbled over to the bar and ordered another drink. As he waited for the prot to mix it, he turned to us, his face suddenly quite serious.

"I keep trying to tell you, gentlemen. This attitude, this loyalty to artificial constructs like 'nations' and 'religion', it's holding us back. What *we're* doing, what this Institute must do, is perfect us! A better sort of human! Not West's tired eugenicist nonsense. I'm talking about a *spiritual* evolution. Unlocking our inner potential! Transcending this crude matter and becoming one with the stars themselves!"

It was a pretty speech. I could tell by their faces that the others had heard it, or variations of it, many times before. I believed Octavian meant it sincerely. It was easy to see how he became the Institute's director, and how he had drawn so many people to him. Even I would have found it somewhat compelling, had it not been for the psychic presence whose imaginary shoes hung by my ear.

Yet, I found one major flaw in his argument.

"You don't have any colored technicians," I said.

My interjection caught them all off-balance. Literally, in Octavian's case. I spoke as he was accepting his fourth gin and tonic. He stumbled, drink sloshing in his glass. He caught himself on the nearest stool, ignoring Traynor's outstretched hand.

"I beg your pardon?" Octavian stammered.

"Your Institute hasn't recruited any colored people. You recognize that women have potential, but only white women. Where are the Negro actives, the Chicanos, the Asians? You say you're disinterested in the flesh, but I'm not so sure. Either you're assuming psychic potential is distributed disproportionately among whites, or you're deliberately ignoring a wide swath of the human population. Either way, you're limiting yourself."

The men stared at me. Voss' face turned red, while Traynor's mouth worked silently, failing to formulate a response. Stewart looked down at his feet, possibly embarrassed. Even Pike stared at me, his attention finally drawn away from his figments. Octavian simply glowered.

"Dr. Adler *is* Jewish," I said. "I suppose you're not entirely blinkered. Or were you unaware of that?"

Traynor finally spat out a response. "That woman's a Jew?"

"I suppose I knew of her heritage," Octavian said slowly, as if suddenly aware of how badly he'd been slurring. He didn't sound entirely confident of that.

"You sound like you have noble goals, Octavian. Maybe you genuinely do. But you're mired in the same mistakes as the society that spawned you."

The atmosphere in the lounge had cooled precipitously. I decided I didn't want to wait for a response. I left my drink on the table and stood to go. The men stared at me as I left. When I reached the door, I looked over my shoulder.

"You'll never perfect anything operating off imperfect premises."

None of them responded; Voss and Traynor watched me leave. Stewart rubbed his chin, as if thinking hard. Pike turned back to his figments. Octavian simply stared into his glass. I wasn't sure whether he was mulling over my words or silently fuming.

10

Everything hinged on Matthew Traynor's experiment. Traynor intended to harness a team of clairvoyant technicians to project their perception further than any human ever had, at least so far as the Institute could prove. Their target was a specific region of space in trans-Neptunian orbit, where the Apollonian Society's records indicated an irregular planetoid lurked.

The project depended on a machine that Traynor had dubbed the Argos Device. I didn't know at the time of the experiment how it worked, but he claimed it would extend a skilled psychic's range. By networking other talents into an array, it would operate on a similar principle to interferometry in radio telescopes. I took his word on that, although psychic emanations are nothing at all like radio waves.

This was the root of the intense competition among his technicians. The one with the highest synchronization rating would take point during the grand experiment and thus reap the lion's share of the glory, apparently. December 14th marked the first of two large-scale operational tests. The three prime candidates would take position in the Argos Device for the first time, trying to yoke all eight other technicians into an array.

It's still funny to me, and also sad, that of the three prime candidates, the one most likely to be selected also cared least about the competition, except insofar as he enjoyed needling Harold and his lackey Richard. At the time I felt that was still a worthy enough motivation until it drove them to do what they did. That's not Norman's fault. I do not blame him for Harold and Richards' actions, or Dr. West's.

Things wouldn't have gone differently if Norman had stepped aside, but antagonizing people like Harold Bates and Richard Seyton rarely has a good outcome.

The afternoon of the first op test, my friends reported early to the laboratory chamber, owing entirely to Irene's efforts. Unlike the lab they'd used for the run up to this experiment, this chamber was underground, on the third sub-level, where the Institute kept its most dangerous experiments. As the others filtered in, the trio hung together by the stairs to the lab's observation chamber.

I wasn't present, of course. Most of this, I observed some years later, trying to piece together how everything had unraveled. Piecing together the Institute's downfall became… not quite an obsession, but certainly more than a hobby. I felt responsible—still do—even though the survivors have insisted there was nothing more I could have done.

Perhaps if I'd spent a little less time in Ravenna's company, I would have been paying better attention. If I hadn't known better—if I thought for a moment Octavian would have considered the possibility—I would think the Institute had maneuvered her in front of me to serve as a distraction. I certainly found her to be one. I spent hours in her company, chatting about this and that—film, theater, arts. Things she'd experienced and I hadn't yet.

I try not to be too hard on my younger self. What queer teenage girl wouldn't have been captivated by an attractive older woman? One who bathed her in attention?

Looking back to find everything I'd missed was difficult. The disaster has its own terrible gravity, yet it threw up a tremendous amount of psychic turbulence. Turning my gaze *back* to this point, I can't help but see the final tragic moments. Looking to the days and weeks around it is far more difficult, all thanks to Traynor's bizarre invention.

The Argos Device took pride of place in the chamber's center, a twelve-foot-long capsule covered in ceramic plates. It was mounted on a single-axis gimbal and a rotating platform. The eight synchronization stations were arranged around the square chamber in two cross shapes, the inner offset at forty-five degrees from the outer. The cardinal points, reserved for the technicians with the next four highest sync ratings, were set twenty feet from the device. The ordinal points, set ten feet back, would hold the rest of the team. I believe the idea was balance—the best technicians would work to extend the array's power while the others would help shore it up. Irene's sync rating guaranteed her a cardinal position, while even with her improvements Lorraine was almost certainly going to have an ordinal seat.

The subsidiary stations were surprisingly simple. Had he waited a few years, Traynor would have upgraded to isolation tanks. Instead, he relied on adjustable hospital beds. Retractable hoods of brass piping and black canvas had been installed at the heads, where they could be lowered to seclude the technicians. Small speakers hung inside the hoods; they were tied to an intercom system operated from the chamber's observation room. Traynor would be able to issue instructions through them, but their main purpose was to play radio static in carefully selected frequencies. Ideally, the set-up would block out most outside sensation, helping the technicians to focus the totality of their psychic talents on the designated psycho-astronomy sequence.

The project's mechanical complexity was embodied in the Argos Device itself, although I couldn't describe most of it. Beneath the plating, six rods of lapis lazuli ran most of the capsule's length. Even looking back, I can't identify much more of its internal mechanisms. Something about its composition produces a great deal of psychic interference. By accident or design, I don't know. I do know that the four large tanks surrounding it contained a thick, pale green fluid with tantalizing organic traces. That fluid would fill the capsule once the pilot was seated, necessitating a watertight seal. The pilot would be completely isolated, relying on a row of indicator lights and their ability to memorize the complex psycho-astronomy sequences.

I had pointed out more than once that a telepathic network would be supremely helpful, but to no avail. Traynor might have been willing to lift ideas from Dr. Stewart, but he had no desire to collaborate with him. Nor to invite my assistance, for that matter. In Stewart's case, he claimed that the telepathy program was not yet far enough along to be of use and didn't want to delay his own experiment until Stewart could catch up. In my case, he insisted the psychic gravity of my presence would overwhelm the clairvoyant array. As much as I hated to admit it, he was probably correct about Stewart's team. I felt his argument against my assistance was more spurious. I couldn't prove it, but I suspected he thought my abilities undermined his efforts. Harold and Richard weren't the only ones afflicted by jealousy.

"Are you nervous about the test?" Lorraine asked.

Norman leaned against the railing, shrugging his thin shoulders. "Should be a breeze, man. Haven't had any problems so far."

Irene favored him with a tight smile. Despite her indignation at being passed over for advancement, she was genuinely proud of our friend. "I expect you'll blow the others out of the water."

"We'll see." Norman made a dismissive wave of his hand. "You're my pals. Of course we sync up. Who knows how things will shake out today?"

"For once, the dope head has a point," Harold said loudly as he and his dormmates walked in. "Do you really think a freak like you is capable of connecting with the rest of us?"

"We're all freaks here, man," Norman said amiably.

"You don't think the squares go stargazing in their dreams, do you, Harry?" Irene said with a sly smile.

"*You* might be freaks." Richard pulled his narrow face into a sneer. "Some of us are just superior."

"Aw, Ricky." Irene pushed out her lip in a mock pout. "Is it 'cause I turned you down?"

"Twelve times?" Lorraine added helpfully.

"Actually, it's thirteen now. He tried getting me to go with him to the Del Sombra autumn formal last month."

"Del Sombra? We don't go there."

"That's what I said. Also that I think he's repulsive."

"He keeps pestering me for dates too!" Patricia called from across the room. "By the way, Richie, the answer's still 'no'."

"Patty's looking for a man, not a weasel," Irene said. "Sorry, darlin'."

"If we could leave our personal lives outside the laboratory, Miss Phillips?" Traynor said as he finally entered the laboratory with a quartet of myrmidons. "I'd prefer to focus on scientific discovery, not canoodling."

"I assure you, Doctor, *no one* is focused on canoodling with Richard," Irene said.

Laughter rippled through the room, touching everyone but the myrmidons. And Richard, of course. Even the doctor had to suppress a chuckle. Richard folded his arms across his chest and fumed, glaring at everyone. He looked to Howard for support, but his hero simply shrugged at him. Richard's face fell, unnoticed as Traynor waved his hand for silence.

"Now that you've gotten it out of your systems, we'll commence today's session. Testing will consist of two rounds, rotating between the three noetic specialists in ten-minute intervals."

Harold smirked, stepping forward and striking what he must have thought was a heroic pose. He flexed his arms, showing off his new Cerulean Blue suit. Irene put a hand to her hip and rolled her eyes at him, unabashedly disdainful.

"My sync rating has been higher than his for weeks." Her tone was mild, her voice just loud enough for everyone to hear.

"As I've warned you before, Miss Phillips, I *will not* have my methods questioned." Traynor's voice was sharp, like a whip crack. "The project follows these lines for a *reason*. Perhaps you'll understand once I publish. *After* our observations produce results."

Irene didn't back down entirely, but she shifted uncomfortably at the rebuke. Richard smirked at her. She rolled her eyes and flashed him a rude gesture after Traynor turned to his clipboard.

"Speaking of," Traynor continued as if he hadn't publicly dressed down one of his best technicians, "I think we've wasted enough time today. Simpson, we'll start with you, followed by Bates and Rogers. For Simpson's first test, configure the array as follows…"

The doctor rattled off their station assignments, and the technicians took their places. As expected, Irene and Norman were given cardinal positions, Lorraine an ordinal. The myrmidons rotated among them, helping the technicians settle in. Each put on a webbed cap fitted with electrodes and sporting a flat quartz disc across the band. The electrodes would allow Traynor to monitor their brain activity, while the disc would amplify their psychic emanations.

With the benefit of hindsight, I wish I'd been more concerned about Traynor's methods. Compared to the Dowling Experiment, it appeared to be safe; they weren't deliberately bringing anything to Earth, they weren't doing it in an inhabited area. Every step was being rigorously tested before they moved on, so far as I could tell. And yet, there was the Argos Device, thrumming mysteriously in the center of the chamber.

We should have known better. *I* should have known better.

While the other technicians strapped in, Eddie followed Traynor's direction to a curtained-off alcove in one corner of the lab. Three new jumpsuits made of a strange, shiny material awaited the specs. Something about their makeup would help them synchronize with the Device, or possibly just make them easier to clean afterward. The suits were *very* slick. Eddie changed suits, then affixed a pump to the valve over his heart to vacuum out the air until it was skin-tight.

That made it difficult to move, but assistance was on-hand. When the secondary technicians were strapped in, two myrmidons helped Eddie into the Argos Device. The pilot's seat was fitted with straps at the chest, thighs and calves to keep him in place as the capsule rotated. His arms would remain free in a surprising display of sense; I wasn't used to mad science with an eye toward safety measures. An aqualung was affixed above his head; one myrmidon helped Eddie fit the mouthpiece and webbed hood. After confirming he was breathing well, the myrmidons sealed the capsule. They opened the valves to the tanks, and the pale green fluid slowly filled the capsule's interior.

From the observation room, Traynor watched the myrmidons' progress with unmistakable excitement. When his indicators told him the capsule was full, he licked his lips and switched on the observation room's recorder. Reels of magnetic tape spun, ready to catch every word he uttered for posterity. He activated the lab's general address circuit and leaned into the microphone until his lips nearly touched it.

"Commencing Argos Device Operational Test One, round one. Test pilot, Edward Simpson. Assistants, clear the chamber."

The myrmidons fell into line and marched up the stairs to the observation chamber. Traynor directed them to their positions monitoring the many readouts. When they were in place, he took a deep breath and turned to the clock hanging above the plate glass window. He switched the intercom to the secondary technicians' circuit.

"On my mark, commence sixty-second countdown. At zero, all secondary technicians will conduct Relay Sequence Alpha."

The clock's second hand slowly ticked forward, inexorably approaching the twelve. Beads of sweat formed on Traynor's forehead. One slid down his brow, around his nose, down his face to the corner of his mouth. He ignored it. He cared only about the seconds.

The hand reached the twelve. Traynor flipped three switches and barked into the microphone.

"Mark!"

The first light in the capsule burned a bright amber. Radio static filled the secondary technicians' ears. As one, they began counting down from sixty.

11

We should have known better. *I* should have known better. After years of dealing with intransigence within the Bureau, after suffering Lucas Dowling's arrogance, I should have anticipated that Dr. West would seek revenge. I couldn't predict that this specific humiliation by the Director would be his final straw, but I should have at least expected a reprisal.

Up to the critical moment, following West's movements in the past is much easier than those of Traynor's technicians. His presence radiates a particular sliminess, a mixture of his odious personality and the aftershocks of his heinous actions. When I look past the disaster's event horizon, I always find him first. Much to my disgust.

Jeffrey West's lab was too small for the equipment he required, making the space cramped and hard to navigate. It was the size of a standard high school classroom, but most of the space was taken up by the counters and the half-dozen cultivation tanks. Each tank was large enough to accommodate a man-sized object, and they usually did. Skeletal frameworks floated within the thick orange nutrient broth, bubbling merrily between ultraviolet lights as complex chemical codes directed tissues to grow around the polymer tubing. The precise method by which DNA passed on genetic information had only just been postulated, but West's techniques had already surpassed that discovery. Unlike Rosalind Frank, Francis Crick, and James Watson, Jeffrey West had no intention of publishing his discovery. The exotic biofluid it depended on inhibited peer review.

"And yet, no one here appreciates my work," he said aloud.

He stood by Gestation Tank 2, the one nearest the door. A half-completed myrmidon floated within. Rapidly developing musculature covered ninety-five percent of its polymer skeleton. Pale skin grew across its back, neck, and shoulders, where the musculature was complete. Its abdominal cavity lay open, exposing partially grown organs. Tubing ran through the open cavity—the myrmidon's development had reached the point where it needed nutrients delivered and waste removed. Most recently, West and Mark had installed the necessary tubing for the myrmidon's thick circulatory fluid. A pump hung from the ceiling, driving the fluid in place of its heart, which wasn't scheduled to be kickstarted for another week. The myrmidon stared blankly up at the ceiling, eyes wide open. It had, as yet, no brain activity. That was a mercy.

West might have thought otherwise. He stared down into the myrmidon's colorless eyes, perhaps mourning the lack of recognition.

"Look at you," he said softly. "Perfect. Or at least as close to perfection as I can make you with these resources. With these hands."

He reached a thick-gloved hand into the blood-warm bath and tenderly stroked the artificial being's exposed cheek.

"We should be entering mass production." He looked over the other tanks, all in the same stage of development, and scowled. "Instead, I have six. Barely half the replacements for your siblings lost at the hospital. With the budget I'm allotted, I won't be able to grow another batch until sometime next year!"

The Institute had sent twenty-two myrmidons into St. Audaeus Hospital on Hallowe'en night to apprehend us. Only seven came back out. I had destroyed the rest to cover my friends' escape.

They hadn't screamed. Even as I tore them apart, they hadn't screamed.

Dr. West turned to the subject in Tank 2. It floated silently, face frozen.

Above it, machinery hissed as it pumped oxygen into brand-new lungs. He slammed his fist against the tank's rim. The nutrient bath rippled. The creature within did not respond, but across the room, Mark turned, his brow furrowed in concern.

"Sir?" Mark was used to his mentor ranting, but striking the equipment was cause for alarm.

"It's nothing, Mark." West straightened, smoothing out the front of his jumpsuit with his dry hand. "Merely woolgathering."

He stripped off his rubber gloves and threw them on the counter. Mark pursed his lips but didn't say anything.

"How fare the specimens today?" West came up behind Mark, looking over his shoulder at the double row of glass capsules hanging from the short wall. The first two batches of cultivated Watcher matter were much the same as before, but the third was thriving. Mark gestured to them proudly.

"Batch 13 has exceeded our expectations by leaps and bounds. You'll recall I implanted these cultures a week ago. This batch has already doubled in size."

"That's a two hundred percent increase in growth rate from Batch 12!" West clapped Mark on the shoulder. "Give or take. Well done, my boy."

"Thank you, sir." Mark grimaced at the familiarity but endured it.

"We need more. Dump Batch 11. Sterilize the tanks. Use the same nutrient mix as Batch 13 and culture another batch." He stroked his chin thoughtfully. "I'm considering purging the twelfth batch as well, or at least putting the specimens in storage. Is there any more to learn from this batch? We could use the tanks."

"But my necrosis observations…"

West paused to consider it, then relented. "We have a spare tank. You may keep one specimen in your personal workspace."

"Thank you, sir."

West beamed. "I can be indulgent when your efforts warrant it."

"Does this mean we're ready for implantation?" Mark waved his arm, encompassing the six cultivation tanks. "This batch was earmarked as replacements, and regardless, they've passed the Eastman Stabilization

Threshold. We can't successfully implant them. I thought you said we weren't going to get the budget to grow another batch this quarter?"

"Let me worry about allocations, Mark." West patted the younger man's arm patronizingly. "You just worry about growing me enough materials."

Mark turned away to hide his sour expression. West took no notice. He whistled as he went to his small private lab, where he kept his most secret experiments.

The main lab was scrupulously clean, with well-organized storage—Mark's efforts. In contrast, West's private lab looked as if a storm had blown through it. Random pieces of equipment were strewn across every available space, mixed with the detritus of abandoned experiments. A large square table took up the center of the space, while a metal desk stood against one corner. A complex hydroponic apparatus covered the desk. Bulbous specimen tanks, each roughly liter sized, hung on chains from the ceiling. Electrical cables and nutrient feed lines spiraled down the chains, making the space look like a wild vineyard of rubber grapevines.

"The Director thinks I'm a fool," West said, seemingly to thin air. "My so-called colleagues think the same, hoping to curry favor. The only person who believes in my work is a single sour-faced would-be aristocrat with mediocre psychic potential."

A large glass canister sat on the table. It was filled with more weird liquid and covered by a metal lid. A round-ish object floated within the murky fluid. West placed his bare palm against the lid.

"Only him… and you."

He grabbed the cylinder and unscrewed the lid. A foul smell wafted up from the open container, at once bitter and honey-sweet. West reached his bare hand into the cylinder and fished out its contents. It was a head, hairless and misshapen, bulging at odd points and sunken in others. Despite its incongruous shape, it was otherwise recognizable as the head of a myrmidon, albeit one marked by age lines. Small incisions covered its skin, unhealed but bloodless. The stump was secured by a metal cap. Its colorless eyes rolled independently of one another, taking in their surroundings and West's face.

"You understand me." West stroked his thumb against the head's withered cheek. "You recognize what's at stake."

West held the head high, turning it back and forth, admiring its contours, its rough complexion. Its mouth moved, but its lips didn't form intelligible words, at least not in a language I understood. Nor did it make a sound, with its windpipe sealed.

"A hundred thousand years of human evolution," West said, "and what do we have to show for it? Heightened endurance? Hyperactive scar tissue? The thumb? All useful, yes, but traits for mastering *this* world. Hardly of any use on our own moon, let alone the next world over. To say nothing about the more exotic environments the universe offers! All novel, all *fantastically* hostile to the human animal.

"That short-sighted fool Traynor thinks he's going to map a new world. What of it? Another world we can't survive? What good is that?"

West tucked the head in the crook of his arm as if he was cradling an infant. He began a slow circuit of the room, pontificating as he went. As he spoke, he stabbed the air with one outstretched finger whenever he thought he'd made a salient point.

"Now, I know what you're going to say. What about tools? Yes, you are correct. Tools *have* aided us, up to a *point*. Man has no claws, so he invents knives. Man cannot outrun a deer or a cheetah, so he domesticates the horse and invents the automobile. Eyes weaken so he grinds lenses, limbs break so he carves crutches.

"What the Director fails to understand is that tools are also a *weakness*. Knives *dull*. Horses *die*. Vehicles run out of *fuel*. The more complicated a tool is, the more points of failure it has. Which would you rather have for underwater exploration—a complex aqualung with a finite oxygen supply or *gills?*"

West held out the head, watching it as if waiting for an answer. They stared at each other for a long moment. Then he nodded enthusiastically.

"Gills, of course! I knew you would understand!"

They had reached the hydroponics table. A dozen different plants grew in shallow trays filled with bright orange fluid. None were likely to be found in a common garden. One boasted lavender fronds like a fern surrounding a nodule of thorny wood. Another grew in long stems covered in thin spines, ending in bulbous red tips. One flowered under an infrared lamp, its glowing bell-shaped blossoms belching out a pale dust full of spores.

Only one plant looked remotely terrestrial. Bland in comparison to the others, it was a simple flowering plant. Its pale green stems sported dagger-like leaflets and a deep red bowl-shaped bloom. Aglaophotis. West set the head down on the table and turned it so it could watch him work.

"That said, we mustn't discount the use of tools entirely. Octavian thinks he can reach the stars with only special diets and meditation exercises. Preposterous!"

He snipped three aglaophotis blooms of their stems and set to grinding them with a mortar and pestle.

"He should recall that where there is a method to *enhance*, there is also a means to *degrade*."

After a few minutes, West had ground the petals into a sticky red paste. He scraped the pungent goo into a flask of distilled water, stirring it until it completely dissolved. When he was satisfied with the fluid's consistency, he poured the thick red fluid into four small vials, capping each with a rubber stopper. He slipped the vials into his breast pocket and smirked. Then, his task complete, he picked up the head and carried it to its cylinder.

"No, no, we can't trust this task to Mark. His perspective is unclear, his personal loyalties divided. It's the dormitory system, you see. It confuses the technicians. Mark may not like his roommates, but he identifies with them. He thinks of them as a *team*. He's unlikely to agree with my plan. We'll simply have to handle this ourselves."

West held the head in both hands and lifted it up, turning it to face him.

"Don't worry," he said softly. "You know I can be discreet."

He pulled the head to him, pressing its lips against his. He closed his eyes and pushed its lips apart with his own, tenderly sliding his tongue into its mouth. He whimpered slightly. When he broke the kiss, a thin line of orange fluid ran between them. He gently dabbed at their lips with a handkerchief, first the head's, then his own.

He smiled down at the head, at once tender and sad. Then he gently placed it in its jar and screwed the lid shut. He folded the handkerchief and placed it on the table next to the canister. He patted the lid once, then left his private room.

In the main lab, Mark was still scrubbing out the specimen tanks in the deep sink. He looked up when West closed the door.

"I have an errand to run," West said. "Finish cleaning and lock up when you're done."

"Of course, doctor."

West patted his breast pocket. He left the lab, whistling.

12

"Like, that gunk is going to be in my hair for days," Norman said.

"Maybe you can finally do something stylish with it," Irene said, her voice light.

"Or just get a proper haircut already," Harold grumbled behind them.

"Oh, go soak your head, Harry." Lorraine tossed her pretty curls at him. "Just 'cause Norman beat you. *Again.*"

With the first op test concluded, the technicians filed out of the laboratory, leaving the quartet of myrmidons to clean up. The test had been a success, at least as far as my friends were concerned. As Lorraine boasted, Norman had once again posted the highest sync rating—significantly below his average, but that was to be expected under the circumstances. Traynor had personally congratulated him after the second round, once Norman had thoroughly cleaned off his hands.

"This doesn't count, you know," Richard said, doggedly sticking up for his hero. "The doc said it himself. The *real* test is on Friday!"

"And I'm sure when Norman posts the highest numbers then, the *real* test will be the big observation," Irene said.

"And then the *real* test will be the repeat experiments," Lorraine added.

"Ten years from now, Doctor Traynor will publish all this in a paper. 'The Realest Test'." Irene gestured dramatically. "Harold's a footnote. Richie's not even in it."

Richard sputtered and fumed, like a record needle skipping over a scratch. He grabbed Harold's sleeve, trying to give and get support at the same time. Harold said something foul and unkind and slapped Richard's hand away.

"Get away from me, you pathetic little worm," he snarled.

Harold shoved his way through the technicians ahead of him, ignoring their protests as he stalked down the hallway, a well-bred thundercloud spreading posh gloom in his wake. The others turned to stare at Richard. He hunched over himself, hands jammed into his pockets. His cheek twitched as he fought back tears. Lorraine looked at him with warm eyes full of pity, then looked to Norman and Irene. They both shrugged, Norman in disinterest, Irene with active distaste. Those bridges had been well and truly burned. Lorraine gave them an exasperated look, then turned to Richard. For a moment, he almost reached out to her. Then he twisted his face into an ugly sneer.

"To Hell with all of you," he spat.

He stalked off in the opposite direction, pushing his way past his other partner. George glared at him in indignation, but didn't bother trying to catch up or demand an explanation. He was even more fed up with Richard's attitude than anyone else on the team. Instead of following, he shook his head and joined the others, attempting amiable conversation.

Richard stormed through the sub-basement, not really caring where he was going. He stared at the tile in front of his feet, mumbling imprecations under his breath. His shoulders hunched up to his ears, his lip quivered, and tears wet his eyes. He hovered on the verge of self-awareness. His mind-state—always unpleasant to see—was particularly disordered. He thought of the easy camaraderie between my friends—the laughs and the inside jokes, the way Lorraine and Irene held each other when one of them was sad, the complete comfort Norman felt around them. He thought of how quickly George left when they weren't on shift, how conversation died when he approached, how Harold never spoke to him unless he wanted something. He very nearly admitted to himself that while he held Harold in the highest regard, the other man saw him as little more than hired help. Less, even; a hired man at least got a wage. That was reciprocity, after a fashion. Richard barely rated an acknowledgement.

Everything would have turned out differently for Richard if he'd gotten another fifteen minutes to think things over before running into Dr. West. I'm not saying he would have ended up as a better person. That would have depended on a number of other variables, not least of which was personal drive on his part. Nor would the worst of it have been averted—West was already set on his plan and would have found another patsy—but Richard's life would have been less immediately tragic.

That's not this timeline.

West initially recoiled when Richard blundered into him. Richard bit back his immediate impulse to say something nasty when he recognized West's dark blue jumpsuit. He mumbled something like an apology and tried to step around the doctor, but West recognized opportunity. He put out a hand to stop Richard from leaving, smiling genially.

"Mister Seyton, yes? From Dr. Traynor's team." He held out his other hand in greeting. "Dr. Jeffrey West, esoteric biology."

Richard shook hands reluctantly, staring past the older man's shoulder. He mumbled something that might have been "Pleased to meet you" and could have been "I didn't do nothin'" but was really an extended nasal whine. If West took offense, he gave no sign of it.

"If I may say, Mr. Seyton, you look rather glum. Did Dr. Traynor's operational test not go well today?"

"Oh, it went fine. For *some*," Richard said, suddenly finding his voice.

West smiled slightly, cocking his head to one side. "Oh?"

"It's my pal, Harold. He ain't getting the recognition he deserves. He ought to be top of the heap, but instead, the doc's acting like that deadbeat Rogers is the star."

"Rogers…ah, yes! I know the type. A wastrel! Chronically lazy, congenitally unserious, entirely unprofessional and incapable of standing up straight. It would be a shame if a noetic savant took a shine to such a man."

Richard, who had never seen a chore he wouldn't pawn off on someone else, nodded enthusiastically. West clapped his shoulder and led him down the hall toward the stairs. With his other hand, he idly patted the vials in his breast pocket.

"We certainly can't leave the reputation of this institute in the ill-manicured hands of a 'deadbeat', can we? Why don't you come with me to my office, Seyton, my boy? I may have the answer to your problem."

In spite of the naked contempt in which the Director held him, West still rated his own office. It was a holdover from the Institute's previous administration, when he was held in higher esteem. Octavian simply hadn't come up with a reason to reallocate the space. West barely used it these days, which was obvious from the visible layer of dust on every surface.

"*Some* of us spend more time pursuing science than bland administrative tasks," he said, seeing Richard's disgusted expression. "Still, can't let just anyone in the lab. Official business only, you understand. I'm sure Traynor has stressed the importance of confidentiality, having entrusted you with his own delicate work. Please, take a seat."

Richard, who knew little more about Traynor's methods than a half-dozen rote psycho-astronomy programs, puffed himself up as he sat in the small chair across from West's narrow desk. Seeing this, the doctor suppressed a smile. He unlocked a cabinet on the side wall and drew the four vials from his pocket.

"Essence of aglaophotis." He held up one of the vials for Richard to see and shook it. The red liquid sloshed thickly. "Fascinating substance. When ingested, it suppresses psychic ability."

Richard perked up and tried to hide it, badly. "That a fact?"

"Indeed. A dose of this and any but the strongest psychic talent would be 'dead in the head', as we used to say, for days."

"I wouldn't think there'd be a whole lotta call for that here."

"Oh, you'd be surprised. It does have a few intriguing side effects. Numbing certain deep structures in the brain acts as an effective defense. The subtle spheres have their dangers, from what I understand, and there are those who would use their psychic gifts unscrupulously. Some find having a defense on hand to be useful." He smiled knowingly, tapping his temple. "*Weak minds*, you know."

His smile widened when Richard nodded enthusiastically. They were on the same page, but only West knew they were reading different books. He withdrew a test tube rack from the cabinet, slipping the tubes into the slots.

"Can't leave something like this lying around, of course! Who knows what mischief the wrong hands might get up to?"

West pushed the rack to the rear of the cabinet. He made a show of locking the door, then dropped the keys ostentatiously into the top drawer of his desk. He very pointedly didn't lock it. Then he sat in his much larger chair and clasped his hands together, leaning forward on his elbows with an avuncular smile.

"There, Mister Seyton! Now you have my *undivided* attention. What is it that troubles you?"

Richard Seyton was loyal, in his own way. To Harold Bates, of course, but also to Dr. Traynor. He was genuinely grateful for the opportunity Traynor had given him to be part of a large endeavor, a great discovery. The problem with his brand of loyalty was that it was easy to make him feel small. Harold did it often, and deliberately, although Richard hadn't yet realized that. Traynor did it as well, although I think less intentionally. He simply regarded Richard as having a minimal role in his project—like Lorraine or Albert— and treated him as such. Traynor only had time for his three specs. Everyone else was just the help.

Meanwhile, here was Jeffrey West, a noetic savant and, as far as Richard knew, of equal standing with Matthew Traynor. A respectable older man, paying attention to Richard's concerns. For all that he adopted the image of the modern silver screen rebel, he desperately sought the approval of men like West. It would have been so much better if he'd found more worthy models, or better, had learned to stand on his own two feet.

"Well, it's like I was saying, Doc." He spread his hands wide, adopting the stance of one mystified by the world's injustice. "Doc Traynor's project hinges on one guy. It *oughta* be my buddy Harold. You know Harold? Harold Bates?"

"Mister Bates? I do indeed." West stroked his chin thoughtfully, eyes on Richard. "A solid man. Honest face. From a good family. Bred for leadership, you might say."

"Yeah, exactly!"

"And now, Dr. Traynor wants to pass him over for that 'deadbeat', Norman Rogers." West shook his head sorrowfully. "What a shame. Such a lapse in judgement is unlike him."

"Yeah... I had a thought about that, actually."

"Do tell?"

"You know that new consultant, Miss Temple?"

"I have had the pleasure of meeting her," West said carefully.

"Well, Rogers is real friendly with her. I keep thinking, maybe that's why the doc's acting like he's hot stuff. He wants to get on Miss Temple's good side."

West nodded sagely. "Ah, office politics. The bane of many a scientific endeavor. I could tell you stories... well, another time, perhaps." He steepled his fingers, resting his lips against his index fingers. "I could speak to Dr. Traynor. Try to help him see how his judgement has been compromised."

"I don't know about that. The doc doesn't seem like the type to appreciate other people messin' around with his work." Realizing too late what he'd said, Richard's eyes went wide. He held out his hands in supplication. "Not that I'm sayin' you're trying to mess it up!"

"Of course not," West said gracefully. "To tell the truth, I'm much the same. I'd want good reason for my colleagues to be dabbling in my work."

"I mean, if it's gonna mess everything up, that's gotta be a good reason," Richard mumbled. "There hasta be some way to make Doc Traynor see

Rogers ain't up to snuff."

He tried not to sneak a glance at the cabinet to his left. West hid a smirk behind his hands. He carefully looked the other way, letting Richard come up with the plan on his own.

"I'm sure you can come up with a way, Mr. Seyton. In the meantime—"

Before he could finish his sentence, there was a knock at the door. West looked up and apologized to Richard before calling for the newcomer to enter. Mark Pressler opened the door and poked his head around it, a stack of multicolored folders tucked under one arm.

"Doctor West? You wanted to discuss Phase Five?"

"Blast, is it that time?" West made a show of glancing at his timepiece, an ornate brass pocket watch emblazoned with the Institute's seal. "I'm very sorry, Mister Seyton, but I'm afraid science calls."

"No worries, Doc," Richard said, rising to his feet. "I think I got what I needed."

Richard was *not* sneaky. He was untrustworthy, of course. He had a stunted and selfish sense of ethics, yes. A combination of his bearing, demeanor, and appearance reminded people of a weasel, absolutely. None of that made him *sneaky*. In fact, he was fairly oafish, obvious in his intentions and unable to hide his emotions.

All of that, in a way, added up to a peculiar form of camouflage. Everyone expected him to do *something* malicious. They just never knew what.

The Institute didn't have an internal curfew. Actives and specs were allowed to go into town on Fridays and Saturdays, provided they returned to the compound by seven p.m., but in the halls there were no lights out. It was simply understood that anyone too sleepy to work in the morning would be quietly but firmly disciplined. Accordingly, there was usually someone in the lounges and other common rooms well into the night, and sometimes in the early morning.

That evening, George and two other dormmates, Oscar Redmond and

Cal Porter, stayed up late playing cards. Richard lay in his bed, eyes screwed shut so he wouldn't have to stare at the boring ceiling, gritting his teeth as he listened to other people having fun. He fumed because they were inconveniencing him. He fumed because they hadn't asked him to play. He fumed because all he really had was his resentment and he played with it like a child with a beloved stuffed bear.

Two weeks ago, the members of my dorm had gathered in the game room to watch Rob and Paul play pool. After a while, Harold, George, and Richard sauntered into the room. Richard suggested he and Harold challenge us to a game. Harold sneered at him and told Richard not to be stupid. Then he and George started playing darts.

Richard sat and watched them for a couple of rounds, sneaking glances at the eight of us whenever someone laughed or cheered. Finally, it got to be too much. He jumped to his feet and stalked across the room. Before anyone could say anything, he loudly challenged Norman to a game of pool.

The fact of the matter was, neither of them were very good at it. The difference was, Norman didn't care. He scratched. He missed the cue ball. He sank one of Richard's balls. Each time he made a mistake, he laughed it off, and we laughed along with him. Richard fumed and swore, to the point that Paul threatened to "sock him one" if he didn't stop using that sort of language around the gals.

(He'd never heard the way Irene spoke when she got angry. As bad as my Luci, that one.)

Richard didn't get any satisfaction out of his victory. He didn't really win; with four balls to go, Norman "sank" the eight ball out of order. As an "aww" went around the table, Norman shrugged and said that was how the cookie crumbled. Rob clapped Richard on the shoulder, Mark congratulated him, and Norman offered his hand. Richard rebuffed all of them before looking at Harold for approval.

He and George had already left the room.

I don't suppose there was any way things could have gone differently after all. West had picked his pigeon well, as Luci would say. Given ample time to do nothing but think, most people would have found a reason to talk themselves out of Richard's plan. He just made himself more resentful, and thus, more committed.

A particularly loud laugh drifted through the wall, and Richard's eyes snapped open. He'd had enough of this. He jumped off his bed and threw his door open, ready to make a foolish decision.

George and the others looked up. George waved, in high spirits.

"Richie! Didn't know you were still up." He gestured to a nearby chair. "Deal you in?"

"It's better with four," Cal said.

"Not in the mood," Richard muttered. He stomped toward the lounge door. "Maybe keep it down? It's late."

"Sorry, pal. No one else said anything," Oscar said.

George peered at Richard's back. "Where are you going?"

Richard yanked the door open. "None of your damn business."

The other men rolled their eyes. Cal made a rude and needlessly biological gesture at Richard's back, and they all laughed. Richard's face screwed up, tears stinging at the corners of his eyes. As he closed the door, he heard Oscar ask whether they could trade him to another dorm.

"I'll show them," he muttered, stomping away.

This late at night, the halls were empty. The prots on custodial duty had made their last rounds hours ago. Even the late-working candle-burners had called it a night, at least on the third floor. A few myrmidons stood guard duty, but all in the sub-basements. Nothing sensitive was kept aboveground. Richard should have remembered that, but as I said, the doctor had picked his pigeon well. A more clever person would have found it suspicious that there were no barriers between him and a cabinet of dangerous chemicals. Not even a door lock. Luci would have recognized the trap immediately. Richard chalked it up to someone else's foolishness.

He was in and out of West's office in a matter of minutes, a vial of red stuff in his pocket. It had briefly occurred to him that his theft might be noticed, but he dismissed the concern. West hadn't even bothered to lock up.

He probably couldn't be bothered to count his stock, either.

Yes, it was arrogance. It's a common trait in the men who fill the conspiracy. They rarely realize that they're not as smart as they think.

Somehow, it's never them who pay the price.

13

Some rogues must surely hesitate before stabbing another person in the back. They might grapple with their consciences, ask themselves what they truly value, and whether their gain was truly worth, say, drugging another person who'd never done them an injury. Not so Richard Seyton. Once he'd taken the bait Dr. West had dangled in front of him, he was committed. His only cause for delay was the necessity of timing; there was no sense administering the drug prior to the day of the second op test.

Traynor's team spent almost every waking hour up to noon of the seventeenth running synchronization drills. The goal for the week was less to measure their sync ratings than to ensure they had the relevant sequences thoroughly memorized. This test was for all the marbles, as they say, and Traynor didn't want anyone fumbling their lines at the dress rehearsal.

At lunch, Richard made an excuse to delay joining his team at the cafeteria. He didn't have to try very hard; Harold really didn't care. While his hero and George headed for lunch, Richard slipped back to their dorm. He expected it to be empty—there was no rule against technicians hanging out in the dorms during work hours, but it was frowned upon—and thus was surprised to see two of his other dormmates sitting in the common room.

His heart sank when he realized who they were. Timothy Binks and James Cole, two other members of Stewart's telepathy project.

Timothy and James, who had thus far strenuously avoided any attempts at shortening their names, looked up when Richard entered. Their faces went blank when they recognized him. Then they put on sincere smiles, in that they sincerely didn't want Richard throwing another tantrum over feeling disrespected.

"Richie!" Timothy said with cloying false charm. "Care to join us? We've figured out a hep game."

"Crosswords!" James held up a pad. The top sheet was half-filled. "Except you don't have the clues."

"One of us does. Whoever does the crossword has to read the clues in the other fella's head."

"Wanna try?" James offered Richard the box with the torn-out clue sheets. "Timothy and I can take turns nabbing clues."

Richard's face went pale. "I'm not letting either of you root around in my head."

James' eyes went wide. He held up his hands. "All right, Richie. Don't flip your lid."

"And my name is Richard. Not Richie."

He stormed into his room and slammed the door behind him. For a moment, he leaned against it, teeth bared, fists jammed against his temples. Tears stung the corners of his eyes. He could hear Timothy and James snickering through the door. About him, of course. Who else would it be? Who else would it ever be?

Richard dragged his hand across his eyes, dashing away the tears. He sucked in a ragged breath, telling himself it was dust. The blasted prots hadn't been cleaning well enough lately. At least that meant they hadn't found his prize.

He yanked out his dresser's bottom drawer and felt through the piles of socks and underwear until his hand closed around a glass vial. He held it up between thumb and forefinger, watching how the aglaophotis extract gleamed red and wet in the light. Snapping his fist closed, he stuffed the vial into his leg pocket. Then he stormed out of the dorm. Timothy and James sat silently as he stalked out. They broke into laughter again as the door closed behind him.

The cafeteria was an automat—a large circular space whose curving walls sported gleaming cabinets dispensing food to the Institute's one hundred junior members. Glass doors across the machines' faces displayed compartments with hot entrees, steaming sides, cool sandwiches, and an assortment of pies and gelatin desserts. Three cabinets at the end offered fresh-drip drinks, selected by turn-knob.

In a stroke of scoundrel's luck, Norman had just finished collecting his lunch selections as Richard entered the cafeteria. The weasel didn't waste any time. He walked right up to Norman, looked him dead in the eye, and shoulder-checked him as he walked past. Norman stumbled to the side, his tray tipping over. He grabbed his entrée before it slid off, but his glass of tea flopped over his arm and went clattering across the floor with his mashed potatoes, greens, and tableware. The spill spread around Norman's feet in a messy splatter. Richard paid him no heed, bellying up to the sandwich machine as if an uproar hadn't erupted behind him.

Some scams can only be pulled off when everyone already knows you're, if you'll pardon the expression, an absolute dick.

As one, my dormmates leapt to their feet, shouting. Norman spluttered, demanding an explanation and trying to grapple with actually being angry. The technicians at the other tables stared in a mix of surprise and disgust. George looked absolutely mortified, and even Harold had the grace to look disgusted.

"Come on, Richie," he said. "That's uncouth."

Patricia grabbed Irene's shoulder to stop her from launching herself over the table. She only slowed Irene a little. She shouted, "You better help clean that!", following it up with a vulgar yet accurate description of his character.

"At least get him a fresh glass, you turkey!" Lorraine said.

Richard glanced briefly over his shoulder, trying to scoff. Instead, he found himself looking directly into Irene Phillips' furious eyes. Irene was a few inches shorter than him, but with Richard's habitual slouch, their eyes were at level. People who didn't know her well tended to dismiss Irene as pretty but bookish, a quiet young woman who needed to be drawn out of herself. More than one arrogant man had elected himself as the person to do that, only to be surprised by the storm inside her. Irene Phillips possessed a furious inner strength, and the Institute had only helped her to nurture it.

In spite of its disproportionately masculine composition, the Institute frowned on psychic conflict, especially in common spaces. It was too dangerous, especially when those rare talents with highly energetic gifts manifested. Everyone in the cafeteria felt it when psychic power began emanating from Irene, focused on Richard Seyton. The glass panels behind him rattled in their compartments. The other actives looked at one another fearfully, wondering who would summon the myrmidons.

Irene didn't care who was watching. "You march yourself over to the beverage cabinet and get Norman a fresh drink."

That had been Richard's entire plan, of course. Nonetheless, he wasn't the sort to do as he was told, especially not by a woman. His odiousness nearly scuttled his entire plan, which would have been a poetic sort of irony. Unfortunately, Irene was entirely too intimidating. His ugly retort died in his weasely throat. A very real flush filled his cheeks. He ducked his head and stomped across the room to the beverage cabinet. Every eye in the room followed him.

Is it ironic that Richard's part in this was facilitated entirely by his repulsive personality? That if at any point he'd been a better person, this wouldn't have happened, at least not this way? Or is it to be expected?

Most of the cafeteria stopped watching after Richard poured a new glass of tea, satisfied that justice had been done. Irene and Lorraine kept their eyes on him the entire time, but he put his back to them particularly. He grabbed a random selection of sweetener packets from a nearby stand. Then, with a deftness that made him a terror of Regina's bars, he emptied the vial into his tea. He stirred it until the red taint disappeared into the brown liquid. He carried the glass to Norman's table, slamming it down in front of him and sloshing some onto his hand.

"Here. Happy?"

Norman locked eyes with Richard and took a big gulp of tea. He finished half the glass in one go, Adam's apple bobbing as the other man scowled. He set the glass down and smacked his lips loudly.

"As a clam, daddy-o."

Richard rolled his eyes and turned away. He scowled as he went to the cabinets, grabbing his own food, trying to project an unearned air of affronted injury despite everyone else deliberately ignoring him. When he sat down at his table, he couldn't suppress a smirk.

I can't see everything. That's the first misconception people have when they learn of my abilities. This has been the genesis of innumerable exasperating arguments. Why did I not know about this thing? How could I have missed that? Why wouldn't I tell someone that this was about to happen?

Beyond the obvious answer that, by now, several methods to confound my perception have been developed, is a more simple explanation. I probably wasn't paying attention.

When you walk into a room, you perceive everything that's inside it, but you don't see all of it. Leaving aside that your eyes can only register less than one percent of the electromagnetic spectrum, and believe me, that's a lot to leave aside, your gaze will be drawn to a small number of particularly striking elements. In fact, the space may be designed to draw your attention to specific points. Everything else becomes background information. In fact, it's probably not what's actually there—your brain will fill in some of the details for you based on memory and what you expect to see.

My brain doesn't do that, thankfully. Frankly, I don't know how you can stand it. My point remains: I don't actually see everything all at once. I may benefit from a broad range of perception, but I still have to focus on details. You see a bookcase, but you don't immediately read every title on the spines. I see a cabinet, but I don't immediately catalogue its contents. Like you, I can only focus on so many things at once. Why was Richard able to drug Norman so easily? Because at the time, I was having tea with Ravenna Adler, and she had my full attention.

It's just polite.

I wanted to keep my relationship with Ravenna—with Dr. Adler—as professional as possible. Despite the fact that I wasn't consulting with her work, I wanted to approach her as a colleague rather than a friend. As I kept having to remind myself, she was still part of the conspiracy, albeit in a very secondary capacity. Ravenna was a woman, and a very charming one at that, but so was Maxine Orr. They had chosen to affiliate themselves with the Chambers Foundation; they were helping it pursue its goals. I couldn't forget that.

Despite that, Ravenna had cleverly managed our relationship such that our interactions consisted of almost nothing but socializing. That Friday morning, her message said she wanted to discuss an upcoming staff meeting. Yet, when I arrived at her lab, she'd already set up the tea service with a plate of cookies. She smiled charmingly at my surprise, and a blush warmed my cheeks.

"I thought you wanted to plan strategy for the Monday meeting." I took the seat opposite hers.

"I see no reason we can't refresh ourselves while we do." She offered me the plate of cookies. "Three sugars?"

"Yes, please."

I took a cookie while she poured my tea. It was soft and slightly chocolatey. The first bite was good enough to make me reconsider my position on socializing.

Adler dropped three cubes into my tea and passed the cup to me. She raised her own cup and blew across it. A light curl of steam rose.

"So," she said companionably, "Dr. Traynor hasn't spoken to me in days."

"Oh?"

"And the other day, Dr. Voss asked if we should do something special for Chanukah."

"Oh?" Realization dawned. "Oh."

"His round little face was so earnest, I didn't have the heart to tell him it's not even one of the High Holy Days."

"Dr. Adler…"

"Ravenna."

"Ravenna, I'm so sorry. I didn't mean—"

She held out her palm for me to stop, smiling gently. "I understand. You mean well. Frankly, you made a point those fools needed to hear, not that they're ready to understand it. That being said…"

Ravenna sat her cup down. A shadow crossed her face. Even though I didn't know her well, I could see in her expression a sorrow and loss that I had never felt. A chill ran up my spine as I realized the risk to which I'd so blithely exposed her. Without paying attention to what I was doing, I reached out and covered her hand with mine. She smiled sadly and turned her hand over, clasping my fingers.

"That being said," she continued, finding her voice, "in the future, ask first. I have good reason to be discreet about my heritage."

"If I've done anything to jeopardize your position here…"

"You haven't. Octavian has his faults, but I don't think he's actively antisemitic. I'm not a fool, I know this organization's history. I wouldn't have been accepted by the previous administration, and I certainly wouldn't have been invited to join its predecessor, for multiple reasons. Still, Octavian is serious about the changes he's made, fumbling half-measures that they are. He genuinely believes this is the start of a 'post-religion' society. My position is secure, for the moment."

She raised her cup to her lips and smiled, livelier now. "Provided my work progresses as it should, of course."

I raised my cup to her. "Here's to that."

Norman leaned back in the pilot's chair as the pale green synaptic fluid filled the capsule. He made himself take slow, easy breaths, trying to trust the aqualung to do its job. This part had come as a surprise during the first op test. The doc really should have let them practice with it beforehand. That explained why Eddie's numbers had been so low. He probably wouldn't be taking up diving as a hobby after this. Neither would Norman, if he was being honest.

The synaptic fluid reached his chin and continued up over his face, over the aqualung's mouthpiece, over his plugged nose, past his eyes and over his hooded hairline. This was a test of Norman's carefully practiced calm. He kept his eyes screwed shut until the fluid completely covered his head. He'd keep them shut for the entire experiment if he could. Norman didn't care what Traynor said, he didn't believe this weird goo was entirely eye safe. It wasn't that he distrusted the doc, exactly; at least, no more than he distrusted any other authority figure. Norman had simply observed how willing the Institute was to jump at untried technology. The savants weren't the ones at risk, after all.

Not for the first time, Norman wondered what he was doing here.

With every bit of chill he could muster, he forced his eyes open. Norman suppressed a flinch when the gel poured into his eyes. Something about the fluid made his brain want to think it stung his eyes, but in truth it was as comfortable as pure, slightly cool water. The Argos Device's operation and his own body heat would cause the temperature within the capsule to gradually rise over the course of the test, but for now it was chilly, even through his special suit. Norman's skin tingled as his nervous system reacted to whatever exotic material was suspended in the fluid. He imagined his nervous system radiating through the liquid around him, like a tesla coil.

The first bulb flicked on, amber light cutting through the gloom. Doc was signaling that the test had begun. Norman began to count down from sixty in his head—not that he had any choice, with the hefty breathing apparatus filling his mouth. He reached zero at precisely the moment the second light burned amber. It was a skill of questionable utility, but Norman had become quite good at keeping time in his head. Maybe after all this he could hire himself out to piano teachers as a metronome, if he ever decided he needed a square job. Norman settled back, quickly running the mental exercise the doc had taught them to clear out stray thoughts. First his mind was busy. Then it was a flat mirror sea. There were no tides, no currents, no breezes. Only pure, placid water beneath a cloudless night sky. No moon marred the night's perfect black, nor stars. Nothing but cold black sky. The water reflected the darkness back to it. The horizon disappeared. There was void above and void below. Void all around. Nothing existed except the count, starting over from thirty. Somewhere, the other technicians were running through the first psycho-astronomy sequence, readying their minds to link with his, ready to join him in the void.

The count reached zero. An amber light pierced the void, the third light of five, winking out as quickly as he acknowledged it. It was Norman's turn. Psycho-Astronomy Sequence Theta, reaching out to the minds ready for him.

Norman didn't understand exactly how the deep structures in his brain worked. That wasn't necessary, any more than he needed to understand how his medulla oblongata controlled his autonomic functions. He only needed to know how to perform the mental exercises that flexed those special nerves, reaching out first to his teammates, then to the Argos Device, and then to the stars. To that particular region of space at the edge of the solar system, where Dr. Traynor assured him that a planet waited to be discovered.

Out of habit, he looked first for Irene. Of the minds he felt closest to, hers was the strongest, the easiest to find in the nothing that surrounded him. With her signal, he would be able to orient himself, finding the other cardinal points before sweeping in to grab the other half of the team. Norman told his mind to expand, to find her, a storm suspended in a glass bottle.

There was nothing.

Irene wasn't there.

He was alone in the void, floating in nothing.

That wasn't

That wasn't possible. Irene was always there. In the previous op test, in the rounds of testing leading up to this, whenever he felt lost or unsure, Irene was always there for him. That's who she was.

No. There was nothing. Nothing but the void, slowly leeching away his heat. He was already going numb, starting from the back of his head and creeping down his spine.

Tension seized his chest, squeezing him like a fish caught in a raptor's talons. His heart sped up. His breath came sharp and fast now.

Norman swept the outer points of the compass, trying to find someone. Eddie, Patricia, Harold. One of them had to be out there. They were all waiting for him. Why couldn't he see them? Where were they?

He pulled inward, hoping to catch one of the ordinal points. Surely he would find Lorraine. He knew her mind as well as he knew Irene's, and she'd come so far. Even if he couldn't reach far enough to find Irene, he had to be able to find Lorraine.

Instead, he found himself floating in a narrow tube, strapped to an uncomfortable chair, the interior inches from his face. Weird fluid filled it from top to bottom, a cold slime pressing against his body, seeping into the gaps of his suit, filling the folds and creases of his skin. He had barely enough room to move. He had barely enough room to breathe.

He stabbed at the emergency button, hitting it again and again until it broke beneath his hand. By the time the myrmidons unsealed the capsule, he had torn his way free of the restraining straps. He'd scrabbled at the seam of the lid until his fingers bled.

When they finally got the aqualung's mouthpiece out, the only thing he could say was "alone", sobbing it over and over again.

I was beginning to hate seeing people in hospital beds. Norman lay beneath a heavy wool blanket, dead to the world. The doctor had kept him sedated since they pulled him out of the capsule. It was the only way to stop him from screaming about the void.

I'll credit the Institute this much—this infirmary was the nicest hospital room I'd ever seen. Granted, I didn't have much to compare it to, but at least I was the only eldritch entity lurking in the vicinity. Instead of the blinding white of the halls, someone had sensibly painted the walls a soothing light blue. Leafy green plants stood in each corner of the room. Speakers set above them played soft instrumental music; not the toe-tapping bop Norman and friends would have preferred, but classical compositions that fostered a sense of calm.

The room held four beds, but only one was occupied. I suppose that spoke well of the Institute's safety record. It also meant our entire dorm could cluster around Norman's bed. No one else had come to visit, but a small bedside table held a few handmade cards from other dorms. It was still Friday night; by the time Monday came around, it would be overflowing with flowers and fancier cards from drug stores and five-and-dimes throughout Regina.

Nearly everyone from the psycho-astronomy team had dropped off some sort of get-well note. Well-wishes from Harold and Richard were conspicuously absent, but at the time we thought nothing of it.

Lorraine and Irene stood at the head of his bed. Lorraine brushed his damp hair while Irene held his bandaged hand. Rob, Paul, and Polly stood on the other side of the bed. Polly laid her head against Rob's shoulder, silently weeping, while Rob held her close. Paul had his hands folded in front of him and his head bowed, unable to look at Norman. I stood at the foot of the bed with Mark. He had been the last to arrive. His usual aura of superiority had entirely evaporated. This was no time for posturing.

"I never would have believed it," Paul said, breaking the silence. Dr. Tucker had left, giving us his official diagnosis. Claustrophobia, apparently.

"I don't remember Norman ever having a problem with tight spaces." Rob rubbed his eyes with his free hand. "Do you?"

"He was fine during Tuesday's test," Lorraine said, her voice almost too soft to be heard. "He was *fine*."

"They really can't expect us to believe this," Mark said. "A case of *nerves*?"

"That's right." I looked at him carefully without taking my eyes off Norman—not digging deeply into his mind but peering at his surface thoughts for his true intentions. "The doctor thinks he panicked from conditions within the Argos Device. Apparently, it's dark and quite a tight fit."

"That's preposterous." Mark scowled, radiating suspicion, cold anger, and a touch of ill-defined guilt. "Rogers is many things, no few of them negative, but he's no coward."

"My father and uncles were in the Pacific Theater," Irene said, her voice quiet and tight. "Dad can't stand fireworks. He's no coward."

Mark's face flushed. He stammered for a few minutes before finding his words. "I misspoke. I didn't mean… I apologize, Irene."

"You're right, though," Rob said. "Anyone can get a case of nerves, but if he was fine before?"

"He was *joking* coming out of the tube," Lorraine said.

Rob shook his head. "This doesn't add up."

"What are you suggesting?" Irene said.

"I don't know. Maybe there was a problem?"

Mark's scowl deepened. He glanced at the open door, seeing that it was empty. Then he leaned forward, his voice low. "Something wrong with the device, perhaps?"

"And they don't want us to know," Irene said.

Rob and Paul shared a look. A mutual idea passed between them, tinged with doubt and shame. Paul broke his gaze, looking down at his feet again. Sighing heavily, Rob tugged at his collar and surrendered to being the one to say it.

"We could try looking into his mind." He cut his eyes to me, fearing my response. "Not *deeply*. Just to his short-term memory. See what happened in there."

"It's not as if he's in a position to tell us," Paul said to his shoes.

My jaw tightened. "We've discussed this. The ethics of your gift."

"I know, Amelia, but under the circumstances…"

"Norman is *incapable* of giving consent. Under the circumstances, we absolutely *cannot* do anything."

"But in an emergency—"

"This *isn't* one. I'm as worried about Norman as any of you. I want to get to the bottom of this, but the medical team is saying he's not in any danger. We have to respect his mental autonomy."

Mark cut his eyes to me. "And you decide this for us?"

I locked eyes with him. "Would you want someone digging around inside *your* head, Mark Pressler?"

He flinched. The guilt coming off him grew stronger, though I wasn't sure why. I couldn't very well pursue it though, could I?

When I began working with Dr. Stewart's team, I was very clear about the ethics of telepathy. Namely, that consent had to be their first and foremost guiding principle. That may be hypocritical of me, to a degree. There's a key distinction, and it has to do with the way my perception works versus telepathy in normal humans.

Yes, to the extent that telepathy in humans can be normal, you're very clever.

My ability to perceive thoughts is inherently passive, like sight or hearing. When you walk into a crowded room, you simply see everyone in it and hear what they are saying—at least, within the limits of your senses and ability to focus. When I interact with people. I perceive their surface thoughts. I have to *choose* to ignore them, just as you may choose not to see someone picking their nose.

Human telepathy is *different*. It's active, like radar, except of course it's nothing like that at all. A human telepath must deliberately create a connection with another mind. They're entering the most intimate part of another person—invading it, if done without consent. A person with minimal psychic potential or without training would be helpless against them.

I wasn't going to turn a horde of Apollonian Society creeps loose with that sort of skill, no matter how many steps removed the Institute was from its origins. The only reason I was willing to help Stewart with his program was that he agreed completely with my concerns. We'd spend as much time drilling ethics into our technicians' heads as we had training them.

I wasn't *disappointed* that Rob and Paul had suggested this step, under the circumstances. They were motivated by a desire to help, not by prurience or personal gain. It was admirable. Nonetheless, it wasn't a step I would permit. Yet.

As if men have ever been willing to listen to me. At least I had some backup.

"Amelia's right," Irene said. "Until they let him wake up and we can ask him, we have to let him be."

The others nodded.

"Maybe then he'll be able to *tell* us," Polly whispered.

The others pulled closer around him and away from me. The atmosphere in the room had shifted irrevocably. They weren't looking at me as a peer anymore, except perhaps for Irene. I wore a different uniform, I held a position of responsibility, which to them might as well have been authority. I may not have genuinely been a member of the Institute, but in their eyes, that didn't matter. We weren't friends anymore. I was a leader. It wasn't a role I was comfortable taking, but it had seemingly been thrust into my hands.

What a birthday week for me.

While we gathered around Norman's bed, the noetic savants had assembled in the staff lounge. By unspoken agreement, they had decided it would be easier to respond to the aftermath of Traynor's disaster if they were inebriated. I'm not sure how that logically followed, but then, I've never created a debacle as large as those the Apollonian Society's descendants regularly left in their wake.

Traynor was there, of course, trying to affect the air of one unbothered by recent events. Voss stood by him, for now. He was already too many drinks in, but still standing upright. Pike sat primly in a leather chair, vaguely aware of everything going on, although in that he was in good company for once. Stewart and Tucker huddled together in deep conversation. They occasionally shot glances at Traynor. They tried to look solicitous, but there was a notable gap between where they were standing and where Traynor and Voss lurked.

The last two savants held themselves apart, as usual. Ravenna sat in a chair off to the side, nursing a martini. West leaned against the far end of the bar, trying to look inscrutable.

"This is a monumental disaster!"

Most of those sitting leapt to their feet when they heard Octavian slam the door behind him. Ravenna rose more slowly, giving him a careful, measured look. West remained standing at the end of the bar, his sardonic smile making it clear he didn't see any of this as *his* problem.

Octavian pushed his way through the men to reach the bar. The bartender, a young prot named Benjamin Foster, had started mixing a gin and tonic the moment Octavian stormed through the door. The Director accepted it with a curt nod. He downed half of it in one angry swallow. Foster immediately began mixing another.

"An absolute foul-up." Octavian's voice was so hot he was nearly belching flames. "I don't mind telling you, gentlemen, that the board is up in arms. A major experiment on the verge of failure. One of our most promising assets in the infirmary. Our entire purpose called into question!" He downed the rest of his drink and snatched the second out of Foster's hand. "At least we have our in-house facilities. Thank God for that!"

"I did warn you about this, Dr. Pretorius," West said. "The human brain simply isn't capable of the feats you're asking of it. It needs improvement."

Octavian rounded on West, one finger stabbing out like a dagger. He gripped his glass so tightly it was in danger of breaking. In spite of himself, West took a step back.

"I am *not* having this conversation with you now, Jeffrey!" Octavian shouted.

West dropped his eyes to his drink, intimidated but not chastened. "You *will* have it, though," he said, loud enough for Octavian to hear but soft enough for him to ignore.

Octavian tried to do just that, but Traynor didn't give him the chance. He stood tall and puffed out his chest, working to keep the Director's ire focused on its preferred target.

"You're being ridiculous, 'Doctor' West. The barbarism of your 'theories' aside, we have ample proof of what the human brain is capable of. Look at what Miss Temple has demonstrated."

Voss chuckled into his drink. "Miss Temple isn't *exactly* human."

"That's an exaggeration!" Ravenna said, indignant.

"Shut up! *All* of you!"

Octavian's eyes blazed. He slapped the bar top, commanding the room to silence. Every eye in the room focused on him. All but Foster, who was carefully cleaning out a glass with his back to the room. Octavian coughed once and set his empty glass down on the bar. It clacked loudly when glass met wood.

"Why don't you take a break, Benjamin? I'm sure these gentlemen are capable of pouring their own drinks for an hour or two."

Foster took the hint and departed through a side door without a word. Once he had left, Voss tried to stammer out an apology, his balding head beet red. Octavian cut him off with a curt wave of his hand.

"Shut up, Charles." He took a hefty drink and grimaced. "Still, you're not exactly incorrect. Amelia isn't entirely human, and please don't interrupt me, Ravenna."

Ravenna swirled her martini at him and curled her lip.

"She has been very helpful," Octavian continued. "She shows us by example what we are capable of becoming. *Not* by stapling bits of weird flesh to our healthy human bodies—"

"I like to think my methods are a little more sophisticated than that," West said to no one in particular.

"—but by developing repeatable methods to advance our preexisting psychic potential. An endeavor *you've* managed to completely cock up, Matthew!"

Traynor glowered indignantly but took a step back, so he was standing partially behind Voss. "Now hold on, Dr. Pretorius—"

Octavian sneered, practically baring his teeth. "You can't possibly be about to defend yourself."

"The project is *on schedule*. Yes, we had a setback. *Every* major endeavor experiences setbacks."

"One of your technicians is in the infirmary," Ravenna said quietly.

Traynor dismissed her with a wave of his hand. "Rogers knew the risks. He's playing with the big boys."

"It's not as if Matthew caused any property damage," Voss said. "That puts us one up on our predecessors."

"Exactly. This is an easy sell to the board, Director. I still have two candidates capable of piloting the device. The observation will continue as planned. You have my word."

"Just how much is that worth?" Octavian took a big gulp of his drink. "That still leaves you down a technician. You were adamant about needing nine trained clairvoyants."

"My team aren't the only clairvoyants in the building." Traynor clapped his colleague on the shoulder. "Dr. Voss can give up one of his."

"Now hold on a minute," Voss said. "I still need to show results too."

"Should have produced them faster. You heard the Director. The Object C Observation is the Institute's highest priority." Traynor grinned, somewhat nastily. "Buck up, Charles. It'll only be for a couple of weeks. I promise to give him back better than I found him."

"Matthew's right, Charles. It's the only way to bring this picture in on time." Octavian raised a warning finger. "You don't have to give up your *best* man, Charles, but he'd better not be your worst." He took another swig and scowled. "I suppose this means delays. You'll have to get the new active up to speed."

"No more than a week!" Traynor said quickly. "I don't need Voss' man to pilot the device. He needs to memorize and execute a handful of psycho-astronomy sequences. If he's dedicated and at all capable, he should pick it up quickly."

"All right," Octavian said. He stroked his beard, mulling it over. He must have hit on an answer he liked, because his face brightened. "All right! We'll see that it's done. Matthew, we're counting on you."

"You can rely on me, sir, I assure you."

Ravenna, who'd been watching this exchange with bright eyes, suddenly stood up. "We should ask Amelia to observe the experiment. If there are any more problems, she can detect them before they get out of hand."

Traynor's face grew indignant, but he tried to laugh it off. "That's unnecessary, really. I appreciate Miss Temple's talents as much as the next man, but I've made my position on this quite clear. I'm afraid her psychic presence will overwhelm the array."

West perked up. He came around the end of the bar to join the others.

"I think Ravenna's right, Matthew. The lion's share of the Institute's budget is tied up in your program. Can we really afford another disaster like today?"

Traynor looked like he was about to object to that—physically—when

Octavian held up his hand for silence.

"No. It's a good idea. We can't afford any more *setbacks* with this project. We brought in Amelia for a reason. Let's not waste the opportunity."

"But her psychic presence—"

"Kenneth, describe Amelia's psychic influence over the past month," Octavian said to Dr. Pike, who was lounging across a pair of leather chairs.

Pike stared at him, eyes unfocused. Then he trembled all over, like a wiry dog shaking off after a bath. He jerked upright, all slender limbs and right angles, and withdrew a small tan notebook from his leg pocket.

"You understand this is a cursory description. More detailed information is available in my weekly report."

"I have been reading it, Kenneth. I suspect Ravenna has as well. Bring Matthew up to speed, if you would."

Pike settled a set of pince-nez on his nose and flipped to the relevant entry. "Miss Temple's noetic shadow is larger than that of any human on record. Nonetheless, on average its intensity has been no greater than the top five percent of our technicians over the period specified. Multidimensionally, she remains a Level One manifestation. No alarms in weeks."

He snapped the notebook shut with an air of finality and removed the pince-nez. He nodded to Octavian in satisfaction. Then his eyes slowly unfocused again. His serious expression gradually melted into a dreamy smile. He sank into his seat, staring at something on the other side of the ceiling. The savants stared at him, dumbfounded. Then Octavian nodded and waved his glass.

"There, you see? Amelia should no more interfere with your experiment than your backup pilot will, assuming he's at all capable."

"Dr. Pretorius, I really must insist!"

Octavian set his drink on the bar. He looked coolly at Traynor. "Please, Matthew. Explain to me exactly what it is about your current position that allows you to make demands?"

Traynor opened his mouth, but no words came. He looked around the room for support and found none. His allies wouldn't meet his eyes, focusing on their drinks or the Director. His rivals, and they numbered nearly every savant in the room, sat casually and smirked. Octavian turned his back on Traynor, retrieving his drink and waving it at the other scientists.

"Now, whose project is the next furthest along? I need something to present to the board in case this ends in catastrophe. Ravenna? Vincent? One of you, dazzle me!"

Traynor shrank into the edge of the group. No one looked at him. No one acknowledged his presence. No one except West, who downed his drink and slipped around the edge of the room. Perhaps he recognized that even if his own project had been far enough along, Octavian would never consider it.

He paused very briefly as he passed Traynor. He couldn't help himself from giving the man a vulpine smile. Nothing that openly declared he was responsible for Traynor's woes. Just enough to make it clear he was relishing the *schadenfreude.*

Crossing his arms and looking away, Traynor moved to let West pass. West let out a dry chuckle. Then he slipped out of the lounge, unnoticed.

15

The Director didn't often walk the Institute grounds. He deliberately held himself apart from the lower ranks, preferring to appear as an aloof authority. Thus, it was a sign of how badly the turbulence around Traynor's experiment had shaken him that he chose to come find me in person.

My friends were with their respective teams, mostly. Irene and Lorraine had claimed time in Traynor's third-floor lab, running through psycho-astronomy drills. Rob and Paul were scheduled for meditation practice with Stewart, while Polly was undergoing artificially induced sleep for an astral expedition. Mark had been even more withdrawn than usual since Norman's accident and was spending most of his time in West's lab.

Norman, of course, was still in the infirmary. Dr. Tucker hadn't allowed him to wake up yet. I couldn't bear to visit him again, although I felt that I should.

I tried distracting myself with a back issue of *Imaginary Tales*. I wanted to lose myself in rockets, stars, and first contact, stories about brave scientific adventurers motivated by the pure desire for discovery. It was childish and naïve, I know, but I needed to convince myself despite everything that people weren't all hidden motives and internecine conflict. That there was more to them than a desire to one-up one another or gain personal power.

I couldn't do it. I couldn't focus on the words. It was all nonsense anyway, a bunch of made-up people having made-up adventures. None of it could affect the real world. The stories were only there to convince a reader to part with a dime or two at the newsstand.

I set the magazine aside and groaned, rubbing my head. It was all getting to be too much. *Have I made a mistake by staying here?* I was grateful for the friends I had made, but what was I doing? Sitting in a library reading magazines, having tea with people who would rightly be considered crackpots in any respectable university?

I ignored, for the moment, that I couldn't leave, that the barrier around the manor kept me pinned in more thoroughly than the Bureau ever had.

When the Director entered the library and made a beeline for me, I felt a mix of gratitude and foreboding. I was glad to have something else to distract me. That quickly faded as I wondered what could possibly be important enough for him to come looking for me himself instead of sending a minion to fetch me.

Octavian didn't waste words. He issued demands before he'd even reached my table. The friendly words didn't match his tone. "Amelia. Care to have a drink in my office?"

I cocked my head to the side, eye quirked quizzically. "I'm surprised you don't want to go to the staff lounge."

He glowered beneath heavy brows. From the bags beneath his eyes, I suspected he hadn't been sleeping well. "Some conversations are better had in private."

Curiosity and a need to do *something* got the better of me. I followed him from the library to his office, marked by its ostentatious brass doors. I'd expected him to take a seat behind his massive mahogany desk, which probably cost an average working person's annual salary on its own. Instead, he fixed himself a gin and tonic and poured me a Coke, then gestured to the reading nook in the opposite corner. Two overstuffed leather chairs and a low table sat before oak bookcases stocked with a variety of esoteric tomes.

Octavian set heavily in the more worn of the two chairs, clutching his glass as if it was a lifeline. He stared at the brass ornamentation hanging behind his desk. It was a bas-relief of Prometheus bringing fire from Olympus, pursued by lightning bolts. I imagined it was how he saw himself.

I took the other chair and sipped my Coke, waiting for him to start talking. It usually didn't take long. If there was anything in this world Octavian loved, it was the sound of his own voice. Yet, the expected speech didn't come. Instead, he stared into this drink as if he might divine the future in its bubbles. The silence stretched out for long minutes as the tick in the grandfather clock on the far wall echoed like a confident woman's high heels on hardwood.

"Lovely weather we're having," I said at last. "I mean, I assume."

"Do you think this is funny?" he snapped.

"What?"

"My people. Our work. Is my Institute a joke to you?"

Without waiting for a response, he downed his drink in a single painful gulp, then hurled the glass across the room. It shattered against the clock, an antique possibly older than the state. Hundreds of thousands of dollars in valuation, lost to a single act of pique.

"I don't have *time* for your snide comments, Amelia!"

Octavian's face twisted into a furious snarl, like a dog about to bite. I stared at him, dumbfounded. Then I narrowed my eyes and leaned forward, letting a hint of anger show on my own face.

"You seem to have forgotten that I *don't work for you*, Octavian." I kept the volume of my voice level, but my tone was frigid. "*You* needed *my* help. I don't see you as an authority, and I certainly am not afraid of you."

I pressed my perception against him. The force of my gaze slid off the mirror-slick defenses wrapped around his mind, but I felt them give. Just a bit. Just enough to make a point. Octavian flinched. He jumped out of his chair, eyes wide and staring. For a moment he stood stock still, muscles trembling beneath his black jumpsuit. Then he jerked around and rushed to the bar, stumbling and from more than the drink.

"I apologize, Amelia." He didn't look back as he mixed another drink. "I've been under a great deal of pressure lately. It's affected my mood."

"Clearly," I said, unmoved.

"A great deal hangs on Matthew's upcoming experiment. I'm not exaggerating when I say it will either be the achievement of the decade or an inexcusable failure." He took a stiff slug of his drink and grimaced. "Right now, it's looking more like the latter."

"I know." I raised a sharp eyebrow. "That's my friend in the infirmary."

He turned to stare at me, as if it had just dawned on him that someone might care about Norman. He approached, one hand spread in a vague sort of apology. "Of course. Of course he is. Please forgive me, I hadn't considered how hard this must be on you."

"Not only me. Our entire dorm is worried about him. So is the rest of Dr. Traynor's team. The doctor himself might even be losing sleep over it."

That was a stretch, I admit.

"Then you'll appreciate what I'm about to ask you." Octavian put his hand on my arm, eyes wide and pleading. "I want you with me in the observation room on Friday. We can't afford another disaster like the one that befell young Norman. I need someone who can see the things we can't, who can tell us if something's going wrong."

I was torn. On the one hand, I'd wanted to be part of the Object C Observation from the beginning; more accurately, I'd wanted to be involved with my new friends' work. I certainly believed that if I'd been in the room yesterday, I could have saved Norman. I felt that I ought to be jumping at the chance to prevent anything from happening to Irene or Lorraine.

Something about all of this rubbed me wrong, though.

I quirked an eyebrow. "Dr. Traynor has been adamant about not wanting me 'interfering' with his experiment."

Octavian smiled. It looked wrong beneath the anger in his eyes. "I've already dealt with that. Unlike you, Matthew *does* work for me."

"Okay." I bit my lip, turning the idea over in my mind. I couldn't think of a reason to object beyond vague misgivings. So, I didn't. "I need something else, though."

Octavian's smile disappeared. I ignored it.

"Weeks ago, you assured me this would be a mutually beneficial relationship. It hasn't felt very *mutual* lately." Octavian opened his mouth to object, but I raised a finger and pressed on. "You promised me information. You've been holding it back even though I've been as helpful as I can, considering your staff's *difficulties*."

I stood quickly, forcing him to take an awkward step away. I put my hands on my hips and gave him the sternest look I could manage. "No more games, Octavian. I want to know where my mother is."

Octavian tried to hold his eyes steady. He failed, dropping his gaze and quickly turning to hide it. He stumbled to his desk, taking another heavy gulp of alcohol. Body language was still difficult for me, but even I could tell how angry he was by the way his hands trembled and teeth ground.

"All right," he said through clenched teeth. "*After* the observation. I'll tell you everything you want to know if it's successful."

I crossed my arms. "And if it's not?"

"Then frankly we'll all have bigger problems than your feelings of abandonment."

My jaw tightened. I very nearly said a foul word. My hands twitched dangerously. I wanted to hurl my glass at his face. *We* would have problems? I couldn't care less for his superiors' opprobrium. Dr. Traynor's entire experiment could fall flat on its face for all it mattered to me.

Octavian felt the tension in the room rise. He quickly moved to put his massive desk between us, for all the good it would have done. He waved his hands, trying vainly to calm me.

"Amelia, I'm sorry," he stammered, the drink starting to slur his words. "I didn't mean—"

"I'll make sure your experiment goes as planned, Octavian," I said, quick and cold. "Then you'll tell me everything you know about my mother. After that, we'll reconsider this partnership."

Octavian stammered something as I stormed out of the room, meaningless apologies and promises of cooperation. I ignored them all. I paused at the door, turning my head only slightly his way.

"You might want to have a big glass of water, Octavian," I said. "The drink is going to your head."

I didn't wait for a response. I slammed the door behind me, leaving the director sulking in his cavernous, empty office. Zeus' lightning bolts loomed over his head. He stared at them, and at Prometheus' burning brand. Maybe he was considering the cost.

Then he downed his drink and went to mix another.

Norman remained heavily sedated. On Tuesday, Tucker had briefly experimented with letting him wake up. He'd come around quickly, meeting the doctor's gaze with his heavily dilated eyes. Tucker addressed him by name, asking how he felt. Norman looked the doctor in the eye for twenty-eight seconds. He blinked once. Then he screamed, a blood-curdling sound that echoed down the hall even through the closed infirmary door. Tucker quickly put him back under, and he stayed that way for another twenty-four hours.

He hadn't said anything coherent. Tucker claimed that was progress. The rest of the savants weren't so sure, but the infirmary was his domain.

The rest of the dorm hadn't stopped visiting Norman, although we hadn't returned in a large group. The others popped by in twos and threes, checking in on him, asking questions about his condition, but gradually giving up hope that he would improve any time soon. Mark and I stayed away. Neither of us had gone to see him since the day after the accident, although no one realized it yet. The guilt over his affliction was eating at us both, although one of us was far more responsible for it.

Rob and Paul had taken my admonition to heart for exactly four days, until the doctor tried waking him. Paul had been on cleaning duty that afternoon. By sheer bad luck, he'd been supervising a group of prots in the halls near the infirmary. He'd heard Norman's screaming. His friend's anguish almost brought him to tears. He'd gone to find Rob immediately after his shift, and they agreed it was time to stop messing around. They were going to sneak into the infirmary that evening.

They only told Polly about their plan, and then only to make sure she kept me engaged. She'd agreed nervously, worried at first that she couldn't keep the secret from me. Frankly, she could barely keep the secret from Irene and Lorraine, and they couldn't casually read minds. She hit upon a solution when she came across a group from Eddie and Patricia's dorm playing cards in the library. I scrupulously ignored everyone's thoughts when we were playing games, even though the distraction tended to degrade my own play. I was many things, but I wasn't a cheat.

Irene and Lorraine jumped at the offer of a game of Black Lady, eager for the diversion. I let them persuade me to join, mostly to avoid disappointing anyone. Once we were three books in, Rob and Paul slipped out. They were sneaky in just the right way—Rob said outright it was their turn to visit Norman. I barely noticed them, focused more on trying to figure out how to get rid of the Queen of Spades.

The infirmary was quiet that late at night. The doctor was out, and Nurse Foster had finished her rounds. She signed the two in and helped them get chairs, then left them to pay their respects. She wouldn't say it aloud, but she didn't see Norman ever leaving that bed on his own power. She turned out to be right about that.

Once they settled in, Ron and Paul gave Nancy a few minutes to return to her duties. They quietly recounted the day's events to our unconscious friend. Then they bowed their heads, as if in prayer, and established a connection.

Rob took the lead, as usual. Centering himself, he reached out to build a link with Paul. They harmonized easily, as they always did. They didn't care that Stewart considered them the weakest links in his team. They saw their psychic gift mainly as a way to share with one another.

Yes, Polly knew. I didn't realize it at the time; she scrupulously avoided thinking about it, to protect them all. It had never been like that between her and Rob; what the three of them were to each other defied easy description. Not that it matters now.

They'd followed my lessons well, visualizing a shared mindscape to support their link. They appeared in an indistinct, washed-out version of our dorm's common room; they'd met at the Institute, and it was the closest thing they had to "their" space. It would help to build their link to Norman as well, but they weren't concerned about that in this moment. This was their little bit of stolen time together. As soon as they both appeared, Paul rushed into Rob's cognitive arms, kissing him the way he'd never been able to in the physical realm. They held each other tightly, love and desire flowing between them, strengthening their psychic link. The common room became more defined—color flowing into the walls and floor, lines on the furniture and fixtures sharpening, names drawing themselves on the spines of books and boxes of board games. They kissed each other the way you can only kiss when you don't have to come up for air, when time is a choice you can make. They kissed as if in some way they understood how fragile everything around us was. Maybe they did. They couldn't see the future, but they were two gay men in the 1950s. Even outside the realm of mad science, everything for them could fall apart in a moment.

Subjective hours later, Rob finally pushed Paul away. The mindscape briefly tinged blue with regret, but they both understood that they had a purpose tonight beyond canoodling. While holding tight to their connection with one another, they each reached out to Norman. His mind drifted a little bit away. It wasn't ready to establish a connection, but in his current state neither was it closed. Unconscious and injured, Norman was incapable of offering any resistance as they slid inside his mind. Guilt flashed through Paul, while Rob tried not to think about it. They were here to help.

Dim light streamed through the gaps around the mindscape's outer door, growing brighter by the second as they strengthened their connection. It took tremendous skill to establish a connection without the other mind's assistance. They were trained well, but at the same time, something about Norman's mind was drawing them in on its own. Before they were ready, the doorknob turned on its own, and the door flew open. They fell forward into Norman's mind.

And they kept falling.

They'd expected to find a coherent mindscape behind the door, like the one they'd built together. That's what I'd taught them to expect. Maybe there would have been, if Norman had been prepared for their intrusion, if he'd invited them inside. Instead, they tumbled through the starless void Norman had visualized during the Argos Device trials. He'd never left it. He was still there, plummeting through the endless nothing, picking up speed as he went. At the bottom of the bottomless void, something waited. Something that spiraled open, a patch of negation in the midst of nothing. Something with countless sharp, gnashing teeth. It howled at them, nightmarish screams and high, mocking laughter echoing through the void. Rob and Paul felt gravity increase as its hunger caught them. They fell faster, falling away from each other, spiraling around the edge of its event horizon. Norman flew around it, screaming. Rob thought he could see colors deep within, streaks and flashes of light that might have once been stars, and behind them all something that might have been a face.

Come to me, fragments of meat and space and time. Let go of flesh. Of thought. Of distinction. Become one with me.

Norman hurled across the psychic event horizon, somehow suspended between the void in his imagination and the void that lurked beneath it. Paul wailed as he flew past him, a screaming comet with a face. Rob plunged after him, howling Paul's name. He felt himself dissolving as he caught up to Paul, pieces of himself ripping away and swirling into the void's maw. He clung to his lover, trying desperately to maintain coherence. Their connection was straining against the void's gravity, but strong for now. It could free them or pull them both under. The way their connection to Norman would.

Rob gave Norman's psychic image one final, desperate look. Then he severed his connection to their friend. He and Paul lurched in their seats, nearly spilling out across the floor as they jerked back to consciousness.

"What happened?" Paul gasped.

They sat in their chairs, shivering. Norman lay on the bed, insensate beneath an itchy wool blanket. In the other room, Nancy's fingers clacked rapidly over a typewriter.

"I don't know," Rob said softly. "I don't know what happened."

"Did we… did we do it? Go into his mind?"

"I don't think so," Rob said. "I don't know if there's anything left to go into."

Their hands found each other beneath the bed. They twined their fingers together, hoping without hope that Rob was wrong. That Norman would recover. Even as a piece of the void ate away at their memories.

Among the specialized equipment in West's main lab was a bizarre communications terminal. It looked like a heavily modified ham radio system, but one tuned to no frequency on the radio spectrum. In place of crystals or vacuum tubes, a tank of carefully grown nerve tissue sat inside. It was West's primary method of communication directly with the myrmidon hive, though he delegated most of that to his assistant. Mark didn't mind. Being the Institute's primary point of contact for directing the myrmidons made him more important than the other specs. It also made his own tasks easier.

Mark adjusted the terminal's frequency, then clicked on the microphone. "Nearest point. Return to nest for maintenance. Repeat. Nearest point. Return to nest for maintenance."

Psychic power radiated from the terminal, instructions pulsing into the hive. Once the signal was sent, Mark shut the machine down and left the main lab for the small adjoining room, grabbing a tank from Batch 13 on the way. A large stand-up tank with an attached container of biofluid dominated the space. A small cabinet full of supplies and a deep sink sat to one side. While he waited, Mark warmed up the biofluid, prepared a batch of nutrient additives, and set out a tray of surgical tools.

After two minutes, a lone myrmidon silently entered the room. Mark didn't look up from his tools.

"It's about time. Disrobe."

The myrmidon removed its white jumpsuit and left it in a puddle on the floor, standing stock still. The room was cold; Mark was shivering slightly, but the myrmidon's pale skin didn't respond. Mark walked a quick circle around it, checking its body for anomalies. As he expected, it was flawless—no moles or freckles or textures of any kind. Like all the others.

"I have good news," he said companionably. "You've been selected for upgrades. This will only take a few hours."

The myrmidon didn't respond, nor did he expect it to. Mark set his tools and materials on the small, wheeled table and rolled it up to the drone. Opening the small cultivation tank, he extracted a squirming tendril of Watcher matter. He left the wriggling thing in a petri dish, letting it flail aimlessly in the cold air. Then he took up his scalpel.

Mark looked up at the myrmidon, which stood a full head taller than him. He carefully measured the incision by eye, a diagonal line running around its right shoulder blade. Then he opened its skin with the scalpel. The myrmidon's back twitched as Mark cut it open, but it didn't move or otherwise respond. Milky white fluid bled down its back. He ignored it. There was no point in cleaning it.

He grabbed a quartet of surgical clamps from the tray and peeled away the pale skin above the myrmidon's trapezius, exposing red muscle. He prodded the fibers with a probe, watching it flex. Then he retrieved the Watcher flesh from the dish. It curled around the forceps like a slimy blueish worm until Mark brought it close to the exposed muscle. It stiffened like a short spear, aimed at the myrmidon's tissues. When it was close enough, the tendril stabbed forward on its own, burying itself in the muscle fibers. Mark carefully laid the tendril along the muscle, pushing it in to help it take root. When he was sure it was secure, he folded the flaps of skin over the infested muscle and sloppily stapled it shut; he didn't need the fasteners to last for long. The skin bulged as the Watcher matter moved beneath it, but the staples held.

"All done," Mark said. "Now, into the tank, if you please."

The myrmidon obeyed, stepping into the tank and turning around. Once he had sealed the tank, Mark turned the valve and flooded it with biofluid. As the tube quickly filled, he attached the small bottle of nutrients to the second hose. It had everything needed to encourage the Watcher matter to grow. West hadn't authorized him to perform implantation on the active units, but Mark had learned from his mentor that science didn't wait for permission.

It would take three hours for the new flesh to cure. That gave him plenty of time to upgrade another unit today, provided he finished his other tasks. Mark whistled as he went to work.

The Argos Device sat quietly in Lab B305. The heart of Traynor's experiment did not beat, but a patient observer with an ear to its side might hear a continual electric hum. This late at night, two days before the observation, no one was inclined to listen. A pair of myrmidons conducted routine maintenance, but they weren't known for their curiosity.

The tanks of synaptic fluid sat empty; they wouldn't be filled until the night before the experiment. Another, smaller tank was tucked up beneath the device's base and had to be kept full to keep the device functioning. It fed the device with necessary resources on top of its hefty electrical power requirements. Myrmidons under West's direction refilled the tank every twelve hours; despite his ongoing feud with the direction, West was the one who controlled the Institute's supply of certain esoteric materials. It made it too easy to surreptitiously introduce something new.

The device might have been dormant, but it was fully operational. It would ruin it to power it down, so Traynor let it sleep. It didn't dream—despite its unique construction, it was a tool. It had no mind with which to think, to wonder, to indulge in flights of fancy. It depended on the will of the pilot to experience the universe, much as the pilot depended on its power to overcome human limitations. Nonetheless, something within it stirred as a myrmidon refilled its nutrient tank. Perhaps it was an echo of the future rippling along the device's timeline. Perhaps it was a remnant of the minds that had tuned to it, or of whatever had happened to Norman in the last operational test. Maybe it was even a sign that the device was becoming something more than it was designed to be, if only it would be allowed time to develop.

Whatever it was, it registered a new impurity in the nutrient flow. The device interrogated West's serum, responding like a body fighting an infection. Its internal temperature rose 2.5 degrees as the serum flowed through its internals. West had anticipated that and included a chemical instruction somewhat like a handshake. After two minutes, those instructions reached the correct receptors and reassured the device that everything was fine. The device relaxed. It had simply received new instructions. That was routine. It took on the new information and set to work.

The serum West had developed slithered through the device's systems, settling in and gradually releasing its new operating instructions. It would take time for the device to execute them, but West had timed everything carefully. The Argos Device would be ready to perform its new purpose the day of the observation.

The myrmidons didn't care. When the bottle was empty, they unhooked it and left the room. The Argos Device sat alone in the dark, asleep and undreaming.

16

◆

As Doctor Traynor promised, the Object C Observation took place one week after the disastrous operations test; on Christmas Eve, not that this mattered within the Institute. Traynor drove his technicians hard over the past week, drilling them on the psycho-astronomy sequences until their execution was flawless. Or so they hoped. Mistakes began to creep in as one sequence bled into another. Lorraine admitted to me that she was beginning to run the sequences in her dreams. Irene, never one for healthy sleep habits to begin with, had been getting no more than three hours a night since Tuesday.

Norman was still in the infirmary. Tucker had allowed him to wake up on Thursday. He didn't scream. He didn't speak. He didn't respond to anything.

Previously, the technicians had meandered to their assigned lab more or less on the dot. On the day of the observation, they began gathering outside the door a full sixty minutes before the scheduled opening. Yet, technically, none of them were early. Traynor was already in the observation room and not alone. I was with him, as arranged. So was Octavian, along with four myrmidons. Another eight drones stood on the lab floor, one beside each of the secondary stations. The Institute was leaving nothing to chance this time, or so it believed.

To say the mood in the hallway was tense would be an understatement. While they habitually gathered by dorm, there had been plenty of cross talk prior to the op tests. Not today. The dormmates clustered together, forming closed units. Irene and Lorrain huddled near the door, whispering quietly. Irene tried to reassure the other woman, despite her own haggard, sleep-deprived face. Harold, Richard, and George stood in a loose triangle. Richard, twitching like a tiny dog who needed walkies, kept trying to strike up conversation with the other two, only to be ignored. Eddie, Patricia, and Albert stood against the wall directly opposite the door, arms folded across their chests, not meeting anyone's eyes. Worst of all was Mitchell Lewis, Norman's replacement. Pulled from the solid middle of Voss' ranks, Mitchell didn't share a dorm with anyone in Traynor's team. They knew of him, vaguely, as he knew of them, but the manner of his joining the project cast a shadow over him. He stood alone at the far end of the hall, his back to his new teammates.

At once together and apart, the clairvoyants quietly counted down to Zero Hour.

Harold was already wearing his shiny synchronization suit. Every so often he would look around the hall, failing to catch anyone's eye but Richard's. Then he would tug at his sleeve or his collar or rub his thumb along the slick material. He hid his anxiety behind his usual haughty stare, but he was wracked with doubt and resentment. How was he to connect with these people under these conditions? Didn't they understand that the entire project was at stake?

If Norman had been piloting, he probably would have made a joke to break the tension. Eddie might have made a little speech. Irene would have gone from group to group, offering support and reassurances. One way or another, they would have tried to bring everyone together. Harold assumed he was owed their attention and could only see that he wasn't getting it. Instead of reaching out, he stood back and stewed. He'd finally achieved his rightful place, had been elevated above them all, and these idiots were going to foul it up.

If the mood outside the lab was the morning of a funeral, the atmosphere inside was the moment before a storm. The four myrmidons monitoring the instrument readouts were placid as ever, but they projected no calm to the rest of us. Traynor flitted between his control console and the readouts, adjusting this, making note of that, and generally trying to make it clear to the Director that he was actively engaged. The show had little effect on its intended audience.

Octavian sat on a metal chair, arms folded, and never once looked at Traynor. His cold blue eyes were fixed on the waiting Argos Device. He stared at it as if he was willing it to function. He didn't have a drink on hand, which was doing nothing for his foul mood.

I leaned against a corner, arms behind my back, trying to watch everything while staying out of Traynor's way.

"It's sort of like we're waiting for the villagers with the pitchforks, isn't it?" Ravenna said cheerfully.

I rolled my eyes at her. "That's how I live my life."

Of course I wasn't alone.

Three days before the observation, Ravenna invited me for tea again. I'd half-expected it was for idle gossip, with the off chance that she was trying to distract me from the sadness hanging over my dorm. In the short amount of time, we'd practically become friends—or so I assumed—although I still wasn't entirely certain what she wanted from me. Did she see me as a protégé? An ally against Octavian? Or something entirely inappropriate? I wasn't sure which I preferred.

Instead, she had a scheme.

"I want to observe Traynor's experiment," she said as soon as I sat down.

That was it. No preamble, no small talk. Directly into her plot. I was grateful that she was the one pouring the tea, because I surely would have made a mess.

"I don't think that's possible. You know how the other savants are better than I. They'd never tolerate a colleague spying on their experiments." I paused, tipping my head to one side, examining Ravenna's face as she handed me a cup. "To be honest, you're the same way."

"True." Ravenna's tone betrayed no shame at the admission. She dropped three sugars into her tea, stirred casually, and took a sip.

"I understand it was something of a fight just to get me into the observation room. I can't imagine what it would take to get another observer inside."

"Less of a fight than you think." Ravenna smiled conspiratorially. "A word in the right ear at the right time. That's all it took."

I selected a cookie. "I bow to your superior persuasive ability, but I still think it'll take more than that to get you in."

"That's the brilliance of it. Yes, Matthew would fight tooth and nail to keep me out *if* he knew I would be there. But he doesn't need to." She leaned across the table and covered my free hand with hers. "Not if you're willing."

A blush rose from my breast to my face, and a tingle ran up my spine. I sat up a bit taller. Then I thought of Luci's lovely face and told my heart to stop beating so fast.

My mouth was suddenly dry. It was tricky to form words, but I managed. "What do you mean, exactly?"

She ran her thumb against the side of my hand. "Let me ride you."

My mouth fell open. It took me a few seconds to speak.

"I beg your pardon."

Her mouth twisted up into a wry smile. "*Telepathically*. I've developed a method. We use it regularly on astral excursions. I'll go into your mind and share your senses."

I couldn't look into her dark eyes for very long. Instead, my gaze slipped down her face to her elegant lips. They were beautiful, the way they made soft curves to form her words. "You want inside my mind?"

"I won't go in *too* deep." She slipped her fingers beneath my hand, clasping it tenderly. "I just want to ride your sensorium. See what you see, hear what you hear—"

"Taste what I taste?"

She raised an eyebrow. Her smile widened. "Now isn't that a thought?"

I regretted saying that. Goosebumps broke out along my arm. No I didn't.

"I need to see what goes on in there, Amelia." Ravenna's expression grew slightly more serious. "I have an unshakeable feeling that this experiment is going to be a bigger disaster than the last test. Matthew hasn't learned anything; he's just moving faster, which means sloppier. I don't want to be out of the loop when this all goes wrong."

"What about Octavian? Can't you warn him?"

She shook her head. "He's losing control of the Institute, and he's the sort who's especially dangerous when he's not in control. He's on the verge of having this whole enterprise taken from him. God knows what he'll do if that happens."

"So we can't let that happen."

"Or at the very least, make sure we've planned for when it does." She squeezed my hand. "Does that mean you're in?"

I hesitated. Ravenna's plan went entirely against the Institute's procedures, but then, I wasn't a member of the Institute. I had no reason to go along with their rules, any more than I did the Bureau's. Yet I couldn't understand why I was so hesitant to break protocol.

I could understand why Ravenna's plan seemed so compelling.

"I suppose we'll need to prepare our connection." I blushed as I said it.

Ravenna pulled my hand a little closer. "Good. Let's experiment."

Thirty minutes before Zero Hour, Traynor issued the order to begin. A myrmidon opened the laboratory doors. One by one, the technicians filed into the room. Most glanced up at the observation window before silently going to their assigned stations. A mix of emotions swirled inside their minds. Fear. Guilt. Sorrow. Mentally, none of them were at their best. Not even Harold, for all that he strode toward the Argos Device like a knight ready to mount his charger. A maelstrom of doubt and resentment raged beneath his arrogant surface.

Richard, sensitive at least to Harold's feelings, followed him to the device platform. He put a hand on Harold's arm, hoping to steady him. Harold actually allowed it for a moment, though he didn't acknowledge Richard's presence. Then he looked up to the observation window and saw Traynor staring down at him. I don't know that Traynor was looking at him particularly, but Harold read judgement in his expression. He flushed with embarrassment, snatching his arm out of Richard's hand.

He whirled on Richard, spitting his words at the only person here loyal to him. "Stop fooling around and get to your station, *Richie*."

Harold's venomous tone echoes around the silent lab. The other technicians stared at them. Richard stumbled away, shocked. His lip trembled and tears threatened to spill from his eyes. Harold turned his back on him, looking pointedly at the Argos Device. Richard glanced around the room. Everyone else deliberately dropped their gaze. Most did it out of pity, not wanting to linger on Richard's humiliation. He didn't take it so kindly. He curled into himself, slouching toward his waiting station, hoping he could hold back his tears until they lowered the canvas hood.

The myrmidons didn't respond to this little drama. Two helped Harold into the capsule. Four strapped the technicians into the cardinal stations, fitting them with their focusing hoods. The last two stood alone, as if on guard. What emergency they expected or how they intended to respond to it, I don't know.

Octavian ground his teeth, thus far unimpressed. "Tell them to get on with it."

"Preparing the experiment takes time." Traynor didn't look up from his instruments. "We're on schedule."

"So impatient," Ravenna said. "As if he can just snap his fingers and make things happen."

"I suppose people in power are always like that," I said.

Her psychic self-image was far more dramatic than I'd expected. She wore a dark violet dress beneath a black cloak, its edges chased with glowing silver embroidery. Her hood was thrown back, allowing her to pile her dark ringlets high in an impossible updo. The white streak rising from her left temple was more like a lightning bolt, running through the thunderhead of her dark hair. She was a head shorter than me in the material, but even without her hair or her high-heeled boots, her psychic self-image would have been taller than me.

Although it wasn't strictly necessary—she was keenly aware of everything in the room—Ravenna walked around the inside of the observation room to examine everything. I suppose it was out of habit; full three-dimensional perception was outside of her experience. I had only granted her access to a portion of my sensorium, both to protect her from being overwhelmed and to hide the extent of my abilities. That portion was still more information than any human could perceive without preparation, such as the sort the technicians below us were undergoing.

"This is amazing. I can see everything down there." She turned and smiled at me, radiating genuine glee. "You truly surpass us."

"I can't carry a tune in a bucket, though."

Her eyes glittered. Quite literally. "No need to be modest. You're a wonder. You've been holding out on us."

"I like to think I've been very helpful."

"You have. And yet." Ravenna followed Traynor on another circuit around the room, peeking over his shoulder with unmistakable amusement. "Makes this set-up seem pointless, doesn't it?"

I twisted my fingers together behind my back. I wished that turning my face away did anything to keep me from seeing someone. "I don't see how."

"No? Octavian has spent two million dollars of various scary people's money to do something you could accomplish from a comfortable chair."

The Watcher didn't project themselves into my perception, but I felt them nudge me in my mind.

This human has a point.

"Shush!"

I had hoped that only they would hear that. That was mostly the case.

Ravenna cocked her head to the side, having detected *something*. Curiosity creased her brow.

"What was that? Are we not alone?"

"It was nothing. A stray thought." I changed the subject hurriedly. "It's not a waste. A bird can fly with nothing more than the wings and feathers she grew herself. That's easier than a human building an airplane and *much* cheaper. That doesn't make piloting a plane a waste."

Octavian jerked his head in my direction, scowling. "Is this boring you, Amelia?"

In the physical world, it must have looked as if I was staring blankly off into space. Others weren't used to that the way Luci and Gloria were. I turned my head his way with an unmistakably annoyed expression. I had volunteered to assist his researchers and their experiments, not serve as Octavian's stress toy.

"I'm examining the greater metaphysical geometry for problems, Octavian." My tone was a calculated mix of boredom and irritation. "As you requested."

He looked away, grumpy and unmollified. "Do you see any?"

"Nothing yet."

It was true. Local space-time had taken on a slight but unmistakable curve—to me—as the technicians began their warm-up exercises, but the Argos Device would compensate for that. I could detect no other issues in the immediate volume. As far as I could tell, nothing external would keep the observation from going off without a hitch.

"T minus ten minutes," Traynor said.

Octavian shifted in his seat, his mental discomfort bleeding over into the physical. "You should have let Charles' team draw up a forecast. I'd like to know what to expect."

"You can expect a successful observation of Object C." Traynor's tone was sharper than it normally would have been when speaking to the Director. Octavian was really getting under his skin. "I have the utmost respect for Dr. Voss and his team, but our disciplines are too similar. A divination into the observation would throw out too much noetic turbulence."

"That was what you said about Amelia. Yet here she is, not causing any problems."

I tossed off a quick, mostly sincere smile.

"That remains to be seen," Traynor muttered under his breath.

"I'm actually with Matthew on this one," Ravenna said. "Charles' research isn't nearly far enough along. You'd get better results from a Magic 8 Ball."

Below us, the myrmidons were sealing Harold into the capsule. While he tried to relax, they began filling it with synaptic fluid. The other six myrmidons on the floor moved to the side walls, standing alert but otherwise out of the way. When the capsule was full, the last two joined them.

"T minus five minutes," Traynor said, his voice brittle with anxiety.

During the op tests, the Argos Device had remained static. Traynor hadn't been testing its orientation mechanisms, only how well his specs interfaced with it. This time, he entered the coordinates for Object C into a set of dials on his control console. The platform shuddered as it slowly rotated, while the gimbal tilted the capsule, aiming it at that volume of space. A jolt of fear shot through Harold. He'd been told the device would move, but not what to expect.

"I'm focusing my attention on Harold now," I said. "He's the pilot."

"I'm well aware, Amelia," Octavian said. I wasn't sure of that.

"Just so you know." I shrugged. "I'm going to look like I'm staring at nothing again. Didn't want to alarm you."

Octavian rolled his eyes. Ravenna smirked, looking like a cat who'd found something intriguing to play with.

"I *like* it when you're catty. It's very charming."

A blush warmed my cheeks. Fortunately, Octavian wasn't looking at me anymore. He'd returned his focus to Traynor, eyes burning holes in the savant's back. I suspected Traynor could feel it. He stood bent over the control console, shoulders hunched up to his ears. He closed his eyes and took a deep breath. He let it out slowly, a soft whistle escaping his lips. Then he switched on the recorder. Reels squeaked quietly as they ran the magnetic tape, the microphone catching every word for posterity. He clicked on the secondary station's intercom circuit.

"Object C Observation, December 24, 1954. On my mark, commence sixty-second countdown. At zero, secondary technicians will conduct Relay Exercise Alpha."

The myrmidons in the observation room focused on their readings. Those inside the chamber stood against the wall, looking like soldiers at ease. Everyone else simply waited. The technicians listened to radio static, clearing their minds, listening for the doctor's instruction. Harold stared at the indicator bulbs, waiting for the first to light, telling himself he was meant for this. Traynor stared at the clock, watching as the second hand ticked toward twelve. Octavian fixed his eyes on Traynor, ready to lunge at the first mistake.

"This had better work, Matthew," he said, quiet but stern.

"It will," Traynor said softly. Then, louder, "Mark!"

The countdown began.

17

This world has been subject to celestial impacts for longer than multicellular life has existed here. These events have altered the course of terrestrial history time and again, often in unexpected ways. Remember the Panspermia Hypothesis? Some scientists have proposed life on this world originated among the stars, that asteroid or comet impacts first brought organic compounds or even single-celled organisms to this planet.

No, I don't know for certain. Nor am I inclined to check. It simply isn't relevant to my interests.

A particular impact *is* relevant. Its after-effects weren't quite so dramatic, although they were transformative. Approximately 13,000 years before present, multiple massive objects struck the planet. The collisions precipitated a sudden change in climate, ending the gradual trend in warming that followed the last glacial maximum. Those objects did not originate in local space-time.

I can't say precisely where or when they came from because I don't know, but they were definitely ultraterrestrial. That's played havoc with geologists' ability to find evidence of them. Historical records can be found if you know where to look.

Of the impacts—there were nine that I'm aware of—one struck in what is now New Mexico, in the Pecos Wilderness region. Humans did dwell there, but the impact of winter forced them to migrate. Tragically, the change in climate ended their civilization entirely. Thus, human records of this event do not originate with any group indigenous to the region. The Clovis culture never discovered what lay in the caverns beneath the mountains, and the Anasazi and later groups never put down roots in the region.

In fact, no human set foot in those caverns until 1913, when Balthazar Vane convinced the Apollonian Society for Illumination to fund an alleged archaeological expedition to the Pecos Wilderness. Although he styled himself as a professor, there's no evidence Vane was ever employed by a university, nor that he had any higher education at all. How he even learned of the Younger Dryas Impacts is still a mystery, although the 1905 volume of his journals offers some clues. Between February and April 1905, he claimed to have seen visions of the impacts and certain subterranean ruins in his dreams. These were accompanied by a faceless entity he identified as "the Stranger", who appears again and again in Vane's journals going forward until his mysterious disappearance in 1941.

Fanciful dreams might seem like an implausible foundation upon which to build a major scientific endeavor, but in the Apollonian Society's defense— words I am certainly not accustomed to saying—Vane brought them far more than just the contents of his dream journal. The second son of wealthy Southern planters—their fortune accumulated via the exploitation of human labor and, despite his many complaints, undiminished by abolition of slavery in the United States—Vane spent his portion of his inheritance scouring Europe and northern Asia for evidence supporting his visions.

His search took seven years. It emptied his coffers, first with travel expenses, then with funding increasingly desperate expeditions, then with bribes. When his family's money ran out, Vane turned to more unsavory methods to secure funding.

It was slow, but gradually he uncovered the evidence he sought. A monastery in the Swiss Alps held a complete set of scrolls dating back to the early Iron Age, detailing a series of caverns in the Greek southern slopes. Within those caverns, he found a map that turned out to depict northern Afghanistan, where in another cave he found shards of metal unknown to any human metallurgist beneath cave paintings depicting a star fall. The symbols etched into the metal shards led, via a series of misadventures, to a highly illegal dig in the Gobi Desert. There he uncovered an underground temple allegedly built by no human hand. Most of the temple's library was now dust, but one surviving book told of an entity Vane's journals name "the Witness."

Vane spent most of 1911 trying to discover who or what the Witness was. That search ended in an isolated village in Nepal that, if his journals are to be believed, harbored a being not of this world. Vane spent himself down to nearly his last dime securing an audience with that entity. The last of his money and every connection he had with the criminals who had funded the last year of his travels. By his own heavily coded admission, Vane received a large sum of money to transport three particular Nepalese children from Kathmandu to a British outpost in northern India, the oldest of whom was estimated at eleven years old. It will not surprise you to learn they never reached India. Money alone wouldn't secure an audience with the mysterious entity. Vane traded each of them, one child per night of his audience. His journals don't describe what happened to them. I hope their fate at least troubled his nightmares.

Likewise, his journals do not describe the being he spoke to, although halfway through the relevant entry he identifies the being as the Witness without further explanation. By his own account, he never actually saw it, only spoke to it through a wooden screen. One might believe Vane—and more importantly, the children he sacrificed—was the victim of a sick hoax, if not for the way he describes it speaking. He claimed it didn't have a voice. Its words dripped into his mind like dirty oil.

The household that served the Witness seems to have been very unusual. In Vane's account, they stood stock still inside the house, like statues or dolls, until the Witness spoke to them. Then they would leap to life, fulfilling whatever task it gave them in jerking, frenzied motions. When it was complete, they would freeze again wherever they stood.

The Witness told Vane many things. He didn't record all of it in his journals (or if he did, those pages were lost) although he does allude to some of it. As Vane wrote, the Witness described the greatest impact site and the caverns that could be found beneath it in such detail that for a moment he believed he saw his dreams again.

Vane arrived at the village with eight people in tow. We know what he did with the children. He doesn't describe what happened to the others. Names pepper his journal entries up to that point. After leaving the village, he describes them only in the past, and only by title or description: a porter, a manservant, a driver, *et cetera*. Then, once he crossed into India, his journal mentions them not at all.

He spent the very last bit of his smuggling money fleeing India for North America, his former associates at his heels. I believe he sought out the Apollonian Society for protection as much as for funding. He would likely have mysteriously disappeared years before he actually did had he not secured Maxwell Thorpe's protection.

It was logical that he would seek out the Apollonian Society specifically. The Apollonian Society for Illumination was the best-known esoteric studies group on the US Eastern Seaboard. Moreover, they were likely the only group that would have given Balthazar Vane the time of day at this point in his obsession. I imagine he must have cut quite the figure while pleading his case in the society's lounge—a vagabond with the accent of a Southern planter. The conspirators would like to believe they cared more about evidence than worldly things, but I suspect it was Vane's plantation roots that truly won Thorpe over. Vane's journals alone wouldn't have gotten him an audience with the Apollonian Society any more than they would have in London, New York City, or Chicago. South of the Mason-Dixon line, however, his heritage still carried respect. He was one of them, so they financed his last expedition. Three society members joined Vane: Fredrick Rust, Kenneth Harris, and Daniel Bernard, along with two dozen hired men of various skills.

Six months of study, comparing his visions against photographs and topographical maps, led Vane and the expedition to the Sangre De Cristos Mountains and the Pecos Wilderness. He chose a spot on the slope of Montana del Lucheza, an otherwise unremarkable peak. Vane was unfamiliar with the legends surrounding that particular mountain—stories from Spanish and Mexican settlers of night-walking spirits, monsters with the faces and voices of women who led travelers astray and feasted on warm blood. Perhaps those stories had something to do with the thing they found beneath the mountain. Perhaps they were something completely different. It's a big, strange world, after all.

Most of the expedition were skeptical when they reached the slope. Vane was vague on how long ago the impact occurred, but even by his wildest estimates there should have been an impact crater. Del Lucheza's slope was rugged, certainly, but nothing to suggest a meteorite had struck. It was more like the rock had closed around itself, like stone wings folding.

Still, the miners dug where Vane told them to dig, and they blasted where they told them to dynamite. After a week's efforts, during which they lost no fewer than six men to misfortune ranging from "misjudged blast radius" to "voices in the night", they uncovered a cavern entrance. Fredrick Rust's journals recount:

"A great exhalation roiled out of the aperture, warm and wet, as if some massive subterranean beast had released a long-held breath. When the wind first wafted over us, I expected it to be foul. To my surprise, the air carried an unusual scent, almost pleasant, like a hint of freshly turned earth mixed with warm blood. That was impossible, of course. Although there was a cavern beneath the mountain, we knew of no other entrances. There could be no life down there.

"The hired men muttered among themselves, uttering oaths and epithets that spoke of superstition. Vane was as giddy as a schoolboy on the eve of his summer holiday. I expected him to upbraid the men, as he'd been quite the tin-pot tyrant during the dig. Instead, he simply paid off the weaker half of the team, claiming we no longer needed so many.

"Before we descended into the darkness, I asked Vane why he had let them go so easily. He said it would make it easier to keep our discovery a secret."

For the first two hundred vertical meters, the explorers descended through what appeared to be completely natural caverns. It was slow-going; the stone walls were rippled, as if the stone had melted and then set, although there was no evidence of vulcanism in the region. Vane, the three society members, and the half-dozen remaining hired men had to navigate a series of switchback trails down steep grades, following the trail of some long-lost molten object. As Rust expected, they found no sign of life within the cavern—no guano, no bones, no snakes or insects. Nothing until they reached the point Rust's journal names "the Antechamber".

Most spelunkers have the honor of naming the chambers they uncover, often with fantastic names. This was no flight of fancy, however. The Antechamber was clearly made of worked stone—the lines were too precise, the curves too regular, to have been formed by anything other than an intelligent hand. Or other maniple.

The entrance was wide and low, barely high enough for a person of average height to pass under without ducking their head. The chamber within was a nearly perfect circle. Its smooth curved wall was decorated with geometric murals in designs that matched no culture the explorers were familiar with, though in fairness, that was not a wide range. The colors were so vibrant that they could have plausibly been painted the day before.

The Antechamber's floor opened into a wide circular pit, which led to a spiral ramp, wide enough for three people to walk abreast. The expedition made camp in the Antechamber that night. In the morning, they continued their descent. The ramp was slightly too steep to be easy going. It was not a simple stair, but a perfectly circular tunnel bored into the rock. Had they delayed the expedition by just a few more years, they might have imagined some manner of "death ray" was responsible. In 1913, they had no concept of what force could have cut a tunnel of such perfection. The flawless smoothness of the walls was broken only by small alcoves spaced every six meters, forming a spiral within the tunnel. They didn't guess the alcoves' function until they had descended another hundred meters, when random alcoves began emitting sporadic light that flickered on and off at random intervals. Harris speculated it was a malfunction. Regardless, in the last hundred meters the lights shone increasingly bright and steady until they reached the bottom.

The tunnel opened onto a wide, bowl-shaped floor beneath a domed ceiling, held up by thick, fluted columns. There, they caught their first glimpse of what was unmistakably a lost city. One whose walls had been raised by no human hand. Possibly not by a hand at all.

A massive cavern chamber stretched out before them. In the heart of the mountain, they should have been swallowed in darkness. Instead, crystals at the tops of the tallest buildings bathed the cavern in pale light. Stepped terraces held squat, trapezoidal buildings that climbed the cavern walls up to its high stone ceiling. Ramps and wide bridges connected them like stone webs. Dark openings in the distance suggested more chambers.

It would have been the work of years to explore that lost city, if not a lifetime. A less focused expedition might have taken a more leisurely approach to that first descent, surveying the initial cavern, cataloguing what they found, trying to gain a sense of the place. Vane did not give them the chance. He drove them through the ruin like a man possessed, following the main thoroughfares deeper and deeper into the alien city. For all its vastness, the city was empty. Except at its deepest point.

As per their usual protocol, the Apollonian Society didn't share what they uncovered in the depths of the Lechuza Cavern. These men weren't archeologists. They weren't looking to study ancient cultures or record the history of life on Earth. They weren't even looking to become famous outside of their rarefied circles. They were looking for something to exploit, and they found it.

When a whale's carcass sinks into the ocean depths, it doesn't decay as rapidly as it would in the shallows. Hydrostatic pressure and cool temperatures keep it preserved for a long time. The carcass becomes the center of a unique local ecosystem, one that can last for decades if not longer.

What the Vane Expedition found deep beneath the mountains wasn't a whale carcass. It may not have been a corpse of any kind. The creature was still bleeding, that massive lump of pale flesh and red bone, her body flayed open where it wasn't pierced by massive skewers made of no material they could identify. Chains that weren't chains bound it in the heart of the cavern, a variant of Prospero's Keys that the expedition never deciphered.

They didn't know what she was, but that didn't stop them from trying to classify her. In Vane's journals, he named her *The Lechuza Leviathan*. His colleague Julian West, himself a student of mythology, labeled her *The American Ymir*. When the Bureau of Extranormal Investigations recovered the expedition's notes, they simply categorized her as *Subject 16*. A former Chambers Foundation researcher, Felix Blake, came closest to understanding her when he proclaimed her to be *The Pecos Madonna* in a paper that was almost immediately declared heretical.

Of all mortal entities, it is unsurprisingly the cosmic researchers known as the Archivists who will describe her the most accurately. Even they will be cribbing from a hundred different sects and cults that proliferated among the stars. Does it interest you to know that one of them will be inspired by Blake's paper? It was suppressed but not lost.

The Archivists named her *Anke zan Ilitu*. In English, that roughly translates to "the Void Mother". Fitting, as she crashed from the stars and birthed a civilization deep within the Lechuza Cavern.

Surprisingly, the Apollonian Society left the leviathan where they found her. Perhaps they didn't trust themselves to recreate the binding seal. If so, they displayed a surprising degree of self-awareness. More likely, it was that they already had their treasure—a sea of ultraterrestrial biofluid, the results of millennia of open, bleeding wounds. Once, this sea of life had been the foundation upon which this lost subterranean civilization had built, a novel ecosystem that had rapidly evolved unseen by the sun or human eyes. The leviathan remained, but her children and grandchildren were long extinct.

The Vane Expedition took samples, of course—skin and flesh and bone and one titanic eye. More importantly, they took gallons of fluid, her blood or bile or milk or some more undefinable product. They didn't know how to exploit it, not in the 1910s, but they knew it was exploitable. It took decades of study.

In 1948, Julian West's son Jeffrey made a breakthrough. Then a whole new trouble began.

18

✦

The second amber lamp cut through the gloom inside the capsule. Harold floated silently in the green synaptic fluid, trying to ignore the tingle in his skin as his nerves synchronized with the bizarre liquid. The process was safe. He was in control, and the doctor had signaled that it was time. That is, assuming the rest of his teammates were doing their part.

In the back of his mind, Harold restarted the count. Thirty, twenty-nine, twenty-eight. He stilled his thoughts, following the exercise Traynor had taught him. The Night Lake Meditation. He stood on the surface of a wide, placid lake. The still water, mirror-smooth, stretched from horizon to horizon. The night sky hung above him, a flawless obsidian dome. The lake reflected the night back to itself, forming a seamless jet-black sphere. Harold stood proudly in the center, the unshakeable axis around which the void spun.

Void. The word stabbed across his consciousness, echoing the blackness. Rogers' word. Rogers' voice. Rogers' fear.

This, he realized with a cold shock, is what had gone wrong. Rogers had fallen into the void. This void. He couldn't climb out, even after the doctor had allowed him to wake up. Harold was stranded in that same void. He could feel its weird gravity pulling at him. Beckoning to him. It would be so easy to let go. Let go of his position. His family's expectations. The weight on his shoulders. The others could never understand the load he bore. They were basically peasants, made to work. They didn't know what it meant to lead, to take on the burden of a great enterprise. He didn't dare falter, and yet it was so tempting.

At the edge of hearing, a voice whispered in his ear. Its words were indistinct, but the void carried their meaning. He could do it. It wouldn't even take a step. He could just let go.

Zero. The third lamp flared, an amber moon desecrating the void's purity. Instinctively, Harold dismissed it with little more than a stray thought, as he'd been taught.

Indignation rose in him like a flame. He'd been trained, *prepared* for this. He wasn't some simpering coward, giving in to the void like Rogers. He was a *leader*. A beacon of stability against chaos. Everyone needed him. Doctor Traynor was *depending* on him.

The fire rose to his mind, his eyes blazing like the lantern room of a lighthouse. The deep structures in his brain roared as he ran Psycho-Astronomy Sequence Theta. His psychic presence shot out, a beam of raw power screaming "I" at the heart of the void.

He swept round the nothingness, searching for the cardinal technicians. He looked for George first. Solid, dependable George, whose psychic shadow bent the cognitive space around him. His noetic gravity caught Harold's beam as it swept by. Their minds synchronized, forming the first point in the array.

Harold continued sweeping around the cardinal points. He looked next for Irene, the brightest point on the compass. Even with her mind distressed and forlorn, he could sense the storm within her. He was drawn to it, though he would never admit it. He yearned to tame it, tame her. He could never, here or in the physical. When his psychic beam reached her presence, a bolt of noetic lightning shot back along it. Irene easily resisted his force, asserting her position in the void. He could not overwhelm her. He could only synchronize his mind to hers, forming the second point in the array.

Psychic energy hummed between George and Irene like a high-tension line, perfectly balanced within Harold's presence. They could maintain this formation indefinitely if they had to, but that wouldn't create a powerful enough lens. Harold had to add the remaining minds, and so came the tricky part.

Eddie's mind shone brightly in the void, a psychic bonfire almost as powerful as Harold himself. He would serve as a decent understudy, if such a thing would ever be necessary. Harold caught Eddie easily, feeding his mental flames into Harold's beacon. Together they formed the third point in the array. Now the whole set-up teetered dangerously. Ironically, without Harold in the middle, this configuration would have been completely stable. Irene, George, and Eddie could have balanced their connection easily. With Harold, the psychic array was irregular, threatening to collapse at any moment. He had to find the fourth cardinal point immediately to rebalance the load.

Sadly, this was the only time Harold ever deliberately reached out to Richard Seyton. Norman's loss had left Richard in the upper half of the rankings. His psychic presence was the weakest of the four cardinal points but also the most eager to connect with the center. Richard's fluid mind surged into a waterspout, leaping out to grab Harold's beam as it swept toward him. They synchronized easily, much to Harold's dismay. He swallowed his contempt for Richard, not that it was necessary. It was their noetic signatures that harmonized, not their full consciousness. Richard could no more feel Harold's contempt for him than Harold could Richard's admiration.

"They've done it," I said. "They've all harmonized with Harold."

Traynor looked up from the readouts, the elation on his face fading into annoyance. "I was about to say that," he said sulkily.

Octavian rolled his eyes. "I don't care who tells me it's working, Matthew, I just want to hear that it is."

"It is," I said. "They've formed the outer part of the array."

"Not yet," Traynor grumbled. He activated the secondary station's intercom circuit again. "Stations One through Four. On my mark, commence Psycho-Astronomy Sequence Beta... mark!"

Below, the cardinal technicians ran the next sequence. The bonds across the array were stable—Irene to George, Eddie to Richard. Now they reached to either side, harmonizing their psychic presences with the remaining cardinal points. Noetic energy whirled round the edge of the chamber, spinning a narrow torus not entirely unlike the energy vortex of a functioning seal. The myrmidons took no note, but immediate space-time took on an even more noticeable curve. Even a normal human with an undeveloped psychic talent might notice something uncanny within the chamber—a touch of vertigo or a persistent feeling that they were being watched.

Within the capsule, the fourth lamp burned amber, signaling to Harold that the outer array was complete. It was time to begin the next sequence. The signal was unnecessary. From his position in the center of the array, Harold could feel the connection between the four cardinal points stabilizing. The flow of psychic power hummed through his nervous system, a bolt of lightning opening points along his spine like blossoms of pure light. His thoughts expanded. His synapses fired through the sync suit into the green fluid. Pulses of electricity illuminated the capsule's interior like a plasma ball. Harold saw by the light of his own thoughts.

The flow of power pulled at his mind, rushing through his gray matter like water through porous stone. He sank into the sensations, washing his fear and doubts away. His resentment of the other pilot candidates, his contempt for the weasel who did his bidding, his desire for the pretty brunette... it drifted apart, washed away into the glittering synaptic fluid. He couldn't remember what the other one had done to provoke him. He couldn't even remember his name.

Like water, it ate at him. It was a new sensation. This wasn't the seductive gravity of the void, the weird psychic vacuum eroding his sense of place. This was a song of dissolution, inviting him into the undifferentiated oneness of their connection. "He" was a thing of transient individual matter, an accident of meat and spark that somehow gave rise to continuity of experience. In the connection between the five minds, there was no "he". There wasn't even a "we". There was only energy transitioning between bits of matter in a ceaseless loop.

No.

The array shivered as the center wrenched a sense of self free of the seductive pull. A miniature lightning storm raged within the capsule. Piece by piece, the center reassembled a "Harold" within the void. The array whirled around him, shaking but holding. More importantly, he could feel himself again. He was floating in the capsule, staring at four amber lamps. He was Harold, Harold Bates of Boston. Scion of a respectable family, heir to a tidy fortune nearly two centuries old, and one of the most promising psychic talents in North America. He wasn't going to dissolve into a cognitive sludge. He was a *Bates*, blast it!

The fourth lamp blinked twice. Harold rolled his eyes. He knew it was time to finish the array, but he needed a moment to orient himself. It's not as if Traynor was the one in here doing this. Harold doubted he was even capable of doing it, assuming he could muster the guts.

His indignation stabilized his sense of self as he fell into the array. Indignation and pride. He conceived of himself as the void's center of gravity. The psychic power spun around him, flowed through him, but he was its master, not a mere component of a greater machine. He felt the array's power, assuring himself that the outer loop remained strong. Then he pulled his attention *inward*, sending his beacon sweeping through the void again. He picked up the ordinal technicians one by one—first Lorraine, then Patricia, then Albert, and finally the new active whose name he hadn't bothered to learn. Their minds synchronized with his, forming a second, weaker array.

The outer array supported itself, for the most part. The four cardinal points kept their bonds stable, holding each other up with minimal effort on his part. The weight of four additional minds, however, threatened to drag him down. He had dismissed the ordinal technicians' minds as being weaker, but the flow of energy had more than doubled. So had the pull of dissolution. He chanted his name like a mantra. Harold Bates. Harold *Bates. Harold* Bates.

"I believe Harold is experiencing some difficulty," I said.

"His sync rating is fluctuating, but it's within tolerances," Traynor said. "In fact, he's setting a personal best right now."

Nine sync meters paneled the wall at his right in a three-by-three grid, labeled with the technicians' stations. On each, a roll of paper scrolled past two wavering needles, which sketched out lines measuring something or another. From inference, one was the technicians' sync ratings. As Traynor said, Harold's was trending upward. Most of their sync ratings were, in fact. I couldn't guess as to the other.

"His sync rating is fluctuating in an inverse relationship to that second measurement."

I joined him at the pane, only remembering at the last second to actually walk across all the space. I stabbed a finger at Harold's graph, where the second reading was trending sharply downward.

"What is that?" I asked, although from Harold's experience in the capsule, I was starting to suspect.

Traynor didn't look at me. "It's Bates' cognitive stability. It measures his sense of self as an individual. More or less."

A red line ran along the graph paper, two inches from the bottom edge. Bates' cognitive stability was approaching that line, as it had done seconds before. In both cases, it corresponded to a spike in his sync rating.

"What's the red line?" It was phrased as a question, but my tone indicated otherwise.

Traynor looked momentarily uncomfortable. "That—*theoretically*—is ego death."

"Ego death."

Traynor's eyes focused intently on the control console. "The point at which he will cease to recognize a distinction between himself and, well, everything."

My mouth tightened into a thin white line. Harold wasn't the only one coming perilously close to ego death. Richard, Mitchell, Albert, and Lorraine were all reaching the red line.

"Are they prepared for this?" I asked. "Do you know what's going to happen to them?"

"More importantly, will it affect the experiment?" Octavian snapped.

"No, no… and no, Dr. Pretorius. Not so long as they can still execute the sequences."

Octavian's brows furrowed. "That sounds perilously close to an 'if', Matthew."

"It's not, I assure you. I've drilled the sequences into their heads. It should be close to instinctive." Traynor shrugged. "If anything, it might make them more successful. Get their conscious minds out of their way."

I stared at the two men, incredulous and furious. "I cannot believe what I'm hearing. You don't know what's going to happen to them, but you don't *think* it'll be a problem? So long as it doesn't interfere with your precious experiment?"

"The Institute operating under its usual standard of scientific rigor," Ravenna said, her voice sour as curdled milk.

Traynor briefly glanced over his shoulder at me before returning his attention to the control console. "It's not as if they'll collapse into a puddle of biofluid, Miss Temple. The technicians will still *be* there. Their brains will still function. They'll simply be experiencing a moment of transcendent awareness."

"Which they might not know how to come back from!"

"We'll cross that bridge when we come to it, Amelia." Octavian slammed his fist against the side of his chair. "Continue, Matthew."

"I intend to." He tossed me a brief patronizing smile. "Don't worry. We knew there would be hiccups. We'll see things start to stabilize once they complete the array."

He clicked the intercom. "Stations Five through Eight. On my mark, commence Psycho-Astronomy Sequence Beta. Stations One through Four. On my mark, commence Psycho-Astronomy Sequence Delta... mark!"

We stared at the readouts. The invisible scars on my right arm burned. Behind my back, my fingers twitched, itching to grab and tear.

"If this starts to go poorly, I'm intervening," I said coldly.

Octavian jerked his head around, his expression fierce and unyielding.

"You'll do no such thing."

"What?"

"You're here to *observe*, not interfere. You'll do nothing that jeopardizes this experiment. Do you understand?"

At his tone, one of the myrmidons turned and looked at me. It had an electric baton in one pocket and a handheld antenna in the other. I stared at Octavian, open-mouthed. Then I turned to the myrmidons lined up in the chamber below. Some signal shivered between them, and they all stared up at me.

In my mind, the Watcher churned coldly, eagerly. I took in a deep breath, but not to calm myself. I straightened and my hands fell loosely to my side. I was about to remind Octavian just how far his authority went when I felt Ravenna's psychic touch on my shoulder.

"Don't. Not yet." Her mental presence was cool and soothing. "Play his game. Let him flex his authority as if it matters. When we move, do it with subtlety."

I glared at her. Ravenna's psychic aura snapped and whirled around me. Beneath her call for patience, I could feel her anger. I nodded, not accepting the need to hold back but agreeing with her for now. I returned to my place in the corner, arms folded across my chest. I didn't look at either of the men, but I watched them as intently as I watched Harold.

Trouble loomed in multidimensional space, turbulence coming from the near future.

The array trembled again, the bonds wobbling dangerously as Harold's psychic presence pulsed arrhythmically from the center. He was creating a stable reference point. The other technicians couldn't understand the content, but it created its own context. This was the pilot. The center. A presence against which to reference themselves. If it was there, so were they.

Following radio instructions, the ordinal technicians reached out to one another, synchronizing and harmonizing their psychic presences. The inner array stabilized, reducing the strain on the pilot. On Harold. His name was Harold. His name was Harold.

At the same time, the cardinal technicians turned their own focus toward the center. Each reached out to two ordinal technicians. They spun a web of psychic bonds, the two arrays weaving together to become one. The nine technicians sang in noetic harmony. The power no longer flowed through Harold. It froze, the array becoming a lens of crystalline power. Harold held their combined potential within his head, feeling his consciousness expand to encompass everything.

It was too much for his mere human mind to contain. The array no longer threatened to fall apart. Now it threatened to tear him to pieces. His body seized, muscles flailing his limbs against the leather straps. He vibrated like a fork after a tuning hit the right frequency. He would tear himself apart in seconds.

Then the fifth amber lamp lit. Harold—for he was Harold, Harold Bates, about to take his place in parapsychological history—grabbed hold of its significance like a life preserver. It was time to run the next sequence. The deep structures activated again, plunging his consciousness *down*. Into the Argos Device, into the strange mechanisms that powered it. Into the miles of actual human nerve tissue that formed complex webs binding the lapis lazuli rods to a dense, twelve-foot-long spinal cord running the capsule's length. This was the Argos Device's secret, a hidden biological layer grown in Jeffrey West's tanks.

This was the synaptic fluid's purpose, to serve as a medium between the Argos Device's nervous system and that of the pilot. Unbeknownst to

Harold or Matthew Traynor or anyone but Jeffrey West, the fluid contained an impurity. It was the serum he had introduced days ago, lurking within the device's tissues. As Harold's synaptic impulses fired along the device's neurons, they woke up the waiting serum and the new instructions it contained.

The Argos Device's nervous system leapt to life as Harold's expanding consciousness filled it. Neurons replicated rapidly in accordance with the serum's instructions. He—they—were more than just a man. More than a piece of equipment. They were something new in the world, a being more than human, with a single perfect eye as large as a moon.

Above Harold's head, the single green lamp burned bright. It was time to run the final psycho-astronomy sequence. Time to open that eye and *see*.

19

Trans-Neptunian space isn't *cluttered*, exactly; it would take a staggering amount of matter to clutter such a vast volume of space. Nonetheless, there are far more objects revolving your sun beyond Neptune's orbit than you realize, particularly in 1954. Contemporary astronomers hypothesized another planet beyond Pluto, but evidence of the many trans-Neptunian objects would be decades away. Even the Institute didn't know for certain Object C existed. Traynor conceived of his experiment using old notes recovered from the defunct Apollonian Society, and their information originated in certain esoteric texts.

The same texts that led Balthazar Vane to Montana de Lucheza.

In the astral realm, Harold rose from the Earth as a giant of brilliant light. His thought-form bore only the roughest resemblance to a humanoid figure. His limbs and torso were simple smooth shapes, and his hairless head was featureless except for a single blazing eye on his brow. Nerve impulses crawled across his surface, tracing the patterns of his nervous system. Tendrils of thought-flesh trailed from his shoulders, his hips and his shining spine like wispy feathers or the fronds of a fern. Two majestic rainbow halos emanated from him, both sporting four nodes with bright eyes. Lightning thoughts sparked between the two halos and to his own thought-form. He—they— hovered in astral space for a moment, reveling in this moment of clarity, in their power and awareness. Then they swung their mighty gaze into realspace, where the object of their desire waited.

Space unfolded before the clairvoyant team. The distance didn't change; their perspective jumped, leaping across thirty astronomical units of uncharted space. Object C sat within a cluster of twenty-one distinct trans-Neptunian objects. Most were no more than a kilometer across their semi-major axis. Object C loomed among them at five hundred times their size, an irregular planetoid that looked as if a rocky sphere was birthing a second, smaller sphere.

It was, on a cosmic scale, a tiny, ugly lump of rock. Its dark surface barely stood out against the blackness of space. Yet the sight of it, a new world millions of kilometers beyond the one they knew, took the technicians' breaths away.

Harold swung their collective vision across the planetoid's surface. It was craggy, with unweathered geological features like rocky webbing stretched across its surface. Vast lakes of ammonia and methane ice sat between the stone ridges. A tenuous atmosphere of nitrogen and helium clung to Object C's surface, gradually being stripped away by the solar winds. The atmosphere was too thin to produce weather effects; that solar radiation was the only source of erosion. Thus, the many impact craters were as fresh as the day the meteors had struck.

Harold would have said this place was inhospitable. No life he could conceive of would survive on this barren lump of frozen rock. Yet, as they scanned the surface, they thrilled to see the unmistakable sharp regular lines of an artificial structure cresting a wide hill.

Some unknown intelligence had stacked black stone upon black stone in a low ziggurat surrounded by concentric rings of standing stone connected by cracked arches. Once, someone had decorated the place with gargoyles.

Angels with the faces of birds and too many legs beneath their robes. I'd seen their like before, in a tiny archive within an equally tiny human village. None of it looked native to the planetoid. Nor could the technicians see any evidence of mining in a quick survey. Someone had brought this stone here, to this barren rock at the edge of the solar system. It was a fascinating puzzle. The solution lurked deep beneath Object C's surface.

As the clairvoyants' psionic energy played across the planetoid, for the first time in millennia a vast intelligence woke up.

A storm of psychic energy spun to life as Harold's presence focused on Object C. Weird radiation whipped across its surface, centered on the temple. The intangible wind tore at his mind. It would have ripped him to shreds if not for the array buttressing his psyche. Harold's scream echoed through the other technicians' minds, his pain replicating along their nervous systems. Nerve impulses like lightning bolts fired across the array, carrying thoughts of pain and fear from node to node. The halos trembled as the technicians instinctively turned their minds inward, trying to protect themselves. Harold poured his will into their bonds, pulling their attention outward again. It was a wordless demand, a call to attend him. It came as naturally to him as breathing.

In response, a psychic scream blasted out from deep within the planetoid. It drowned out their song, a hundred voices raised at once. There was no harmony among them, only fury. It filled the humans' minds with raw emotion, with incomprehensible truth, with the glory of the cosmos. It was the raw pain and fury and glory of an entity that had traversed the universe for eons, a psychic pressure the size of a star. It subjected them to concepts they lacked names for, never mind context. Despite all that, this being had been trapped in this prison since before their species had adopted language.

One hundred thousand years ago, while humans were still spreading out from Africa, another intelligent species arrived in this star system. They called themselves the Ixikan; I don't know whether that was their name for their species, civilization, or just this particular polity. Their physiology was unlike anything indigenous to Earth, although not to the Jovian moons. Their closest terrestrial analogue was to the insect kingdom, although they were larger than any insects seen on Earth since the Carboniferous Period. They had evolved to survive anaerobic, low-gravity environments such as those on the small trans-Neptunian objects.

Accordingly, they established their foothold in the star system's outer regions—specifically, on the planetoid the Institute labeled "Object C". Today, no trace of their civilization exists in this system other than the temple that once stood at the heart of their city and a handful of artifacts recovered in the Andes, Himalayas, and Greenland. These artifacts, which display similarities to the ruins on Object C, imply the Ixikan did travel sunward at one point. The Bureau recovered some of these artifacts in the 1930s, labeled their creators *Subject 21*, and promptly forgot about them.

I don't know what happened to the Ixikan or their kin but I know what brought them to this region of space-time. They were seeking their gods, and they found them.

Despite the archaeological record proving their presence on Earth, history suggests the Ixikan never had an interest in humans. I can't say the same for Object C's *second* inhabitants, a group of astral invaders calling themselves the Zi-Thra. They inhabited the planetoid, which they named Kor-Mitra, between eight and four thousand years ago. Evidence of their presence on Earth survives into the modern era. Stories of their predation exist in various cultures' oral histories, but highly distorted. It's not just due to repeated retellings; many cultures, such as the aboriginal Australians, maintain highly accurate oral records. Something about the Zi-Thra affects human minds, resists accurate retelling. Humans are vulnerable to them.

Yet, they were here. I don't know what they were looking for in this system, but they found five inhabited worlds—yes, *five*—and something very much like a god lurking in the void. Maybe their predation on Earth, Mars, and Europa was about appeasing the entity beneath the Ixikan temple. Maybe it was about supplication, or keeping it bound. I only know that they left a scar across your collective legends thousands of years wide. Until, perhaps, your ancestors had enough. Or at least someone did. Around the time the Xia Dynasty was established in China, the Middle Kingdom reunited Egypt, and the wooly mammoth went extinct, the Zi-Thra were driven from Object C.

Balthazar Vane followed their legends to the mountain; they may have had a connection to the entity he called the Witness. Other than that, the Zi-Thra do not come back into this narrative for some time. This is about the Institute's Object C Observation and what happened afterward.

The nine objects of the Younger Dryas Impacts weren't the only ones in that cluster. I don't know what sent those objects flying sunward. I know the Ixikan weren't responsible; they had abandoned the planetoid by then or died out. Likewise, it had nothing to do with the Zi-Thra; they arrived well after. It's possible it was just a cosmic accident, like the ones that created your moon or exterminated the Utsoggthua. Sometimes events have a cause, not a reason.

Other times, the reason is neglect and imprudence.

It was all simply too much. The clairvoyants struggled to maintain cognitive stability in the face of the entity's fury. They couldn't hold on to themselves and the array. The bonds holding the inner and outer arrays together shattered beneath the scream's force, motes and flickers of psychic energy flashing briefly like sparks from a bonfire.

Harold, his brain enhanced by the Argos Device's growing nervous system, tried to stand firm against the assault. The others abandoned him one by one, retreating into themselves in a desperate attempt to protect their individuality. The array lost equilibrium, the many psychic bonds becoming too much to bear. He couldn't balance the load and withstand the imprisoned god's assault. The inner array collapsed first, the clairvoyants' minds washing into incoherence amid a stream of flaw and delusion. The outer array followed, the stronger technicians fleeing, their psychic awareness spinning off in random directions in the astral realm. They should have been capable of recovering from this, but astral navigation was not among the skills Traynor had drilled into them. They were trapped in whatever vision random chance placed in their way.

Harold felt the last of his team fall out of the array, a sensation akin to limbs falling numb one by one. Anger rose within him. How dare they abandon him, leave him to face this thing alone? He knew they were weak, but he'd expected at least together they might match him. Now it was up to him. Well, he'd show them all.

Harold screamed defiance into the psychic storm, his will and fury forming a windbreak in a wide arc in front of him. The storm raged on, revealing a wide eye centered on the temple's astral reflection. For a moment, he felt coherence return to his astral form. Then the entity within Object C screamed again, a train whistle shriek that pierced his cortex. The astral equivalent of gravity warped around the planetoid, dragging Harold in. He flung his many cognitive limbs and tendrils out, digging into the ethereal substance of the astral realm, trying to brace himself against nothing. What he at first thought was lightning flashed through the storm, until the first bolts pierced the vortex. They were wings made of neural impulses, vast and terrible, titanic thoughts that encompassed an entire catechism of occult secrets. A second pair joined them, and then a third. Six dogmatic wing-sermons, describing the breadth and depth of the entity's psychic presence, singing its name. *Amn-Zuhad*. Harold caught glimpses of a cyclopean form beneath the storm, an astral presence like a many-limbed giant made of light against which Harold's thought form resembled a doll.

The wings spread, reaching toward Harold like a spider's legs. The giant of light crawled up from the temple, moving hand over hand across the planetoid's surface. Harold saw hints of its immense form reflected in its noetic song. The thick coils, as big around as a house. The many-jointed limbs—six or eight or more, extending and retracting from its trunk as needed. The smooth pale skin, lit from within by the lightning bursts of its vast intellect. He told himself that it wasn't real, that it was all imaginary, a shadow play cast against the walls of his own mind. He tried to imagine himself as larger, as a being of equal stature to this angelic alien intelligence. It was no use. He couldn't approach its magnificence. The winds of its stray thoughts tore at him, the wings of its canons overturning his core beliefs with every beat.

Despair clawed at him. The light of his thought-form disintegrated. He saw himself kneeling at the being's altar, offering obeisance in exchange for ordination. He wore robes of a shiny scarlet material. A fiery halo burned above his head. His hands leaked bright orange fluid from jagged rents—a blessing for the fields and beds. It hurt, but the pain was a prayer in and of itself. He was made for this pain. It was a fit enough position for such as him. Gods always had a use for priests.

No. Harold grasped desperately for a rejoinder. He found a half-remembered quotation in the depths of his memory. "I have sworn upon the altar of God, eternal hostility against every form of tyranny over the mind of man." The words were Thomas Jefferson's, but he heard them in his father's voice. This motto had guided him through life, from the early days of his education all the way to the Nova Anima Institute. He was a free thinker, as his father had taught him to be. Unbound by the chains and fetters of superstition that hampered lesser men. His own will to power had propelled him here, to the edge of space, where he faced nothing more than an arrogant boggart clinging to a speck of space dust.

He laughed cruelly, and now he stood in his father's study. The air smelled of wood smoke, old leather, and expensive bourbon. As a boy, he'd spent many evenings here, tracing the family tree with his father. His father had conducted his business in front of Harold, imparting the lessons of courage and leadership. Instilling him with the values that made him who he was.

Striking him across the face. Lashing his bare back and buttocks with his belt. Screaming incoherently at him, about his habits, about his choices, about his mother. Harold tasted his own blood in his mouth, smelled his father's breath stinking of whiskey and cigar smoke. Saw the tumors growing in his father's lungs, heard them chewing at his father's flesh. Watched his father gradually wither away until he had one foot in the grave. Worms would eat him. Worms would eat Harold, too. They crawled up and through him, eating at his flesh until it fell apart. He was nothing. Dust. Meat.

Harold wrestled free of the deception, seeing again the temple standing amid the psychic storm. Nothing? Harold Bates, *nothing?* He was a man of privilege, of *accomplishment*. He leapt from the temple floor into another memory. He stood on the stage at Harvard, just a year ago, accepting a degree from one of the most prestigious institutions in the country. It was an accomplishment to be proud of. He swelled from the approval in the presenter's eye. They exchanged a firm handshake, and the presenter handed him his scroll. Harold looked out at the audience, his classmates and their families, basking in their approval as the great and good of New England applauded him.

Of course, Father wasn't there. He'd been too ill, and if he hadn't been, he'd have been too busy. Even though it was his name and his money that put Harold here. He was a lackluster student; he'd never have merited admission to Harvard on his own, let alone graduated. The dean might as well have just handed him his diploma the moment he'd set foot on campus and saved them all the trouble. Let Harold busy himself with drinking and gambling and women. He'd certainly done that more than study. He was the true wastrel. A simple puppet fit only for carrying out other's expectations. He'd spent his life following his father's path. He might as well continue now. It was what he was made for.

That was a ridiculous thought. Father hadn't sent him to the Institute. He knew nothing of the greater human potential, the occult world just outside blinkered human perception. Father would have dismissed the Institute's goals as base superstition. He would never stand here, piloting this wondrous deice, expanding the limits of human potential.

Of course, Harold was only here because Rogers had failed. He was never the first choice. He was an understudy. A backup. A living spare tire, pulled out of storage because the real thing had failed. Did he really think he was up to the task? He couldn't even earn his companions' respect, let alone lead them into the unknown.

Harold saw the infirmary, only it was him in the hospital bed. He was emaciated, gasping against a breathing tube as more pipes ran in and out of his orifices. His hair was falling out, his eyes had lost their color. His bleeding gums pulled back from his rotten teeth. He tried to lift his head from the pillow, call out to his doctor and friends, but there was no one in the room. No one stood by him. No one left gifts or well-wishes. No one cared that he lay here in his soiled hospital gown, dying by inches as his flesh turned against him.

The psychic storm intensified. The eye widened as the noetic maelstrom grew to encompass half the planetoid. The behemoth screamed again as it rose from the gaping eye. The weight of its gaze pinned Harold like a hand on a slender wrist, holding him fast. His will drained out of him, evaporating under the behemoth's heat. He was nothing but a tool. An object to be used.

The behemoth's wings flashed at him, six titanic numinous daggers striking him at once, burning everything that was Harold out of his brain.

20

Electricity arced from the Argos Device to the ceiling. The lights in the lab and observation room flickered wildly. The Institute compound shook at its very foundations. Gravity tilted sickeningly as something immense moved through space and time at right angles to everything.

Octavian leapt from his chair, shouting, "What the devil is happening, Matthew?"

Traynor stared at the readings. All the blood drained from his face. Harold's cognitive stability had fallen below the red line, flat as a leather strap, while his sync rate climbed so high the needle snapped under the pressure. The other technicians' cognitive stability readings were also plummeting, but unlike Harold, their sync ratings dropped too. Three had already crossed the red line—Lorraine, Richard, and Mitchell—with two more soon to follow.

"I... I don't know."

The Argos Device shuddered violently, as if it was trying to free itself from the platform. Rents opened along its surface, shooting jets of pressurized synaptic fluid across the lab. A tube ripped free of the capsule, gushing more luminescent fluid in a thick gout that splashed across George's station. He didn't respond. His own cognitive stability hovered above the red line.

"Shut it down!" I cried.

Ravenna shook her head. "It's too late for that. Can't you feel it?"

The psychic array had collapsed, but the space around the lab was still noetically active. The air thickened. It was even denser on the lab floor. A sphere of psychic power emanated from the Argos Device. Octavian stumbled drunkenly, blood spurting from his nose. Ravenna's psychic image flickered in and out, almost like a scrambled television signal. Traynor clutched his head, digging his fingers so far into the base of his skull they drew blood.

As one, every myrmidon threw its head back and screamed.

"What are they doing now?" Octavian asked around bloody fingers.

"Oh no," was all I could say.

Something was filling the echo of their minds. Something old and cold and implacable. Like a flood of psychic goo, the strange presence that occupied the Argos Device forced itself into the myrmidons' minds. It filled them with fearsome purpose.

Before I could shout a warning, the myrmidon closest to Traynor grabbed him by the neck and smashed him face-first into the observation window. Cracks spiderwebbed across the pane. It held. Traynor's skull did not.

The myrmidon threw his body to the floor. He was already dying, but the force that controlled the drone didn't intend to wait. It lunged at him, smashing its fists into the ruin of his face again and again and again. Blood and other fluids geysered from Traynor's body, coating the walls and the myrmidon, yet its expression remained as placid as ever. It was like a machine that had been set to perform a single repetitive task; in this case, beating a man into jelly.

Ravenna's scream was cut off when I slammed our psychic connection shut. I could feel the Object C entity pressing against my mind. *Amn-Zuhad.* I was sure my will would hold it off, but I couldn't be completely sure. Better to not risk it entering her mind through a break in mine. The thought of the behemoth hollowing out her magnificent mind filled me with horror.

A second myrmidon grabbed Octavian's arm. I tried striking it with my other limbs, no plan, no skill, just pure power and instinct. Space *jerked.*

Strange energy burst around us, scarring space-time. Pain screamed through me, a violent bolt of feedback. Everyone stumbled to the side as if we were standing on a boat that had hit a swell. The myrmidon was unhurt.

I very nearly said something vulgar.

It was the seal. The barrier around the Institute compound that was supposed to keep ultraterrestrial entities out and incidentally kept me trapped inside. It had clearly failed against whatever monster was taking over the Argos Device, but infuriatingly it held firm against me.

A sick feeling dropped in the pit of my stomach as understanding struck me. It had followed the path they laid. They had effectively invited it in.

I stared into the Device. The entity's psychic immensity kept me from seeing it clearly, but I could make out vague shapes and impressions. The synaptic fluid was roiling as nervous tissue sheathed in weird flesh grew into Harold's limp body. It ran through the capsule and into him like the roots of a tree. Or a cocoon of spider silk.

The myrmidon wrenched Octavian's arm high behind his back. The Director screamed in pain, which was quickly cut off when the drone's other hand clamped around his throat. The other two myrmidons turned on me. I clenched my slender hands into fists despite knowing I was no match for them. Instead, I lashed out psychically, driving my presence into their minds as a blow. The closest myrmidon hunched over, hands flying to its head as milky fluid gushed from its orifices. The entity struck from the other myrmidon's brain. It was as if a shark lunged into my brain, powerful jaws rending and tearing at my mind. I screamed, feeling myself give way under its assault. I'd never faced anything this powerful. This entity was my equal, maybe even my superior.

Was that thought mine or its?

I dug into the space around me, trying to find something to brace myself against. The assault continued, but it didn't penetrate any further. I could hold steady but not push it out. I had no idea how long I could maintain this stalemate, but all the entity had to do was repurpose another myrmidon to strike back physically.

As soon as I had the thought, the myrmidon astride Traynor stood and looked at me, the scientist's blood dripping from its pale fists.

Amelia wasn't strong enough for this. I had told myself I could manifest my apocalyptic form if I really had to. Now I wasn't so sure, but there was no other way.

I tried to rotate the Amelia facet out of this segment of space-time while simultaneously rotating in a larger, more monstrous aspect of my being. This time she didn't fight me, but it didn't matter. Weird energy flared around me, showering the room with charged particles in wide arcs that fell far outside either end of the visible light spectrum. Space-time around me *wrenched* as if it was a can being crushed by a giant hand. The observation window shattered, glass blowing outward and raining down on the lab floor. Lights burst and instrument panels blew sparks from the walls. Steel supports screamed as the floor lilted downward, sending Octavian and I tumbling through the open window to the hard floor below.

It was only a ten-foot drop, but in an uncontrolled fall that would have been enough to hurt. Instinctively, I jumped *through* space; I couldn't move through the barrier, but I had complete freedom of movement inside it. I suddenly appeared on the steel floor, sliding across it as I burned off the little momentum I'd built up. My jumpsuit tore on my left side, but thankfully it protected my skin.

Octavian wasn't so lucky. Yes, it was only a ten-foot drop. Ten feet is enough to break a human neck, especially if the body lands on a metal surface face-first. The crack of Octavian's vertebrae breaking echoed across the room like the snap of a whip. The myrmidon that had been trying to tear his arm off landed two feet away from him on its left shoulder. Arms and ribs snapped under its weight, but the entity that propelled it did not register its pain. It forced the myrmidon to its feet. The drone stood over Octavian's broken body, staring down at him. Then it lifted one foot and brought it down hard on Octavian's head. Again and again and again.

It all happened in less than two minutes.

There was no chance to intervene on Octavian's behalf, not that it would have mattered if I did. Now on the lab floor, my focus encompassed the other myrmidons. Two of the eight remained in the lab. They were pulling the technicians out of their cradles. They had already dropped five—Lorraine, Patricia, Richard, Albert, and Mitchell—into the expanding pool of synaptic fluid at the Argos Device's base. They lay insensate, their cognitive stability having collapsed along with the array. The stinking green fluid soaked into their jumpsuits and their skin. Electrical impulses leapt through the fluid from the device and into them. Their hearts were still beating, they were still breathing, but nothing happened inside their minds until the sparks struck them. Then their brains were momentarily illuminated by the entity's titanic thoughts.

With the sharp crack of fracturing ceramic, more rents opened along the capsule's side. Pale white tendrils wriggled their way through them, growing along the electrical impulses' paths. They branched and spread like roots. Or nerves. The tips pierced the unconscious technicians' skin, opening bloodless holes into their necks and sides. My stomach lurched as I watched the tendrils grow into them, leaving pulsing furrows in their flesh. At least they didn't cry out. There was nothing left of them to feel pain.

Not so the others. A myrmidon yanked Eddie out of his cradle, wrenching his arm out of its socket as it pulled him free of the leather straps. He screamed in pain, and the myrmidon silenced him by clamping its hand around his throat. Without thinking, I tried to lash out at the drone, only to double over in pain as the barrier again denied me.

The myrmidon dropped Eddie. All those in the lab turned to stare at me—the two from the floor, the one that was killing Octavian, and the one left in the observation room. I felt the pressure of the entity's gaze fall on me like a boulder the size of the Moon. With nothing to support me, I buckled under its weight. Whatever this entity was, it was nothing like the Watchers Above or the fragment of the Gaze That Chains I had faced in the hospital. This behemoth was something far greater. More powerful, more "there".

More like me, a stray part of me whispered.

Except the greater part of me was locked behind a wall of eldritch fire.

The entity saw me. I saw it. A vast torrent of churning thoughts tore through space-time, terminating in the capsule. The Argos Device's nervous system, fed by alien biofluid, programmed by Jeffrey West's malice and animated by alien thought, had gone into overdrive. The spiderweb of nervous tissue had become a cocoon, rapidly transforming Harold's body into something that could support a fraction of the entity's presence. The giant of light glared at me through its many blazing eyes, six wings of thought emanating from its spine. Its attention burned against my mind, but I saw through it. Across the vastness of space, where its body lurked within the frozen planetoid, in a red stone prison beneath the abandoned temple. It was a massive knot of corpse-pale coils, thick around as ancient redwoods, writhing in the darkness of the planetoid's caverns. Triple-jointed limbs sprouted at random points, ending in uncomfortably human hands with a thumb on either side. Two massive lances pierced its titanic body, pinning it to the chamber's spherical interior. What I presumed was its head, a massive lump of blunt-tipped tendrils ending in luminescent spots, lolled uselessly, dripping a florescent fluid that hissed and smoked where it struck the chamber's surface. Deep pits and rivulets spoke to millennia of erosion that had brought the behemoth no closer to freedom. Not the way Harold's body could.

The astral giant bent low, its smooth alien face falling like a meteor until it hung above my own astral presence. Its central eye transfixed me, a dozen oval-shaped pupils swirling within its yellow light. I felt its scrutiny press against me, a blazing dry heat. I wasn't one of the others. I was familiar. I hated that.

In the physical realm, I mustered what remaining strength I had and climbed to my feet. Their names echoed in my mind; those of the people I cared for and those I didn't. Lorraine. Eddie. Patricia. Octavian. Richard. I might not have appreciated some of them, but they were human, they *mattered*, and in an instant, they were gone.

I was bare yards from Irene's station, either by chance or instinct. Hoping my physical form was still beneath the behemoth's notice, I walked slowly across the lab. The myrmidons followed me with their eyes, heads turning slowly, but they didn't move toward me. I put one hand on her arm, slipped my other hand into hers. She was deep within the clairvoyant trance, but she was *there*. The storm within her had dimmed, but I could feel it churning. After a second, her fingers squeezed mine lightly. She was coming back.

They weren't going to take them all.

In the astral realm, I drew myself up high. Though I could not summon my apocalyptic form, I could feel it within/without/behind me. The ephemeral sphere shook under my power.

"My name is Amelia Temple," I said, "and I am not afraid of you."

The behemoth roared. Its psychic force struck me like the winds of a hurricane, showering me with rage and hate and shame. I saw myself as a germ, a tiny lump of protoplasm and rudimentary responses, crawling across a chuck of rock drifting aimlessly through the void. *SHE* towered over me, a leviathan, vast, ancient, incomprehensible. *SHE* descended upon the rock, vomiting forth blood-warm orange fluid. The ooze flooded the rock's surface, suffusing it, reshaping it in accordance with the leviathan's will. Stars flickered as time spun around us. The flood of ooze receded, sinking into stone-turned-soil, evaporating into an atmosphere. Life grew in its wake. Specks such as myself could either change to accommodate it or be destroyed, as was right and proper.

First came strange plants grasping at the open air for sunlight, trees and bushes and flowers spreading across the once-barren surface. Then small creatures, beasts with six or eight or no legs, emerged from the shady grasses, creatures of scale and skin and sharp-burred hide. They fed on the grass and leaves and grew in size and number. Then new beasts emerged from the caves and rivers, feeding on the first. After minutes and millennia, one set of beasts rose from the others. They stood on four legs and built things with their hands. Their long, narrow heads were studded with sensory tendrils, covering round mouths full of sharp teeth. They hunted the beasts, then corralled some for food and labor. They cultivated the plants, allowing them to support greater numbers. They built huts of wood and stone that became villages, then cities. They built tall towers, beacons that pierced the sky and the astral realm, singing praises to the being that made this world for them.

Eventually the prayers reached a critical mass, enough for the behemoth to hear from across space and time. The great beast, angel to the leviathan, journeyed to the lonely, now-lush planet. The people rejoiced to see the messenger descend from the heavens. They threw ecstatic festivals in its honor, offering up flesh and fruit in its name. In response, the behemoth ran riot across the world, devouring everything from its youngest worshipper to the oldest tree. When it was done, the rock was barren again. It curled up in the ruin of an ancient metropolis and slept for a time. Then another world's prayers awakened it, and it returned to the void.

I felt small. Disgusting. I was worthless. I was an accident. I was something that wasn't supposed to exist.

My head hung low. I sank to my knees, clinging to Irene's arm. The myrmidons closed in, ready to restrain me. The behemoth loomed over me in the astral, radiating satisfaction and triumph, and beneath that, an oily taint of vengeance.

Against me.

The behemoth wanted revenge against *me*.

A memory flickered across my mind. Mine or the behemoth's, I didn't know, but I saw the great beast on another ruined world. Seven entities descended from the void, falling on it like raptors. They were winged beings, creatures or machines or something in-between, leaving blazing trails of psionic energy and wielding lances made of light and fury. Within each, a crew of six combined their own noetic might to pilot the things. They were the scions of seven different worlds, utterly unlike each other but united in purpose. Yet they only directed the vessels. Their power came from the combined prayers and anger of billions, thousands of light-years away. Whole worlds prayed as one, bringing vengeance against the behemoth.

Above/behind/beyond them, I waited. The Opener of the Way. The Gate and the Guide. That who shows no favor or preference but may be propitiated. *Teshu Ung Maya.*

They had begged me, they had sacrificed to me, and I had opened the way to the behemoth's current lair. It was a one-way trip—they had not asked me to bring them back, and I had not offered—but I waited anyway, watching. Perhaps I was curious as to the outcome. This was a new thing, after all, mortals striking back against the Elder. Perhaps, though, something about me found the behemoth distasteful. A small part, one as yet unborn and yet as eternal as the rest of me. Perhaps that wanted to be certain that the thing was done.

The battle was fierce. In its rage, the behemoth destroyed three of the vessels, killing not just their pilots but those who supported them, billions of minds snuffed out by psychic feedback. Nonetheless, the four vessels that remained were victorious. Using metaphysical methods of tremendous power, they bound the behemoth to a worldlet, built a prison in the heart of the void, and left it to rot. It could not die, but neither could it escape. The vessels remained behind, silent sentries to ensure its sentence was carried out.

How it had ended up in this solar system, how its mistress had landed on Earth, I did not know. I had nothing to do with that. Not that it mattered to the behemoth. It knew of my part in its imprisonment. It had not anticipated finding me here, but it would happily take advantage of the opportunity.

No, it would not.

I was Amelia Temple. I was *Teshu Ung Maya.* I might be contained for now, but I was unbound. And I could still freely move within the compound.

I could only save one person right now. I grabbed onto Irene with both hands and *leapt.* Beneath us, the behemoth roared. The myrmidons ran from the lab, pursuing us.

21

The violence within lab B305 spilled into the rest of the compound. In labs, in workspaces, in halls and common rooms, the myrmidons turned on their supposed betters without warning. The Institute had measures in place to protect itself against violence, of course—from hostile ultraterrestrial intelligences, from the Bureau of Extranormal Investigations, even from disgruntled prots.

All those plans hinged on the myrmidons. They were ubiquitous throughout the compound, providing security and performing whatever tasks couldn't be entrusted to prots. No one felt entirely comfortable with them, but after a few months on the compound, they became familiar. They faded into the background, a slightly unusual but helpful fixture of Institute life. Up until the moment one grabbed your lab partner's head and smashed it across the rim of a counter.

The Institute boasted one hundred and eight members across five levels of development. Within one hour of the behemoth's invasion, that number dropped to forty-five.

The attacks were random but hideously effective. The behemoth didn't target a specific group or subset of the Institute, didn't try to decapitate the leadership before working its way down. It couldn't; it didn't know how the Institute was organized and almost certainly didn't care. It simply sent its appendages swarming into groups of people wherever it found them.

Nonetheless, the savants didn't escape the violence. Their work required several extra hands. They surrounded themselves with myrmidons and prots. Thus, when the myrmidons turned on them, the massacre took the Institute's highest and lowest levels alike.

By the evening of December 24th, the only senior personnel left standing were Ravenna Adler and Jeffrey West.

Kenneth Pike entered the multidimensional monitoring station before the alarms started going blaring. His finely tuned psychic senses had already warned him that something was off within the compound. It wasn't as impressive a talent as those of his colleagues; a rollicking great headache made for a poor party trick. Nonetheless, it had served him well up until today.

"We're about to have an emergency," he said by way of greeting to the techs on monitor duty. "You'd better be prepared."

At that moment, lights on the monitor console flashed red. An angry beeping poured out of the speakers. The right-hand monitor, Bill Palmer, had just turned in his seat to stare at his suddenly present supervisor. When he turned to read the indicators on the console, his face went pale.

"Level Four manifestation! Second sub-basement, southwest quadrant!"

Pike made a tsking sound. "And Miss Temple had been so cooperative. Well, we have pre-planned responses for a reason. Sound the alarm and let's get it contained."

"I don't think it's Temple." The left-hand monitor, James Potts, pointed to the readouts. "Look at that signature. It's nothing like her previous activity."

Pike snatched the printout from Bill's hand, tearing it from the printer. He stared at the measurements with a deep frown, stroking his narrow chin. Skepticism quickly became confusion, which gave way to fear.

"You're right," he said at last. "Then what the devil is going on down there? Is the barrier still in place?"

James kicked the wall, sliding his chair across the narrow room to the second monitoring station. "Looks like it is. I'm seeing weird spikes here and there, but it seems to be holding. Power flow is uninterrupted, temporal-spatial distortion is within normal tolerances." He stared over his shoulder at the others. "This shouldn't be happening."

"Evidently it is." Pike's scowl deepened.

All three men jumped as a second alarm blared in opposite time to the first. A different set of measurements spiked across the printouts. James rolled back to his station. He stabbed his finger at the new lines.

"*That's* Temple."

"Sound the alarms," Pike said, his mouth dry. It must have been the only thing he could think to do. "We have to… we have to secure the facility."

Bill and James didn't argue. Bill flipped open a glass panel on the console, revealing a large red button. He slammed his fist against it. Klaxons echoed through the gleaming halls, warning everyone on the compound of the danger. Far too late for those already dead and dying.

This alarm triggered more than sirens and warning lights. It was the Institute's ultimate failsafe, a security measure specifically for uncontrolled, high-level ultraterrestrial manifestations. Across the building, thick shutters slammed into place on every exterior door, every window. Each was a steel sandwich, containing metal panels inscribed with warding seals connected to the mansion's electrical system. A lattice of smaller barriers snapped into place inside the original. Every soul currently in the compound was now trapped there.

It did no good for Pike and his team. Moments after they triggered the alarm, the door to the monitor room fell inward. A half-dozen myrmidons swarmed like wasps. They seized Pike and his monitors, beating them brutally against their own equipment until the whole room was a bloody, sparking ruin. Then they dispersed, looking for their next targets.

Doctor Paul Tucker was in his office in the infirmary when the myrmidons attacked. Officially, he was studying his patient's treatment plans. That shouldn't have taken much time at all, considering he only had the one. In actuality, he was having a quiet afternoon drink with young Nancy Foster.

Nancy would have preferred being anywhere else. Even with only one patient, she had a tremendous amount of work to do. In addition to her nursing duties, she doubled as Tucker's secretary and general aide. The man left almost all his drudge work to her, giving cursory attention to whatever prots were assigned to the infirmary this month and focusing almost exclusively on his medical experiments. He was running a drug trial with a half-dozen prots right now; Nancy quietly expected the infirmary to fill up before the end of the next week.

Now, though, Tucker's attention was focused entirely on her right knee, and thus, so was hers. His hand sat just above it. She suppressed a grimace when he gave it a squeeze, grateful that the Institute required her to wear the blue jumpsuit instead of a traditional nurse uniform. She couldn't stand the feeling of his skin against hers, when his fingers brushed the back of her hand or neck, as they did far too often. She wanted nothing more than to bash her untouched tumbler of bourbon into his smug face, glass and all. Instead, she faked a laugh at his latest inappropriate comment and wished she could escape from this room, this building.

Nancy didn't realize it was too late when the alarms went off and the infirmary's door splintered inward.

Two myrmidons stepped through the door. They paused briefly to survey the room. The light streaming beneath the closed office door caught their attention. One drone crossed the infirmary in four smooth strides. With a quick jerk of the wrist, it broke the lock and yanked the door open.

Tucker leapt to his feet. "What is the meaning of this? I didn't call for you. Get out this instant!"

Nancy saw the blood dripping from the myrmidon's hands and screamed.

It ignored her, charging the doctor. The myrmidon grabbed Tucker by the throat with both hands, lifting him off his feet and slamming the back of his head against the wall. Tucker let out a weak groan and fell forward, blood streaming through his thinning hair. The myrmidon brought its fists down onto his spine in a double overhand blow. The doctor collapsed against the floor, sending his chair tumbling over as he fell across it. The myrmidon followed him down, slamming its fists into his back over and over.

Nancy didn't wait for her turn. As soon as the myrmidon grabbed the doctor, she fled the office, running pell-mell through the infirmary and into the outstretched arm of the second myrmidon. It caught her below the throat, knocking her off her feet and sending her crashing to the floor. Her lungs gasped desperately for air until the myrmidon brought its foot down on her face.

Norman lay perfectly still in the bed, staring at the boring ceiling, ignoring the sounds of bloody destruction all around him.

The first myrmidon emerged from the office, white jumpsuit stained with Doctor Tucker's vital fluids. The second straightened, its suit soiled by Nancy. They looked around the room again. Their eyes passed over Norman, seeing nothing. Then they turned on their heels and left the infirmary. Norman, or whatever was inside of him, continued to observe the ceiling.

Charles Voss was in the staff lounge, already three drinks in at two in the afternoon. He was regaling Frank Abbott, the prot working as bartender, with a ribald and highly improbable tale about his sexual exploits when five myrmidons burst through the door. They surveyed the room, clearly expecting to have encountered more people. Seeing the space nearly empty, the three drones in the back rank whirled around and went in search of their next target. The remaining two charged the bar.

"What's this, then?" Voss sputtered.

Frank, who'd lived a rough life before wandering into an Institute testing fair, immediately recognized trouble. He smashed a glass against Voss' head and fled. Vaulting the bar, he ran for the side door with a myrmidon hot on his heels. The other myrmidon grabbed Voss by the shoulder and slammed the back of his head against the bar's edge until it split open. It dropped him, letting the ruin of his body tumble off the barstool and land wetly on the floor.

Then, helpfully, the alarms went off.

Frank didn't know where he was running. He turned to the right without thinking as soon as he left the door, looking to put distance between himself and his assailants. Unfortunately, the way to the staircase was on the left. His panic took him to the maze of third floor offices and four different dead ends. The myrmidon would have caught up with him shortly if a door beside him hadn't shot open, whereupon two hands yanked him inside.

The stranger spun him around, holding him tight with one hand clamped over his mouth. The other pushed a syringe into his neck, though not hard enough to break the skin. Yet.

"Quiet now. Quiet," the stranger said softly. His voice held a malicious humor. "We don't want to draw attention to ourselves, do we?"

As if to punctuate the stranger's words, a door cracked open down the hallway. The myrmidon had come to a dead end and was now searching the surrounding offices. Frank let out a pitiful whimper.

"Now, we have two options ahead of us, yes? I can use *this*—" The stranger pressed the needle in further, now pricking Frank's skin, "—and knock you out, leaving you for *them* to find while I make my escape. That would be the *easy* way."

Frank shook his head slightly, trying to convey how little he liked that idea without sticking the needle deeper into his neck.

"However, I find myself in need of a strong back. My usual help seems to have gotten himself… well, let's just say I'm well practiced in sacrificing lab assistants to cover my exit."

Another door smashed open, this one closer. They could hear the myrmidon throwing furniture around, looking for anyone hiding.

"I'll help you," Frank whispered into the stranger's fingers. "I'll help you!"

"Good man," the stranger said. "And what is your name?"

"Frank. Frank Abbot."

"Charmed to meet you, Frank Abbot," Jeffrey West said.

He let Frank go, capping the syringe and returning it to his breast pocket. Then he turned to the open cabinet next to him, speaking over his shoulder as he rummaged through it. "A prot. I don't suppose you've displayed a talent, then?"

Frank stared at the door, waiting for the myrmidon to start bashing it in. He stammered out, "I scored well in telepathy, sir."

"Interesting. Not my field in the slightest. You could be what I need, though."

"What's that?"

"Manual labor, at the moment."

West withdrew a ten-liter tank of luminescent orange biofluid. It sloshed thickly as he shoved it into Frank's arms, not waiting to ensure the tech had it before stepping around his desk. He reached underneath and triggered a hidden switch. A panel on the wall slid open, revealing a secret passageway.

"I might have need for more skilled labor if we survive this."

"*If?*"

"Well, this all went in a rather unexpected direction. Not sure how it will play out. Still, we'll make the best of it."

The door shook as a fist hammered on it. Frank flinched but didn't drop the tank. West looked unconcerned, even as the wood bowed inward, straining against the brass lock.

"So glad we didn't invest in the glass doors after all," he said cheerfully. "Come, come, step lively. We've one more stop to make before we can leave."

West grabbed a canister off the desk, which contained a severed head, and pushed the other man into the passageway. He stopped briefly to slide the panel shut moments before the myrmidon smashed into the room. Then he stepped around Frank, leading him into the darkness within the building.

Vincent Stewart sat with his team in Lab 303. Despite the gleaming white walls, it was a cozy space with all nine members of his team plus himself. That was one of the things he liked about it. The close quarters encouraged a sense of unity, of oneness.

That, in Stewart's mind, was what the Institute was all about. A true believer, or at least so he seemed in conversation, Stewart tried not to be upset that Matthew Traynor had clearly been plagiarizing his work. They were in this together, after all. So what if it was Stewart's method of harmonizing minds that formed the foundation of Traynor's psychic array? That just proved the Institute's way was working. After this afternoon's success, he'd congratulate Traynor and then quietly remind the Director whose shoulders Traynor had been standing on. The Director was a reasonable man. He'd ensure Stewart received a reasonable amount of credit. If not, well. Stewart would simply have to take steps. Jeffrey West thought no one knew about his horror show downstairs. A whisper in the right ear—or a nudge in the right mind, as the case may be—would work wonders.

The ten telepaths sat in lotus position in a close pyramid, with Stewart at the center. Each telepath had linked minds, forming a delicate array of interlocking triangles. Timothy and James, from Harold and Richard's dorm, sat in the middle ring, linked directly to Stewart and three other telepaths. Rob and Paul were two of the three points, which held two connections each. Psychic energy pulsed among them, buttressing their minds against any strangeness they might encounter. Their thoughts were gradually becoming one.

Stewart frowned, and that frown rippled through the room. He chided himself gently. Letting his stray thoughts leak into lesser minds was bad form. Stewart stilled his thoughts, emanating calm through the connections. His expression relaxed back to tranquility. Around him, his team's faces did the same. Harmony washed through the lab, out to the pyramid's points before flowing to the center. All was one. All was calm.

The alarms ripping through the air didn't disturb their harmony. Neither did the trio of myrmidons who bashed open the door. Stewart read their hostile intent immediately. The decade of telepaths turned on the intruders as one. They lashed out with their collective strength. The myrmidons stumbled back, stunned. Together, they might have been enough to face down the intruders. Perhaps even the entire myrmidon hive, if they had to.

But there was a flaw.

At the core of the suborned hive, the behemoth recoiled as if it had been stung by a hornet. It roared and lashed out, venting its fury through the myrmidons' brains and into the telepathic array. Blood vessels burst under the strain as they switched to defense, relying on the links to strengthen each individual node.

Then the void within Rob and Paul reached out. They barely had a second to register the sudden mental cold before it devoured their conscious minds. Their links collapsed, their minds going blank. The telepaths connected to them stumbled, suddenly missing a support. Weakness rippled through the array. It crumbled beneath the behemoth's assault. They had faced it as one, but they died as ten, nervous systems burning out one at a time. Stewart was last, following over in the midst of his students, blood leaking from eyes and ears.

The three myrmidons had no more survived the attack than had their victims. Their marvelous brains had collapsed under the strain, gray matter splattering into goo inside their weird, artificial skulls. They fell in a small companion pyramid by the door.

A no-score draw, as Paul might have said.

If suddenly being thrown out of my mind had affected Ravenna, she did a good job of hiding it. Where everyone else panicked, she approached the Institute's fall with a disturbing degree of calm. When I shut down our psychic connection, she immediately rose from the reclining chair in her office. A still-steaming cup of tea sat on the desk next to her; she swallowed its contents in a single pained gulp. Then she reached beneath the desk to open her own secret door.

Her office was on the opposite side of the manor from West's, so the two did not cross paths as they slipped through the secret passages. Fortunately, for one of them; I'm not sure who. Nevertheless, she was far from out of danger. She could hear the rampaging myrmidons through the thin walls, brutally murdering whatever Institute personnel they encountered. Her expression remained placid as she made her way across the third floor, but her eyes twitched every time she heard a scream or the wet sound of flesh being brutalized.

I wish I knew what went through Ravenna's mind as she made her way along the Institute's labyrinth of secret passages. Had she expected something like this to happen? Was she satisfied to see Traynor's fall, for the current institution to be dismantled and dismembered? Was she horrified by the viciousness? Was she planning some way to stop the behemoth's invasion or solely her escape?

I can say with certainty that she wasn't motivated only to save herself. Her path led to her third-floor lab. There, her small team was trying and failing to hold off a trio of myrmidons with the help of their pet. Free of its crystal cage, the astral creature appeared as a ribbon of mysterious light swimming through the air. Half of Ravenna's girls had already fallen, leaving Polly and two others. They were trying to give the creature commands but couldn't agree on how to fight the myrmidons. The creature writhed angrily, whipping back and forth between contradictory telepathic commands. It hissed, throwing out random bursts of harsh light.

The three myrmidons sported burns but continued to advance. They formed a triangle around the creature and drew their antennae. Previously, the myrmidons had used them to focus energy from Institute-designed transmitters; it was how they'd captured me at the hospital on Hallowe'en. Now, they channeled the terrible thoughts emanating from the Argos Device. The behemoth's mental commands redefined space around the creature. It shrank, turning in on itself in an elaborate knot as its luminescence faded. It howled pitifully, a cry for help in radio static. Then a myrmidon grabbed the diminished creature and crushed it. The astral beast burst, bright goo and harsh radiation burning the drone's hand and arm down to artificial bone. It paid no attention to the damage, nor to the noxious smoke wafting from its scorched limb.

As one, the myrmidons turned on Ravenna's girls, ready to finish their murderous task. Two of the women froze, staring at the carnage in horror. Polly grabbed them by the shoulders and pulled them back. They stumbled against the wall, not knowing where to go. The myrmidons stood between them and the only door they knew of.

Salvation came when the hidden passage opened behind them. Ravenna stepped through, eyes shining with weird light. One of the women shrieked, but Polly grabbed her hand and pulled her through the exit. As the last woman followed, Ravenna smiled.

"Sit tight, girls. I'll be with you in a minute."

The myrmidons recognized nothing dangerous about her, but the thing animating them recoiled ever so slightly. The animals in this place had already surprised it more than once. Now one approached it without fear.

"You killed my students. And their pet," she said, her voice steady as steel. "That was a mistake."

She spread her arms as the myrmidons advanced again. The lights in the lab flickered. The air whirled around her.

"Fortunately, I keep my own on the inside."

Ravenna's eyes rolled back as the creature within her unfurled. Weird light emanated from her, bathing the walls and drones in shifting colors. A half-dozen tentacles unfolded from her back, covered in bulbous nodules. They lashed at the myrmidons, striking them again and again. Their bodies smoked where they struck, but the true damage was within their hollow minds. Flashes of nightmare danced across the myrmidon hive, visions of fang and poison and deep currents as Ravenna's pet laid eggs in their rudimentary psyches.

In creatures with more individual minds, the eggs would rapidly hatch into fast-growing nightmares, parasitic personalities that would fight their host and one another until only one remained in control of the body. The nightmare child would grow until it was strong enough to return to the deep currents of the astral realm, where schools of such creatures floated.

The psychic eggs could not quicken in the myrmidons, instead leaving swaths of cauterized nerve tissue as they failed and melted. The three myrmidons collapsed, their brains dissolving from the venom. Across the hive, other myrmidons faltered, recoiling from the psychic backlash. Prots and actives under threat took the opportunity to flee for whatever safety there was.

Ravenna pulled her familiar inside and smiled down at the fallen drones, momentarily satisfied. Then she withdrew, gathering up her remaining students. They were huddled together in the secret passage a few feet from the door. Ravenna didn't stop, simply walked past expecting them to follow.

"Come along, girls," she said. "Let's go find Miss Temple."

West's scheming made the slaughter happen. Ironically, it also kept it from being complete. After the incident at St. Audaeus, the Institute retained forty-three active myrmidons. The neurons within the Argos Device—seeded with myrmidon tissue as well as human—gave the behemoth access to the myrmidon hive. Yet its control wasn't complete. Under West's orders, Mark had begun the implantation process. He'd seeded the six myrmidons currently in the generation tanks with Watcher matter. Fearing for the project's future, he hadn't stopped there. Mark had implanted another dozen myrmidons with Watcher matter under the guise of "maintenance". The alien matter had altered their psyches enough to create a divergence within the network. When the behemoth invaded, the hive split in two. The "loyalist" myrmidons were outnumbered almost three to one, but by a quirk of fate or intent they were concentrated on the second floor.

When a pair of turned myrmidons burst into the cafeteria, three loyalists were waiting for them. Immediately recognizing a threat, the loyalists charged their kin before the watching technicians could react. Two loyalists seized the first infected drone, slamming it against the wall and holding it fast, while the third engaged its partner. The two dozen technicians who'd gathered for lunch, mostly prots, screamed and hid behind flipped tables, not knowing what to do.

The drones fought without restraint, slamming fists into one another with no heed for their personal well-being. The loyalist shoulder-checked the infected drone into a wall. The infected responded with a brutal overhand blow that cracked one of the loyalist's shoulder blades. When the loyalist doubled over, the infected picked it up by the waist and hurled it across the room, sending it crashing into a supporting column with a bone-snapping crack as the nearby technicians screamed. The infected rushed to the fallen loyalist, face still unnervingly blank. It smashed its fist into the fallen drone again and again, arms hammering like pistons, as its milky fluid splashed across the floor. It didn't stop, even when the fallen drone was a ruin, until two sets of hands grabbed its shoulders from behind. Before it could react, a dozen tendrils of blue-green matter stabbed into its arms and neck.

Responding to a bizarre signal, the Watcher matter within the loyalists had activated. Tendrils of weird flesh had torn free of their once-pristine white jumpsuits, waving in the air like alien anemones. Where they stung, they implanted the infected drone with more Watcher matter. It grew rapidly, twisting the drone's nervous system away from compatibility with the original hive. The first two loyalists had already suborned the first infected. Blue-green tumors were growing across its face and arm, surrounded by spiderwebs of dark, infested blood vessels. Now they rescued another sibling. Thus was their hive restored.

While physical battle raged through the Institute, a psychic war churned in the astral realm. The behemoth and the core of the myrmidon hive struggled for control of the corrupted network. As an order of being, the behemoth was greater and more powerful but locally limited by the Argos Device's physical form. The core was more familiar with local conditions but hampered by its stunted development and the weirdness of the Watcher infection. The resulting stalemate gave the behemoth the advantage. It could only be resolved in the physical realm, where the behemoth's forces outnumbered its enemy three to one.

As it gained understanding of the situation, the behemoth redirected four of its drones to West's primary lab, where the resources necessary to assist its growth were stored. It sent the rest charging down to the deepest sub-basement, where its enemy lurked. Recognizing the weakness of its own position, the hive core pulled the drones back to defend it.

In the cafeteria, the only thing the technicians knew was that the four myrmidons suddenly withdrew, leaving the wreck of their fallen behind. The survivors stared at the open doors from behind overturned tables for long seconds, shivering with shock. Then Vernon Calloway, the first to regain control of his nerves, pulled himself shaking to his feet.

"Don't just sit there!" he cried through chattering teeth. "We need to block the doors!"

Without waiting for a response, Vernon grabbed a table by the leg and started dragging it toward the doorway. After a moment, two more prots rose to help him. Then another three. In a slow chain reaction, the numb technicians joined their fellows in twos and threes, wordlessly stacking tables and chairs into a rough barricade in front of the doorway. One of the doors hung by its lower hinges; they propped it up and tied the doors together with ropes made of torn-off sleeves. When the door was as secure as it could be, Vernon and four others fell into the kitchen. They locked the door that led to the supply rooms and loading dock, then knocked over an industrial freezer to block the way. They were trapped, as far as they knew, but at least that meant the monsters were stuck outside. They hoped.

The two dozen techs, only five of them noetically active, gathered on the bare cafeteria floor. They huddled together for warmth and comfort, looking from one face to another, asking without words what they were to do next. Their eyes kept turning to Vernon, who'd inadvertently appointed himself their leader.

He swallowed hard, not sure what to say. He opened his mouth to speak. No words came.

Then space ripped. I fell in the middle of them, cradling Irene in my arms.

22

❖

Irene Phillips drifted in time and space. The psychic array's violent collapse had been a horrific shock to her nervous system. It had left her insensate for who knows how long, her mind buffeted by the noetic winds of a god's fury. She awoke to a sensation her distant nervous system could only dimly recognize as motion—the horrible feeling of falling in a dream, times a thousand. Some unimaginable gravity had caught her and pulled her *down*, plummeting through Object C's wispy atmosphere before sending her crashing into its frozen surface.

As she came to, her psyche instinctively coalesced into a self-image. She wore an ethereal grown, gauzy orange fabric draped across her like a chiton. Pale yellow ribbons wrapped around her limbs, and she wore a floral crown. In better circumstances, she would have been a vision; now, the psychic storm tore at her dress, slowly rending the fabric apart. She could feel it raging around her; if she turned her head just *so*, she could see the storm clouds high above her. If she turned the other way, the storm was gone, and the temple was far from abandoned. Irene knew, as one knows things in dreams, that she had fallen into the planetoid's distant past.

Object C's noösphere buzzed with psionic signals. In between craters, a small city of shell-like buildings stretched across the frozen plain. Strange matter like tree roots made of resin or spider silk grew between them, forming twisted, covered roads. The city's architecture was utterly unlike that of the temple—whoever lived here now, they were not Object C's first inhabitants. Irene could *feel* thousands of minds milling about the city and hundreds more inside the temple. A name floated to the top of her mind, propelled by thousands of thoughts: *Kor-Mitra.*

A strange object hung in the thin air above the temple. It resembled an upside-down hill, perhaps a quarter of the size of the one that hosted the temple. Perhaps, instead, it was the roots of such a hill, ripped out of the ground and hung high in the sky by some unknown force. A massive tree grew atop it, with thick roots similar to those that connected the shell-like buildings winding through the earth and dangling in empty air. More of the strange shells clustered around the tree's huge trunk and hung from its branches amid razor-sharp metallic leaves.

The psychic wind picked up. In the present, the psychic storm pulled in around the temple, spraying Irene's astral form with black sand and ice at flesh-ripping speeds. She stumbled up the low, wide steps that led to the temple, seeking shelter and answers. Her far-away body went numb where the debris tore at her. Memories faded and became confused. The pigment leached out of her gown as she forgot her favorite color. Snatches of her childhood blew away in the wind. She forgot how she came here, where she had come from, why she had come here and where "here" even was. She only knew her name for certain and whispered it to herself as a mantra while she climbed the steps. *Irene.* One step. *Phillips.* One step. *Irene.* One step. *Phillips.* One step. Over and over, as she climbed the five hundred and twelve steps that lead to the temple.

If the pure, focused will that was Irene's psyche expected salvation within the structure, she was to be disappointed. The thick black stone walls sheltered her from the behemoth's fury, but new dangers lurked within. Irene fell to her knees on the stone floor, exhausted, barely registering the intricate geometric patterns etched shallowly across the broad, flat stones. The gaping doorway opened onto a long, wide narthex with a low ceiling. Bowl-like sconces were carved into the walls, each glowing with violet light. Larger flames illuminated the nave, which swarmed with strange creatures.

It hurt Irene's faraway head to look at them. They were amorphous, like clouds of multicolored gas and static. They were chanting in a sibilant, hissing language, at once beautiful and terrible. Their voices, purely mental communication, struck her mind like thorns.

A tall, flat icon made of gleaming metal hung from the chamber's back wall, behind a wide altar. Two heavy censers stood on either side, filling the air with acrid smoke. Six of the creatures were spread out in an oblong around it. Irene could feel the psychic pressure emanating from them, directed at a trio of beings chained atop the altar in agonizing positions. The smoke cleared briefly, and Irene screamed when she saw the sacrifices, their faces frozen in pure terror. They were unmistakably human.

At the sound, the alien congregation turned to find the intrusion. They screamed—in rage at the violation or in joy for another sacrifice or in service of some alien emotion—and rose *en masse*. Their bodies shivered, resolving into coherent forms—tall, hairless, with long fins sprouting from faces and heads and all-black eyes, their mouths filled with rows of shark teeth. It was the closest to mercy she would find here. They charged, singing the song of her annihilation. Irene fell back, scrambling for the door, but there was no safety in the storm.

Strange light flared all around her, and I was there. Wind whipped at my hair and dress. I held out my hand, pleading for her to take it.

"Irene! I found you! You must come with me!"

She didn't recognize me. Nonetheless, even in this state, honed down to her most basic responses, Irene realized I was her best option. She leapt for me, flinging her arms around my waist. I *pulled* and the alien temple fell away from us.

Irene's eyes fluttered open. She was lying in my arms on the floor of the Institute's cafeteria. A dozen techs surrounded us. She didn't yet realize that they were holding mops and brooms out as weapons. I pointedly chose to ignore that, for now.

"Amelia?" she said softly. "Is that you?"

I laughed, tears stinging my eyes, and kissed her forehead. "Yes, it's me. I'm so glad you're here."

"Where am I? Wait, is this the cafeteria? How did we get here?"

Now that her psyche was firmly seated in her body, Irene's identity and memories were returning. Both would be shaky for a while—her consciousness had traveled further and suffered greater psychic trauma than any human in modern history—but she would be fine so long as she didn't engage in astral travel for a few months. Or years. I didn't think it would be likely, but in this moment, I took nothing for granted.

"Everything's gone wrong, Irene. Doctor Traynor's experiment was a disaster."

Irene's brow furrowed. "I remember there was something out there. It attacked us."

"It followed you. The lab is destroyed. I got us out, but…"

"Us?" She sat up and looked around. "Where are the others? Where's Lorraine?"

I looked away, not that it helped me escape the despair on her face. "I saved who I could."

Her face collapsed into tears as she realized what I was saying. I pulled her close, pressing my cheek against her forehead. As she sobbed into my arms, I wished there was someone to comfort *me*. I ached for Luci. I missed her touch, her voice. I wanted nothing more than to sink into her arms the way Irene was curled up in mine. I briefly closed my eyes and *wanted*, but I didn't have time to cry.

Irene recognized that neither did she. She was devastated, but strong as ever. She allowed herself one minute to cry before gently pushing herself away from me. She wiped her hands across her eyes, sniffling. Then she pulled herself to her feet.

"You said we escaped?" Irene shook her head, fixing her ponytail as she tamped her fear and sorrow down. "How?"

Vernon stepped forward, brandishing the dead myrmidon's stun baton. "We'd like to know that too."

I glared at the baton, then at Vernon. Old pain briefly flared in my right arm. I hadn't felt the baton's shock before, but I wasn't eager to find out how it compared. "I've had experiences with electric shocks, Vernon Calloway. Now is *not* the time to provoke me."

Vernon's broad face flushed bright red. He puffed out his skinny chest, trying to maintain what small amount of authority he'd fallen backwards into. "I'm not letting anyone else hurt these folks."

I bristled. In spite of the barrier, I felt myself reaching for my other limbs. "Neither am I. Which means you'd better get that thing out of my face."

The young prot wouldn't let himself be intimidated, but neither was he in control. The baton's tip swung wildly. His thumb was dangerously close to the trigger. "You just popped out of *thin air*. You're just like those other things. You ain't *human*."

That struck me like a fist in the stomach. My eyes flew wide and my face contorted into a snarl. I slowly rose to my feet as a grumble of agreement rippled across the ring of survivors. A couple of them stepped closer, broken handles held out like spears. I kept my attention focused on Vernon, hands curling into claws. Irene clung to me, for her safety as much as mine.

"Vernon, you need to think about this."

Vernon's mind burned hot and bright and defenseless. I looked past his bravado into his fear. It lurked just below the surface, sharp and spiky. Turned against him, his fear would tear him up as easily as it would me. If he pushed this, things would be over quicker than he thought. He looked intent on pushing me.

Thankfully, it didn't come to that. A voice rang out behind me. "Oh, for pity's stake, stop playing around."

Everyone turned to see Ravenna Adler emerge from a sudden opening in the cafeteria wall, Polly and two other women in tow. Irene let out a happy cry and pushed her way through the ring of survivors to hug Polly. The two held each other, crying in relief to see a friend had survived. Ravenna paid them no mind, moving through the ring of survivors. They spread to give her room. She was the highest authority in the area, after all. They desperately wanted leadership.

Ravenna looked me up and down with a satisfied expression. She gave my arm a lingering squeeze. Then she turned to Vernon and rolled her eyes.

"Put that thing down before you hurt yourself."

Vernon gulped and lowered the baton. He didn't drop it, but his thumb was now far from the trigger. That was something, at least.

Ravenna turned slowly in a circle, taking in the scene inside the cafeteria. From the way her eyes widened, I suspected she was impressed. Things were a mess, but the barricades were a sign the prots had tried *something*. She gave them a brief, approving nod.

"You've done well," she said, "but this isn't going to last. Sooner or later, Dr. West's creatures are going to come back to clean up. We need to evacuate the facility."

"Easier said than done," I said. "The barrier that's supposed to keep ultraterrestrial entities out is keeping me trapped inside."

"I don't see how that's our problem," Vernon said hotly.

I looked at the little ingrate coldly. "If you think you can escape this nightmare without my assistance, by all means, be my guest."

"We can't." Ravenna's voice was firm, brooking no dissent. "We're all trapped now."

She gestured to the speakers, still blaring a klaxon that had faded into the background.

"This isn't just any alarm. It's specifically for uncontrolled, high-level ultraterrestrial manifestations. It's supposed to mean that the multidimensional barrier has failed. When it's triggered, it automatically activates the Institute's ultimate failsafe, physically sealing the building. *Every* exit is sealed, hopefully containing whatever monster is loose."

"The only way for any of us to get out is to cut power to the building," I said. "That will take down all the wards, and I can move us all out. There's only one problem."

"If the wards are down, that means that *thing* can get out, too," Irene said, her voice soft but firm.

"Isn't that a problem for later?" Vernon's face dripped with sweat, and he trembled like a rat terrier. "I think getting everyone out safely is the most important thing right now."

"There's no safety anywhere if the behemoth escapes," I said. "I don't know what it is, but…"

I reached into my mind, giving the Watcher Within a psychic nudge. They were curled up in a corner of my mind. For a moment, I thought they were sulking. Then I realized they were terrified.

Hey. Wake up. I need information.

The Watcher uncurled slightly, radiating fear and refusal. All they wanted was to flee. Instead, they were trapped with me and the Institute swarm, and they were utterly convinced we were all going to die.

No, *we're* not. *I can save us all, but first I need to know what we're up against. You obviously know* something. *Spill it.*

Reluctantly, the Watcher obeyed. They unfurled, leaking themselves into my sensorium. In my perception, the Watcher-As-Lucas stepped around Irene. Their borrowed air of Lucas Dowling's infuriating nonchalance had entirely evaporated.

"The monster in the basement. What exactly *is* it?"

The Watcher shrugged, the fear rippling through their form as if it was jelly. "We only know legends, but based on what you say, we believe it is an entity called *Amn-Zuhad*. It is an order of being unlike anything you have experienced. Other than yourself."

"I'm not exactly myself lately."

"We have noticed. That may be a good thing. If the barrier is preventing you from manifesting your full majesty, it may be doing the same to *Amn-Zuhad*."

"You're telling me what to call it, not what it is."

Irene looked from me to what looked to her like the empty space I was conversing with. "Amelia? Honey? You're talking to yourself."

Momentary annoyance flashed through me. "What? Oh, for pity's sake. Ravenna, I need you to open your mind to me."

The moment she did, I grabbed her and Irene and pulled them into my mindscape. We all appeared in the star-strewn replica of my dorm room on the Bureau campus—mostly. One corner was a piece of Ravenna's lab; instead of her lost astral pet, her device's spherical tank held the Watcher Within's murky fluid form. The opposite corner was festooned with flowering plants and hanging ivy, with a hand-carved wooden bench in the middle—a piece of the mindscape Irene had crafted.

Ravenna and Irene appeared in their respective corners. The Watcher-As-Lucas sat on one of my two steel folding chairs, hunched over themself and twisting their long-fingered hands together. I stood at my kitchen counter, heating my kettle for tea. It was purely conceptual, a manifestation of soothing thoughts to keep everyone calm.

"Sorry for the lack of warning," I said, trying to sound chipper, "but it's an emergency."

I poured the boiling water into four cups, over tea bags. I didn't add sugar, feeling that would take the pantomime a step too far into absurdity. I waved away the tea bags and passed the cups around. Irene took a hesitant sip of hers, then blinked in surprise.

"This is *really* good," she said. "What is it?"

"A memory of the best cup of tea I ever had, plus two lumps of the first time I felt safe and secure."

She nodded, confused but impressed. She took another sip. "So, who's Luci?"

Of *course* that memory involved her. I blushed and looked down at my feet, smiling like a fool. "Lucille Sweeney. She's my girlfriend. I think you'll like her."

Irene's eyebrows shot up. The mindscape didn't allow for the confusion of word games; she understood exactly what I meant by that. She was surprised and disbelieving, but not hateful.

"Your *girlfriend?*"

"That's right. She's my, um, my steady? Is that right?"

"They do the mouth thing and all," the Watcher-As-Lucas said, pressing the tips of their fingers together.

Irene blinked, processing this. "Is that an option?"

"Oh, my dear. You have so much to learn," Ravenna said with a half-grin. "Sadly, we have bigger revelations to grapple with today. Such as, who is this?"

She nodded to the Watcher.

"This is," I released a burst of radio static and chemical scent. "They're a horrible monster from beyond the stars who lives in my brain. They're not as bad as the horrible monster from beyond the stars who is taking over the basement, though."

The Watcher-As-Lucas lifted their chin stiffly. "We shall take that as a compliment."

"It was actually almost meant as one."

"They've been inside your *brain* this entire time?" Ravenna asked.

The Watcher quirked an eyebrow. "We don't appear to be the only one."

Ravenna's familiar flickered in and out of view behind her as it tried to monitor what was happening in the shared mindscape. She smiled and coaxed it into revealing itself. Slowly, a few bits at a time, it unfurled from its den in her psyche. Irene let out a small gasp and covered her mouth with her hands.

"She's *beautiful.*"

It was true. The living nightmare was unlike any creature that had ever lived on Earth. Yet, it borrowed elements from a dozen of them, or perhaps that was just the mind's attempt to correlate her with something familiar. She was like a coral crossed with a jellyfish or squid. Her body hung from a great amorphous envelope, which grew fleshy branches every which way. Long and short tendrils trailed beneath it, wafting gently in the cognitive air—seven or nine or thirteen, it was hard to tell. Their number changed every time I looked, but it was always odd. They were spaced unevenly around a round, stubby head studded with large pearlescent eyes and a fringe of wispy fins.

Her body was primarily black and purple, but veins of green luminescence shot up her tendrils and across her envelope. Irene cooed at her, reaching out to pet her without asking Ravenna. Before either of us could stop her, she was stroking the nearest branch of the nightmare's envelope. The familiar wrapped three tendrils around her. Those tentacles had destroyed a trio of myrmidons not long ago, but they simply caressed Irene gently. A strange resonance emanated from the familiar, like the memory of a lazy summer day from a childhood much happier than mine.

"I think she's purring," I said.

"Yes." Ravenna smiled. "I think she likes you, Miss Phillips."

"I like her back." Irene laughed as a tendril wrapped around her face. "What is she?"

"*Zedu heth mahr*," the Watcher-As-Lucas said, impressed despite themself. "A creature of the astral realms. They parasitize dreamers, breed in nightmares. We're amazed to see one so domesticated."

"She's *not* a parasite," Irene said, stroking the nightmare's tendrils. "She's a lovebug. Aren't you, girl?"

"That nodule you're stroking is an egg sac that contains—"

"We're not here for this metaphysical biology lesson," I said quickly, as much to spare Irene's feelings as to move things along. "We're here for a completely *different* metaphysical biology lesson. The thing in the basement— what the heck is it?"

The Watcher-As-Lucas turned their attention from Irene and her new friend. They reached up to a vine that was suddenly hanging above them and retrieved one of the objects affixed to its leafy length. It was a broad, flat stone inlayed with a shiny mosaic. It depicted a coiled serpent with multiple limbs and a tentacled head—an abstract representation of the behemoth at the heart of Object C.

"I know that creature," I said, more to myself than anyone else.

"We would prefer to avoid this particular conversational branch, as it causes you to yell at us," the Watcher said stiffly. "This is *Amn-Zuhad*, of the *Zuhad Ithon*. The Dragons of Order, the Progenitors. The Firstborn, or so legends call them. They're possibly the first intelligent life in this iteration of the universe."

Ravenna cocked her head to one side, disbelieving. "One of the first intelligent beings in the universe and it's *here*?"

"There are legends and then there are legends." The Watcher-As-Lucas shrugged. "It's possible that's pure speculation, inspired by their acts. The *Zuhad Ithon* are certainly ancient, more ancient than anything we know. Their legends predate any civilization we're familiar with… and usually involve ending them."

The Watcher let the mosaic piece go. It floated in space for a moment. Then the dorm room disappeared. The five of us stood atop a high ridge beneath a stormy sky. Violet lightning erupted between the dark clouds as a pale, wormlike creature descended from the void, falling upon a wide city of bright, jewel-toned buildings. They had been grown, not built. Each was a single massive tree, some the size of skyscrapers. Temples within the city offered up prayers to the behemoth; it was a festival day. The last they would ever know.

I looked across the ridge and was unsurprised to see a familiar fleshy tower growing miles away. Root-like tendrils as thick around as a mature tree dug into the ridge, while large tentacles hung from a wide flat cap at the tower's top. A thick chemical haze tainted the air around the Watcher's terrestrial body for miles. Small groups of plants, a cross between trees and coral, grew along the ridge, displacing the natural vegetation.

I turned to the Watcher-As-Lucas with a sour expression. "You?"

"No," the Watcher said. "This tragedy occurred long before our spawning. This is a much, much older colony who thankfully escaped this world's destruction, spreading the memory through the swarm as a warning."

Space and time warped above the Watcher as an entity of immense power and gravity opened the way from the local sphere. The tower collapsed like a giant that had suddenly lost its bones as the Watcher's consciousness rapidly vacated this plane. I shivered, recognizing the resonance of the entity lurking in the tunnel through space-time.

Teshu ung Maya.

Me.

The memoryscape dissolved around us with the other Watcher's departure. We found ourselves once again in my cognitive dorm. Irene stared at us, trying to take in the sudden rush of information. Ravenna hung back, looking thoughtful.

"Let's return to the physical realm, Amelia. Miss Phillips looks a little overwhelmed."

I nodded. Her and Irene's psychic self-image faded from my mindscape. Before I followed, I turned to the Watcher.

"That was helpful. Thank you."

The Watcher-As-Lucas smiled wearily. "It didn't even hurt you to say that."

I returned my attention to the physical realm. Only seconds had passed, leaving us little to explain to the jumpy prots. They stared at us, expecting some sort of answer.

"*Amn-Zuhad,*" Ravenna said. "We have to stop it."

"We have one major advantage," I said. "It's not fully manifested. If I had to make a guess, it needs to build itself a body big enough to support it, but it doesn't have enough materials yet."

"Not to be crude…" Irene looked around the cafeteria. "…but there's an awful lot of biomass here for it to collect."

"And an entire laboratory dedicated to exactly that sort of nonsense," Ravenna said, cursing Jeffrey West. "How do we keep his experiments out of *Amn-Zuhad's* hands?"

"I believe I can help with that," a new voice said.

Mark Pressler emerged from the secret passage. His jumpsuit was torn in several places, where it wasn't scorched. Four long scratches ran down his right cheek. His eyes burned with an intensity that spoke of a man pushed to his absolute limits.

"I know what the hive is after," he said, "and I know how to stop it."

23

That morning, Jeffrey West had given Mark a list of tasks to accomplish in his main lab. Most were routine: monitor conditions in the generation tanks, take note of tissue growth progress, inventory and restock supplies. In other words, it was an utterly normal workday. Doctor West had been in and out of the lab all day, both the main space and his private room. If anything about his demeanor seemed unusual, Mark thought nothing of it. West was an unusual man, after all.

The doctor returned to the lab at the hour the Object C Observation was scheduled, although at the time Mark didn't realize it was significant. He was adjusting the temperature of Tank Five when West entered. He double-checked the thermometer, then respectfully greeted his mentor.

West didn't return the greeting. "What's our progress on implantation?"

Mark didn't miss a beat. He was accustomed to West's moods. "Despite my fears, the six units in production have all accepted the implants. Musculature is ten percent donor tissue, on average. Epidermis is twenty percent. No spread to organs yet. Nothing visible in five units; Unit 16-3 will probably need gloves."

West frowned. "I told you to be careful with the implantation."

"I was, sir." Mark gestured to the myrmidon in Tank Five. Three knots of

Watcher matter grew across its chest and abdomen, surrounded by traceries of infected veins. "I picked the same implantation points on each unit—right pectoral, rectus abdominus, right inferior trapezius. However, growth has been far from uniform. In 16-3, the tissue in the pectoral and trapezius spread almost exclusively along the right arm."

West bent over Tank 3, inspecting the myrmidon with a stern expression. "There are three fingers on this hand, Mark."

"I don't think that middle digit *is* a finger, sir."

The offending digit, twice as long as its companion, twisted bonelessly in the orange goo. "Do you really think a *glove* will help hide that?"

"No, sir. I'm sorry. I was trying to be amusing."

"Well, stop it." West straightened, tugging at his lapel with a scowl. "I suppose it doesn't matter. What about the active units? How is your progress there?"

Mark's face went pale. He stared at a point just over the doctor's shoulder, not wanting to meet his eyes. "I don't know what you mean."

West tilted his head to one side and smiled condescendingly. "Oh, Mark. I know you think I don't pay attention to day-to-day matters, but I'm well aware the assets don't need maintenance that frequently."

Mark started to stammer something between an excuse and an explanation, but West held up his hand for silence.

"It's all right, Mark. I'm not opposed to a little initiative. I was always going to move into implanting the live models if things went well with this batch. However, events appear to have overtaken us."

He turned his head to the side, briefly staring into space. Then he shook his head sharply and smiled uncomfortably wide. "Now. How many?"

"I've implanted a dozen live units with alien tissue. No rejections so far."

"I wouldn't think so. Not with this wonderful substance to play with." West dipped his hand into the tank, dabbling his fingers in the blood-warm goo. "Fascinating, isn't it? A miracle of biological engineering and we didn't even create it. Did you know that, Mark? Did you ever wonder about its provenance?"

"I… of course I did, doctor." Mark took a step backward. He suddenly found the gleam in West's eyes unsettling. "I assumed you'd discovered it. It's named after you, isn't it? I thought you'd share the formula with me when you thought I was ready."

"When I thought you were ready. How touching." West moved closer, sliding his hand along the tank's rim. "You really have been very loyal, haven't you, Mark?"

"Yes, sir. Of course I have, sir." Mark backed up farther, trying not to take his eyes off West.

"That's good, Mark. That's what we—I—will need, going forward." He kept moving closer, staring through Mark's head. "What is the progress on those units? How far has the growth progressed?"

"It's hard to say, sir." Mark ran into the wall, one of the small cultivation tanks ramming into the small of his back. Alien tissue writhed behind his head, aware of his nearness. "I only used one implantation point on the live units. Inferior trapezius. Epidermal conversion is ten percent, on average. I can't tell internal growth without exploratory surgery."

"Exploratory surgery. Yes, that would be time-consuming and potentially costly, resource wise." He was standing nearly nose to nose with Mark. "More difficult to hide from me, as well."

Mark swallowed hard. "Yes, sir. I had considered that."

"Well. Twelve units." West rolled his eyes ceiling-ward, as if performing a mental calculation. "That will have to do."

He abruptly stepped away from Mark, turning on his heel and staring at the clock on the wall, just above the door to his private lab. Mark let out a held breath as quietly as he could, trying not to let the doctor hear his relief. He slid away from the wall, moving toward the farthest corner from the doctor.

West didn't look at Mark when he spoke again. "Meet me in the utility room in two hours. In the meantime, carry on with your tasks."

"Of course, doctor."

Mark said nothing when West pulled one of the small tanks from the wall and carried it into his private lab. He leaned against the counter and closed his eyes, letting his body tremble away its tension. The doctor was unusually intense today. He thought he was used to West's mercuriality, but this was something else entirely. It provoked a response. He hated that the body reacted this way, in defiance of his mind's intent, but he'd learned that it was no good denying it when it happened. Best to let the body respond, get it out of the way so he could return to work when it was done.

Once the trembling stopped and his heart rate lowered, he followed West's last instruction. He continued his checks on the generative tanks, ensuring everything was nominal. He bustled around the storage cabinets, double-checking the inventory and making notes for what needed to be restocked and what needed to be disposed of. He filled out the supply requests that West could never be bothered with, deftly forging the good doctor's signature where required. He scrubbed the lab from top to bottom, trying to maintain a sterile space.

He was halfway through mopping the floors when a blood-curdling scream erupted from the side room.

The horrific racket was muffled by the fluid-filled tank, but it was enough to set Mark's hair on end. He ran into the room to see what was happening. Bradley Finch, the dorm's long-missing "dropout", was pressing his palms flat against his tank wall, head thrown back to scream into the bright goo. Every muscle tensed, as if an electric current ran through his body. His eyes bulged. Before Mark could act, Bradley lunged forward and smashed his head against the glass. Cracks spiderwebbed across the tube's interior. He leaned back and rammed his head into the tube again. Mark let out a wordless cry and ran to the tank, not sure what to do. He reached it just as Bradley forced his head through the tube, sending near-boiling liquid splashing into Mark's face.

Like the biofluid, Mark had wondered at the provenance of the flesh the myrmidons had been grown from but had never asked what "Subject 16" actually was.

He stepped backward, slipping on the slick floor and falling hard. Bradley tore free of his restraints and ripped the tank open, paying no attention to the deep cuts in his hands as he forced his way free. Mark scrambled toward the main lab, hoping to find something to defend himself with. He was too slow. Bradley grabbed him by the throat and lifted him off the ground. Mark kicked wildly, slamming his heels into his former friend's abdomen. Bradley ignored the blows. His grip remained strong. The room swum around Mark, blackness creeping in at the edges of his vision as his oxygen-starved brain slowly died.

Salvation came when the half-grown myrmidon lunged out of Tank 3 and grabbed Bradley's arm. He dropped Mark to the floor like a sack of flour and swung wildly at the creature, smashing a fist into its skinless head. It noticed the damage no more than Bradley had. Its fingers dug into his arm, the tendril of Watcher matter that replaced its middle fingers trying to pierce his skin. Bradley grabbed the myrmidon's arm with both hands and yanked, ripping the limb out of its socket. A gout of milk-white fluid splashed across his bare torso.

More of the half-formed myrmidons struggled against the tubing running through them, trying to free themselves from their tanks. Tendrils of Watcher matter lashed at the air like scorpion stings. Mark ignored them. He crawled across the floor to the fire extinguisher hanging from the wall. While Bradley tore Unit 16-3 apart, Mark yanked it from the box with numb hands. When Bradley turned at the noise, Mark bashed the fire extinguisher across his head. He hit Bradley again and again until his mutated friend fell to the floor, head split open and leaking milk-white fluid across the tiles. Mark stood over his still body, breathing heavily, and let the fire extinguisher fall from his hands.

He barely noticed when the alarms started going off.

"I know what's happened to the myrmidons," Mark said.

Everyone in the cafeteria stared at him. He took no notice. I wasn't sure if he really knew where he was or if he'd simply gone to the first source of light and voices.

"So do we," I said. "An ultraterrestrial entity has taken over the hive mind."

"Not all of them," Vernon said. "Some of them are fighting each other. They've got weird stuff growing out of them, like big worms."

"That may have been our doing," Mark said. "We've been conducting an experiment with the myrmidons. Upgrading them."

"What do you mean?" Irene asked, far too calmly.

I didn't wait for his explanation. I dove into his mind, sifting through his memories. I didn't have to dig far. My eyes widened when I found a memory of three days ago, when West summoned him to the room in the deepest basement. The one where they kept the poor tortured creature at the heart of the myrmidon hive. Where he and West cooked up the serum that had made the Argos Device the perfect host for the behemoth.

"You… you *bastard!*" I shouted.

Without thinking, I lashed out with one of my outer limbs, or tried to. I was so angry I ignored the burning pain that stabbed from the base of my skull down my spine. The survivors screamed as lights exploded above us, coronas of weird light blazing around me as the barrier reacted. The space between Mark and me *twisted*, hurling him to the floor.

I grabbed his psyche and ripped it from his mind. We flew across the compound, down through the subbasements to Lab B305. The fragment of *Amn-Zuhad* had burst the Argos Device's seams, pallid flesh bulging in a sinuous mass that fell across the platform. Wormy tumors the size of a person pulsed sickeningly, growing in a roughly serpentine shape.

Myrmidons trooped in and out of the lab, carrying large tanks of biofluid or the bodies of the people they'd murdered. They laid the dead out in a loose scaffolding for *Amn-Zuhad*'s growing body. They dumped the biofluid over its existing form, bathing it in stinking goo. Sucking toothless orifices opened along its length wherever the fluid ran, slurping it down greedily.

I couldn't see the bodies of Traynor's team anymore, nor of the doctor himself or the Director. They had all been consumed, raw materials for the behemoth's new body. Harold, too, had utterly disappeared. His body had become a hundred wriggling tentacles inside the split capsule, a rudimentary new head that lurked quietly in the dark, although far from quiescent.

Amn-Zuhad ignored my psychic intrusion. The battle was still raging in the astral realm. Even from realspace, I could feel the aftershocks of its struggle against the being at the heart of the rival hive. What had been a stalemate was gradually coming to an end. As its body grew, it could concentrate more of its presence, its power, into this space. It was gaining the upper hand.

The beast was massive yet still small. All the people in the building wouldn't provide enough mass to support *Amn-Zuhad*'s vast consciousness, but that didn't matter. We couldn't be far from Regina.

"There are nearly a *million* people in the city!" I shouted. "What do you think it's going to do to them?"

Mark screamed. He wasn't trained for astral travel or remote viewing; disembodiment was terrifying enough without facing my fury or the hunger of a growing god-monster. Disgusted, I flung him back into his body, leaving him shivering and weeping.

Steady, Ravenna sent. A burst of calm followed her words. I ignored it. I stood over him like a vengeful fury. One hand clutched at my head, trying to steady myself against the mounting pain. The other clenched into a fist.

"This is *his* fault!" I shouted. "His and Jeffrey West's! They sabotaged the Argos Device, made it into something the monster could use! It never could have taken Harold's body if they hadn't infected it with their *filth!*"

"I didn't know!" Tears streamed down Mark's face. "He didn't tell me what we were doing! He was lying to me the whole time!"

"Amelia," Irene said softly. She laid a gentle hand on my shoulder. "This isn't you."

"You have no idea what I am," I said, but the anger drained out of my voice.

Mark lay on the ground before me, sobbing, one arm curled protectively over his head. He was pathetic and far from blameless, but he wasn't lying to me. I was too exhausted to maintain my fury. It was still there, acid roiling in my stomach, ready to vomit forth without warning, but I held it in.

The Watcher-As-Lucas stood behind Mark, glaring down at him.

Izulz? they asked, with a casualness that defied their affront.

I took a deep breath, forcing my fist to unclench.

No. Not yet.

I turned my back on Mark, more to express my displeasure than to avoid seeing him. I took three steps away. Irene followed me, still touching my shoulder. I covered her hand with mine and gave her a small smile I didn't feel. The fight with *Amn-Zuhad* had already taken a lot out of me, but it had also taken a toll on her. If Irene could keep her anger I check—and I could feel it through her palm, the storm inside her whipping up into a hurricane—then so could I.

The Watcher didn't bother to hide their distaste. *This animal used us as raw materials. We* demand *satisfaction.*

"I thought you didn't care about that body?" I said aloud.

We find that we've changed our minds.

"Hm. Feels bad, doesn't it? You'll get your satisfaction but not like this."

I ignored the confusion rippling through the cafeteria. I was starting to develop a plan. It was dangerous, but only to me. That was acceptable.

"You introduced alien matter into the myrmidons," I said, working it out aloud. "That's what split the hive."

"That's right," Mark said, still on the edge of hyperventilating. "We were trying to innovate a method of enhancing the human body. We—"

"I could not possibly care less what you thought you were doing," I said sharply. "That creature I saw in your memory. It's controlling the loyal myrmidons?"

"More like they're a part of it, but yes. It's the core of the hive."

"Not for long. It's fighting a psychic battle with *Amn-Zuhad,* and it's losing."

Irene paled. "The fighting must be what's keeping them all busy. If it takes control…"

"It will kill us all. Then it will break free," Ravenna said.

"At which point, it will run riot over Regina," I said. "We can't let that happen. I think I have an idea to stop it, but I'm going to need help."

"What do you need from us?" Irene asked without hesitation.

"The electrical supply to the building. Does anyone know where it is?"

"I do," Vernon said. "There's a generator room in the basement. I've done maintenance on it. Most of us have."

About a third of the survivors nodded.

"Okay. I need you to take a group of people—four or so, just to be safe— and shut the generators off."

"That will set *Amn-Zuhad* free," Ravenna warned.

"It will also let me get everyone out," I said. "It'll take careful timing. You'll have to wait for my signal."

"What'll that be?" Vernon asked.

"Unmistakable."

"Is this safe?" He frowned. "What about the monsters?"

"Don't worry. Their attention will be elsewhere."

"What about me?" Irene asked.

I hesitated. "Does anyone have a pen?"

Instinctively, a half-dozen hands went to their breast pockets and offered their pens. I grabbed the nearest one and fetched a napkin. Jotting down the number to the Lane Diner, I folded it in half and handed it to Irene.

"Plan A is that I get everyone out the same way I got us out of the lab. Plan B is for you to take everyone to the vans and drive. In that event, call this number as soon as you're somewhere safe and ask for Gloria Lane. Tell her… tell her Amelia needs help and to bring her bag. She'll understand."

"Are you going to need her?" Irene asked softly.

"I hope not." I caught her in a tight hug. Then I turned back to Mark. "I can see almost everything in this building. Your 'utility room' is part of the 'almost'. Where is it?"

"The deepest subbasement." My expression must have turned suddenly fearsome, because he quickly added, "I can take you there!"

"Good. We don't have a lot of time." I turned to Ravenna. "Keep them safe."

"Tell me what the plan is, Amelia," she said. "I can help you!"

I shook my head. "I have everything I need. I don't want to risk you."

I didn't add that I also didn't entirely trust her. She'd been helpful, yes. She'd also been willingly part of the Institute—not just a technician, but a researcher. Ravenna claimed to have been using them to advance her own agenda. Maxine Orr, who'd enabled Lucas Dowling, had done the same thing.

"Yet you'll risk me?" Mark said.

I grabbed his arm and yanked him to his feet. "Yes. I will."

"Seems pretty fair," Irene said, folding her arms.

"I can't take us directly into the utility room," I said. "We have to go just outside it. Picture it in your mind."

I saw it then: a nondescript stretch of hallway in the third sub-basement. An elevator hid behind a white wall panel. Looking down, I could see that the hallway was no longer quite so unassuming, but we would deal with that in a moment.

I glanced at Vernon. "Take your team and go. Now!"

Before anyone could say anything else, I *jumped*.

I hated lying to Irene, but I didn't have time to argue.

There was no Plan A.

24

The passageway was a horror show.

A half-dozen bodies were strewn from one end of the hall to the other. They'd been brutally beaten, heads and limbs and torsos crushed or bent at sickening angles. The myrmidons' milk-white internal fluid was splattered across every surface, floor to ceiling, mixed with the Watcher matter's blue-green ichor. A splash of orange and brown joined the puddle at our feet; Mark vomited up his lunch at his first sight of the carnage.

Despite the slaughter, the loyalist myrmidons hadn't fallen yet. Their numbers were holding firm; for every loyalist *Amn-Zuhad*'s forces dispatched, they infected another. The suborned myrmidons had fallen back fifty meters to the nearest stairwell, waiting for reinforcements from above. The loyalists stood guard on either end of this hallway, six at each intersection. They turned in eerie sync when they heard us arrive. Three from each side charged, registering us as new threats.

I reached out to the hive, trying to pour friendly intent into their echoing collective consciousness. It was true, to an extent. I was aligned against their enemy, at least. My plan meant nothing good for the hive, but they didn't need to know that.

The approaching myrmidons slowed but didn't stop. I picked up skepticism and wary curiosity. That was a start. I kicked Mark, still crouched beside me and voiding his stomach across the floor.

"Mark!" I hissed. "Tell them we're friendly."

He climbed shakily to his feet, wiping his sleeve across his mouth. Standing up as straight as he could, he held out his hands and commanded the myrmidons to stop.

They didn't.

He frowned, staring at me. Then he stepped away and took a sharp breath. Deepening his voice, he shouted, "All points—cease activity and await further instruction!"

Four of the myrmidons stopped. Two others, one on either side, continued their approach. I felt unsettled emotions flow back and forth between them, jagged and new. Fear. Anger. Wonder. Confusion.

Mark gasped. "They've broken their conditioning." He sounded far more excited than I thought appropriate, under the circumstances.

"How is that a *good* thing?"

"The hive is becoming independent. Between the physical changes and the psychic stress, I think it's developed an identity."

Normally, that would have been thrilling. Unfortunately, my plan depended heavily on not thinking of the myrmidons as people… or as a person, as was more accurate. I needed the hive to be a tool, like the Argos Device, to justify what I was going to do to it.

Unbidden, I saw Agent Pickman leering down at me, a nasty smile on his pinched face.

"We're running out of time." My words were hollow. I told myself I didn't care.

"What?"

"Nothing."

I turned to the myrmidon on my right, palms held out. "You know who I am. I'm Amelia Temple. I'm with the Institute. Sort of. I'm here to help."

I sent the hive a vision of the entire troop of myrmidons charging *Amn-*

Zuhad as one, overwhelming it and beating it to death. I followed that with an image of Mark and me in the utility room, backing them up. I poured vague assurance and feelings of friendship into the hive, hoping it would be enough to earn its trust.

We have the same enemy, I sent. *We can make you strong enough to fight it. Trust me.*

I don't think it would have worked if I'd had the hive's full attention. It probably would have picked up my true intentions behind the half-truths. If nothing else, it likely would have demanded details. As it was, the bulk of its attention was devoted to fighting the behemoth, which had redoubled its assault on the astral realm. It only had the attention span to make a snap decision, and some of its conditioning still held. It knew Mark. It trusted him.

The hive sent back its assent before abruptly shutting off communications. The six myrmidons pulled back, returning to their positions. I didn't relax, but I let myself feel a moment's relief.

"I think we have an agreement," I said. "Get us inside."

Mark withdrew a thin, flat tool from his pocket and selected a wall panel that looked like any other. Grimacing at the sticky mess clinging to the wall, he fit the tool into the seam between panels and pushed. A hidden mechanism clicked loudly, and the panel slid to the side, revealing a small, glass-doored elevator. I let out a heavy sigh and suppressed a shudder. Mark gave me a questioning look.

"I had a bad experience with elevators recently," I said.

I declined to explain further. Mark shook his head and opened the door, gesturing for me to go first. I frowned and stepped inside. He followed, closing the door and pulling the lever; it only traveled between two floors. The elevator shuddered, then slid down the shaft. I leaned back against the wall, arms folded across my chest, waiting to pass through the seal hiding the last level from my senses. I hoped there wasn't also a ward. I didn't have time to be writhing in agony.

The Watcher-As-Lucas appeared before me again. Their liquid eyes locked with mine. Their facial expression was unreadable, but I could feel their disapproval. It was like a current of cold water swirling through my mind.

"We do not believe you have a 'Plan A'."

I looked up at them through half-lidded eyes. I was so tired. Tired of carrying them, tired of fighting monsters like me and reckless men like Mark Pressler. Mostly, though, I was physically *tired*. The struggle against *Amn-Zuhad* had left me utterly worn out in a way I'd never felt before. Maybe it was a side-effect of the barrier cutting me off from the rest of myself. I was simply Amelia Temple now, and Amelia Temple was almost entirely a human teenager.

This, in the parlance of the times, was a total drip.

I shrugged at the Watcher, lacking the energy to argue, and said, "So what?"

"We have a vested interest in your well-being."

I rolled my eyes. "I do have a plan. You'll be fine."

The Watcher-As-Lucas radiated distress. "We will be very upset if you come to harm."

I managed a weak smile. "Don't be sweet. Not now. It's weird."

A shudder rippled through the Watcher's image. I sighed and tried to send it reassurance. "This *is* going to be a little dicey. I need you to promise to look out for the others, okay?"

Mark glanced at me, tears still drying on his dirty face. "Miss Temple, are you talking to me or to yourself?"

"Shut up, Mark."

The elevator shuddered to a stop. I couldn't help but let out a sigh of relief when there wasn't a new monster waiting in front of the door. It slid open, freezing air pouring into the small space. Mark immediately started shivering and grabbed one of the clean-suit coats hanging beside the door. I ignored them. I stepped into the room, taking it all in.

A huge column of metal scaffolding dominated the room. It was surrounded by large glass and metal tanks, most filled with either the same yellow-orange biofluid as West's generation tanks or the myrmidons' milk-white circulatory fluid. Tubes ran from the tanks to the creature hanging from the scaffolding. It was twelve feet tall. It looked something like a myrmidon stretched out to scale, but the resemblance was faint. Most of its naked skin was pale, like the belly of a cave-dwelling fish that had never known the sun, except where the tubes entered it. There, spiderwebs of angry red spread from tortured flesh, which hung loosely from withered muscles.

The rest of its flesh was blue-green with implanted Watcher matter. Of course they'd started here. The infection had spread across almost half of its body, a forest of alien anemones waving from its left arm and torso, tendrils climbing up the tubes. It twitched and trembled as it struggled against the behemoth's power.

Seven nodules, cerulean orbs like spider's eyes, dotted the forehead and cheeks of its hairless head. They ranged in size from a marble to a fist. Each hand had four fingers and two very human thumbs, one on either side, but its feet had two toes. It didn't have nipples, genitalia, or a belly button. I don't know why I found that comforting. Perhaps it proved that whatever it was, West had grown it in a tank instead of using other methods.

"This is it," Mark breathed reverently. "This is the heart of the Myrmidon Program."

Its face was slack, but its wonderous brain was busy. It was thinking for twelve other bodies, after all. The room was so noetically active that anything not bolted down was hovering in the frigid air. Hundreds of punch cards orbited the creature in a double helix that would mean nothing to Mark for another year or so. The rivulets of milky fluid mixed with dark ichor leaking from every orifice suggested how well the psychic battle was going without me having to look into the astral realm. Blood vessels throughout its body were bursting under the strain. It was only a matter of time before it suffered a fatal aneurism.

I leaned against a nearby worktable, struggling to ignore my sudden fatigue. Mark shrugged into the coat, breath steaming. The Watcher ignored us both. They approached the scaffolding and stared up at the creature with a mix of awe and terror.

"Do you know what this is?" they asked, their voice hushed. "Do you know what these animals have done?"

"Something horrible, I'm sure." I rubbed my hand across my face, not keeping the irritation out of my voice. "It's nothing human. I've known that since I… since I *encountered* the first ones. It's some kind of alien?"

"In a manner of speaking," Mark said, falling into the habit of the long-suffering assistant. "It's native to Earth—Doctor West grew it here—but the tissue he used is certainly alien."

"He did grow it?" I said, aghast.

"Impossible. Blasphemous, if possible," the Watcher said in a scandalized whisper.

"What *is* it?" I asked.

"I don't really know," Mark said, as the Watcher intoned, "Magna Mater." I don't know whether they meant it as a prayer, a description, or a curse.

"Explain," I said.

Mark started to object until he realized I wasn't looking at him. The Watcher paid him no attention, continuing, "*Amn-Zuhad* is one of seven. They are—they were—they *are* similar, yet distinct. Legends have them traveling the universe, altering and destroying life at their whim. They were bound, eventually. It's a long and complicated story."

"I was there for some of it," I murmured.

The Watcher nodded. "So legends say."

"What is it doing here?"

"*Amn-Zuhad's* prison found its way to this solar system. It must not have been the only one."

"Then this is, what, a clone? Like a plant? Using something alien as a cultivar?"

"I don't *know*," Mark said, irritated. "I only know it's West's creation. He thought of it as a prototype."

"You're correct," the Watcher said. "This is not the form of the *Zuhad Ithon*, but it *is* of their flesh. The myrmidons must be hybrids. We don't know why we didn't see it before."

"How could he have accomplished this?" I asked. "This isn't science, it's alchemy."

"With this." Mark placed a gloved hand against one of the large tanks of biofluid feeding the creature. "It's the foundation of our—of his—work. It's like super-blood. The primordial soup itself."

"*Zuhad-Isseth*," the Watcher intoned. "*Anke zan Ilitu.* The Void Mother. The legends also say they served another. Or perhaps they only followed her, like lesser predators feeding off the scraps of the apex. It was she who seeded life across the cosmos. Some of it, anyway. This liquid is her blood. Her amniotic fluid. Her semen. It quickens and nourishes life where there was none."

"Okay. We can do something with that," I said. "How much do we have?"

"Thousands of gallons," Mark said. "Two tanks are hooked up to the creature, with six more in reserve. This is where we store most of it."

"That's what they really want. Even more than to destroy this," I said. "*Amn-Zuhad* is using it to fuel its own growth. It's probably used up whatever you had in your main lab."

"I tried to stop them," Mark said. "They were too many."

"Here's your chance to make up for your failure," I said. "Start hooking the tanks up. All of them. I want you to feed every drop of that goo into the creature."

"What? Why?"

"Because I need it to grow. Quickly." I turned to the Watcher. "I'm keeping my promise."

The Watcher-As-Lucas stared at me as understanding dawned. "Amelia…"

"Look at it." I gestured at the Watcher matter growing on and through the creature. "It's almost a third you already. Or your encounter suit, anyway. You'll be compatible with it."

As if to punctuate my words, the Watcher tendrils reached toward them, drawn by their presence. I could feel the Watcher yearning for that weird flesh. It was familiar to them in a way my human-ish brain never could be.

Mark ignored me, slipping fully into his role as a mad scientist's assistant. He ran back and forth between the scaffolding and the various tanks, hooking up hoses and splicing them together with duct tape. It was going to be messy, but that was okay. If everything worked, this whole room was going to get a whole lot messier very quickly.

"You want us to take over the hive," the Watcher said.

I nodded. "I'm betting on you being better at controlling the myrmidons than the behemoth. It's the sort of thing you do."

Doubt radiated from them. "*Amn-Zuhad* is a god. We very much are not."

"It's a piece of a god, if that. *Amn-Zuhad* is still trapped at the edge of the solar system, trying to pilot that body by remote. If we can destroy that body before it gets large enough to inhabit, if we break the connection, then we'll be safe."

I shook my head, laughing bitterly. "At least, until the next crisis."

The Watcher didn't laugh with me. Instead, a suspicious look crossed their face. "We'll have you to help us?"

I bit my lip. "No."

"*What?*"

"Mark, are you almost ready?"

"I have three tanks hooked up," he called from the back of the room. "That's a thousand gallons apiece. I still have three more to go."

"Open the valves now. Hook the others up as quickly as you can. Then take cover."

"What do you mean, no?" the Watcher demanded.

I sighed, then smiled sadly. "Seals require power. The barrier around this building uses electricity. The ward locking you up in my head runs on my own metabolism."

Silence passed between us. Silence and sadness.

"There's a reason I wouldn't let Irene come with us," I whispered.

"You can't!"

"I'm about to."

The Watcher continued shouting objections, but I ignored them. I focused my attention inward. I couldn't look across space, not from inside the sealed utility room. I could only hope Vernon and his team had reached the generators. If not… well, everyone would still be trapped inside the building. Hopefully the Watcher could smash open a wall.

Vernon! I sent as strongly as I could. *Cut the juice now!*

Then it was a matter of shutting off my own autonomic functions. I always knew I could do it. I never had any reason to. About three minutes, and the seal imprisoning the Watcher would collapse.

After that, it was out of my hands.

I closed my eyes and said, "Be good."

25

Discontinuity

26

❖

Lightning burned through my body, erupting from my heels all the way up to the base of my skull. I was suddenly intimately familiar with every cell in my nervous system as the entire delicate tracery screamed at once. My eyes flew open, and I sucked in a loud, desperate breath.

My body bent in a tall arc atop a large, flat surface—*a table, I was lying on a wooden dining table*—while a vortex of wild energy swirled around me. It rose in a sparking, arcing funnel before plunging into me. A familiar voice called my name. Another voice shouted at her to stay back, it wasn't safe.

I fell onto the table, shaking it so hard it nearly split. I jerked forward into a sitting position, doubling over as my aching lungs tried to remember how to breathe. As my chest seized, I stared at the room around me. I was in a simple dining room, white walls and wood floors, with three women and dozens of candles. I recognized Irene and Polly right away. I burst into tears when I saw the third—a beautiful Black woman who was clearly in charge.

"Shut it down!" Gloria Lane shouted. "Put the candles out!"

Polly grabbed a pitcher of water from a side table and started filling cups. Before she could pass the first, I whipped my other limbs out, snapping the candles out all at once. The energy vortex collapsed, giving me relief from the pain. My body still ached all over, but my nerves stopped screaming. In truth, I was grateful for the pain. It was good to feel anything at all, under the circumstances.

Irene and Polly leapt forward to hug me, crying along with me. I clung to them, trying to anchor myself to something familiar. I'd been gone for a while, and I wasn't sure how long. This was far worse than when the Institute had captured me. Then, I'd simply skipped over a week. Now, I had the disconcerting feeling of having been *somewhere*, but also *nowhere*.

With some difficulty, I freed myself from my new friends' grasp and slid to the edge of the table. When I reached out to Gloria, she smiled and shook her head, amazed at both me and herself, and took it. I pulled her close, resting my head atop hers. She pressed her cheek against my head and stroked my neck, cooing softly as I cried.

"Amelia Whatever-Your-Middle-Name-Is Temple," she said, at once loving and stern, "you had better never make me do anything like that again."

I laughed through my tears. "What's a middle name?"

Gloria just squeezed me tighter.

I was about to ask her what had happened when awareness flooded my mind. For the briefest second, I was no longer just sitting atop a dining room table in a humble bungalow in the Merryweather neighborhood of Regina's southwest side. I was everywhere and everywhen, a vast undifferentiated "I" threading through and around universes spanning a dozen geometric dimensions. I knew everything, everywhere.

I only had to look.

Like a fluid under pressure jetting through a gap in its container, the Watcher's consciousness flew out of my body. They hated to abandon me, but my dying brain would take them down with it. They couldn't exist as a bodiless psychic matrix on this plane, nor could they return to the aether without my help. Seizing the nearest compatible substrate, they dove into the web of alien matter growing within West's creation. By itself, the biomass wasn't sufficient to support their vast confluence, the memories of a billion minds across millennia. Fortunately, the creature was suffused with the impossibly nutrient-rich biofluid. The Watcher cells fed greedily, multiplying at an alarming rate. Months ago, the Watcher had rapidly grown themselves a body using only the compressed remains of a previous form. This sudden growth made that development look positively languid. The creature's body buckled as dense alien tumors emerged from its back and chest in a matter of minutes. The scaffolding shuddered as the mass it supported increased exponentially, the racket of steel rods squealing and creaking drowning out the sound of stretching flesh. The mass tore free of its restraints when the Watcher matter bulged and erupted upward, fountaining up into a twisting tower of flesh. Thick roots sprouted from the base of the mass, snaking across the frigid floor and digging into the concrete pad to anchor itself. Hoses and tubes tore free, spraying steaming fluid across the room, but questing roots quickly found the tanks. Sharp tendrils pierced the metal walls, sucking down more of the biofluid.

Within the body's twisting, expanding nervous system, the Watcher and the creature fought for control. The battle was short-lived. The creature was already spent from its struggle against *Amn-Zuhad*. The Watcher was fresh, and enraged, and well accustomed to dominating lesser minds. Their invasive chorus overwhelmed the hive mind, enveloping and quickly consuming it. The nascent identity sank into the depths of the Watcher colony, dissolving into oneness. Perhaps it would retain enough individuality to survive as a coherent facet, like the piece of Lucas Dowling. Perhaps not. The Watcher didn't care.

One level up, the behemoth felt its rival fade away and roared in triumph. The psychic blast shook the building to its foundations. It took no notice when the lights all went out at once. Sinking further into its new form, *Amn-Zuhad* commanded its minions to harvest the rest of the building's biomass.

The behemoth's dominance was short-lived. The biofluid didn't supercharge only the Watcher matter's growth. The Watcher's expanding body had initially incorporated more flesh cultivated from *Zuhad-Isseth* than their own. As they tried to build their encounter suit along familiar lines, they found it changing despite their directions. The tower's fleshy top bulged and split, but it did not form a familiar flat cap. Half a pallid, hairless head jutted from the Watcher's shaft, studded with sapphire eyes as big as beachballs, its half-mouth yawning silently. Eight long, thick arms tipped with double-thumbed hands sprouted from the trunk just beneath the head. The Watcher lashed out with the arms, trying to master their new body. The rest of the scaffolding fell around it. Equipment toppled and smashed beneath their arms. They grabbed a tank and crushed it beneath their grip, and then they found that their new form was good. The Watcher pressed all eight hands against the ceiling, tearing the basement open, exposing rooms and hallways of the level above.

The half-visible mouth opened wider, revealing teeth like a whale's baleen, and vomited forth a geyser of ichor. The stinking mass spread through the sub-basement like thick fog, splattering loyalist and suborned myrmidons alike with a cloud of sticky spores. The myrmidons, three dozen in total, collapsed in a pile. They rose again moments later. Boils and tumors of weird flesh tore through their white jumpsuits as the Watcher infected their bodies and minds, converting them into the sort of servitors they understood. The neurons in their novel brains rewired, forming new structures and issuing new commands. They stood silently, quivering as the Watcher's infection ran rampant through their bodies. Then they charged, a small horde rushing into Lab B305.

The Watcher's growth slowed but didn't stop. It ceased its wild flailing. Pieces of ceiling tile crashed to the floor, but otherwise the utility room was silent. Mark Pressler crawled out from beneath the worktable, shoving aside a piece of fallen scaffolding to make a gap. With the lights out, he couldn't see, and he couldn't hear any more destruction. The myrmidon horde had already left. For a moment, he thought he might be able to escape.

Then the Watcher's massive hand grabbed him and pulled him close.

Mark gibbered as the many spider-like eyes stared at him. A long rent opened down the length of the Watcher's trunk. As he opened his mouth to scream, the Watcher spat a wad of stinking ichor into his face. He coughed and spluttered while the black-green goo worked its way into his nose and throat. The Watcher tossed him through the gap in the ceiling. He landed hard on a hallway floor and rolled three meters before running into a wall. The Watcher left him there, chemical commands burrowing into his brain.

As one, twenty-nine myrmidons stormed the lab. They represented the majority of the surviving drones. Steering so many bodies at once was unlike the Watcher's usual methods; typically the infection built new structures in the host, giving it new instincts, but these creatures had less identity than the most rudimentary animal. They had no instincts to follow, nothing to add to the colony besides mass. No matter. The Watcher needed only their hands, and that only for a few minutes more.

Seven myrmidons remained under the behemoths' control. The Watcher's horde showed them no mercy. They had no need to convert the rest. They simply needed to remove an obstacle, and they did so with brutal efficiency. It was horrifying to watch, and even more terrible to realize the Watcher cared little for their lack of personhood. They would have murdered the surviving technicians with as much brutality had they decided the humans were disposable.

Amn-Zuhad still lurked on the Argos Device platform, its pallid, tumorous mass coiling around the distressed capsule. Its body was still sessile, its rudimentary limbs far from ready to support its mass. Nonetheless, it was still puissant. When the myrmidons crashed into the room, the capsule shattered, shards of ceramic and lapis lazuli flying across the room as the huge tentacle-covered head tore free. *Amn-Zuhad* screamed, spitting corrosive bile across the Watcher's horde. A half-dozen myrmidons in the first rank collapsed, Watcher matter dissolving, cultured leviathan flesh warping and metamorphizing in response to new chemical commands. It was too late. The rest of the horde swarmed the behemoth like ants covering an earthworm.

Still, the real battle was again in the astral realm. As soon as the myrmidons entered its lair, *Amn-Zuhad* recognized a new enemy had emerged. The giant of light reared up inside the tapestry of Earthly dreams, roaring out its dominance to the universe. The Watcher bubbled up beneath it, a psychic fungal infection growing beneath the surface, spreading and digging in until it was too entrenched to tear out. Fruiting bodies sprouted around the behemoth, releasing nightmare spores that covered the giant. The behemoth roared again, blasting the Watcher with raw psychic power, burning it with undiluted splendor. It burned holes in the Watcher's psychic presence again and again, but still the Watcher spread.

Amn-Zuhad was a god, but the Watcher was a legion.

The Watcher's collective billions launched themselves at the behemoth's psyche, a horde of mnemonic Lilliputians swarming the eldritch Gulliver. Countless millions of the Watcher's long-lost ancestors, the memory of the Utsoggthua and a dozen other extinct civilizations, even snatches of a hundred-ish human dreamers screamed "WE" in the face of divinity.

They could never have won a long battle, but they didn't need to. Bifurcated and overwhelmed, the behemoth couldn't dominate on either front and so lost both. The myrmidon horde tore its body to pieces, destroying the behemoth's toehold on Earth. As the last of its new nerves splattered beneath a myrmidon's foot, *Amn-Zuhad* felt its awareness of the hot, wet planet go dark. It screamed helplessly from within its trans-Neptunian prison, once again impotent and alone.

Thirty feet above the carnage, two dozen survivors huddled around the vans as the few who retained hope struggled to pry open the garage's shutters. Killing the power had shut down the wards; it had also shut down the mechanisms that would open the manor's barricades. As far as the survivors knew, they were no less trapped than they had been in the cafeteria. Clinging together in twos and threes, they stared dully as Irene led an effort to pry up one of the barriers.

Vernon had scrounged up a long metal rod. Using a stack of cement blocks as a fulcrum, he'd wedged it beneath the shutter. He, Irene, and four others were straining with all their might to lever the shutter up. They only needed to push it up seven feet; that would be enough clearance for the vans. So far, they'd managed six inches.

"Forget seven feet." Irene panted hard, every muscle in her arms screaming. "I'd settle for one. We could squeeze through a one-foot gap, right?"

"All of us?" Sweat poured down Vernon's face, beet-red with the strain. "What, then we hoof it to town?"

"It's only a couple of miles."

"More like ten."

"See? That's nothing."

Metal groaned loudly as they threw themselves against the lever. The shutter creaked up another inch. Then the pipe bent nearly in half, sending the six of them sprawling. Irene spat out a foul word, but it was drowned out by Polly's screams.

A trio of myrmidons shuffled into the garage. The Watcher infection had warped their bodies beyond recognition. Only the tattered remains of their once-white jumpsuits suggested their former existence. That, and the bundle the central drone carried. It held my body in its arms, limbs dangling loosely.

The three myrmidons approached the van closest to the shutters and stopped. They stared at the survivors expectantly, waiting for someone to act. Most of the technicians shrank against the walls, finding whatever cover they could and waiting for the carnage to begin again. Vernon grabbed the bent lever and held it out like a spear. Irene put a hand on the rod and gently pushed it down, giving him a warning look. Then she slowly approached the van, staring at them —at me—as if she was in a dream. Gingerly, she put her hand against my forehead, wincing at how cold I was. Her other hand found her pocket, closing around the napkin with Gloria's phone number. She bit her lip nervously. Then she nodded.

Irene opened the van's side door and gestured at the seats. Wordlessly, the central myrmidon pushed past her and carefully laid me across the middle seat. The survivors watched, numb, as the three myrmidons then huddled around the shutter. Grasping its lip, they began to lift. They strained, weird muscles bulging as they forced it up. The dense metal plate resisted passively, the thick steel protesting with the screech of metal scraping against metal. It drew blood even as they gained feet. Six muscles in the left-most myrmidons arm burst, splattering nearby surfaces with ichor. The right-most myrmidon's leg snapped, sending it toppling to its side. The middle myrmidon's body warped, alien matter consuming the rest of its original flesh to fuel its growth. It grew another three feet, shoving the shutter up into the ceiling. Then it collapsed, ichor spewing out of a dozen rents in its flesh.

The survivors stared at the fallen monsters, unsure what to do next. Then Irene shouted for them to get in the vans. That broke the spell. They ran to the vehicles, briefly scuffling at the doors until everyone had acquired a seat. Some sat on one another's laps, but no one protested the intimacy. They just wanted out of this nightmare.

Meanwhile, Irene rallied Vernon and two others to help drag the myrmidons out of the way. They lay in a pile, staring silently at nothing at all. Whatever commanded them had abandoned them. For now. She didn't intend to wait for them to reawaken. Once the exit was clear, Irene shooed the three into the van. Then she clambered into the first van's driver's seat. Without bothering to signal the others, she fired up the engine and stomped on the gas pedal. Her van shot out of the garage, down the long driveway and toward the big city. Hopefully they would find safety there. Failing that, a shower and a clean bed for the night.

When the third van had departed, another trio of myrmidons shuffled into the garage. They each grabbed one of their fellows and dragged them inside, down to the depths of the manor, to the deepest point. The Watcher Below waited for them.

"Miss Adler disappeared on us when the lights went out," Irene said. "She left me a note with this address. It's a boarding house. Miss Catalina was expecting us."

"What, all of you?"

We had moved into the living room, an airy, open space hung with

Spanish tapestries. Sleek modern furniture sat upon a shockingly teal carpet. Our host was nowhere to be seen, but Polly had wrangled a pitcher of iced tea and a plate of cheese and crackers. It was taking all of my considerable reserve not to fall on them and devour the whole lot. It felt like I hadn't eaten for a week. That turned out to be the case.

"I dropped almost everyone off at the first bus station I found. I said where I was taking you and then told them to sort themselves out." Irene shrugged. "Polly stayed. I guess the rest didn't want to take their chances with one of Miss Adler's friends."

"Or it could have been the dead body in the middle seat," Polly said, far more chipper than she felt.

"Well, I wasn't going to let you go."

"They called me the next day," Gloria said. She fixed herself a small plate of cheese and crackers and set it to the side. Then she dumped two large handfuls onto another plate and handed it to me. I smiled gratefully, then started shoving food into my mouth with no grace whatsoever.

"It took me a day to figure out what was wrong with you. Another six to figure out how to fix it." She smiled with absolutely no mirth whatsoever. "If you would kindly never make me do that again? Because it was awful."

"Sorry," I said around a mouthful of cheese. I wiped my hand across my face. "Desperate measures."

"You didn't tell me you were going to *die*," Irene said.

I shrugged. "It would have taken too long to explain."

"Welcome to the team," Gloria said with a rueful smile. "We get ourselves into impossible situations and take big risks to get ourselves out of them."

Idly, without really meaning to, Gloria placed a hand against her stomach. She hadn't touched her plate. I didn't take note of it then. My mind was elsewhere.

"Where's Luci?" I asked around another mouthful.

Gloria glanced at the sunburst clock on the wall. "Explaining to her mother why she didn't come home for Christmas, most likely."

"You didn't tell her?"

She stared at me, at once incredulous and annoyed. "Didn't tell her what? That I finally found her missing girlfriend and she's lying dead on a stranger's dining room table? No, Amelia Temple, I *didn't* tell her that. *You* get to have that conversation with her."

I flushed, guilty about the trouble I'd put everyone through. Imagining how Luci would respond to my story made me realize just how awful it must have been for my other friends to see me like that. I started to stammer out an apology, but Gloria waved it off.

"Stop. You're here safe. That's what's important," she said. "I would like to know where you've been for two months, but that can wait until you're stronger."

"Thank you. There's a lot to tell. Not a lot of it good."

I leaned against the couch, staring at nothing in particular. I'd dropped out of that feeling of *oneness* almost immediately, but I could feel *myself* again, waiting out there in a direction that lacked a name on this planet. I flexed my other arms, comfortably tucked away at right angles to realspace. I picked up Gloria's candles in the dining room, where Polly and Irene couldn't see, and put them away for her. It was wonderful, being able to move normally again. I was back to normal. My normal.

Back to square one.

Without warning, I burst into tears, burying my face in my hands as I realized what I had lost. Gloria called my name, alarmed, and Irene put her arms around me.

"Amelia, what's wrong?" she cried.

"He's dead," I sobbed. "The Director. Octavian. He's gone."

Irene stared at the other women, utterly lost. Polly shook her head, and Gloria raised her arms in bewilderment.

"Were you close?" Irene asked carefully.

"No. It's not like that." I sniffed noisily. "He had information I needed. That's why I was helping the Institute. He died—they killed him—before he could share it."

I looked at Gloria, helpless. "He knew who my mother is."

Her hand flew to her mouth, eyes wide. "Oh, baby."

Irene moved aside to let Gloria hold me. I sobbed into her neck. Polly put a comforting hand on my back, cooing. Gloria mumbled something soothing into my ear, while Irene first slapped her pockets, then ran out of the room.

After a minute, my tears ceased. I hiccupped and sat up, mostly straight. Polly fetched me a cloth to wipe my face. Gloria took my other hand, rubbing my arm with sisterly affection.

"It's fine," I said with a humorless laugh. "I'd given up on her until now. I told myself it was a mystery I'd never solve until he dangled her in front of me like a carrot."

"Maybe he was lying," Gloria said softly, not sure whether she was helping but unable to not try. "You know what those men are like. They'll say anything to get what they want."

"Maybe." I hiccupped again. "Maybe I lost her all over again."

"Maybe not!" Irene ran into the room, waving a piece of paper triumphantly. "Miss Adler left me *two* letters. This one has your name on it… and an address."

I stared at her, barely believing her until she held it out to me. It was indeed from Ravenna and addressed to me. Gingerly, I took it from her. Gloria shooed Polly away so I could read privately, although she burned with curiosity herself.

Amelia,

I don't know what your plan is, but I hope it succeeds. I won't be sticking around to see, one way or the other. By now, you've probably figured out that my own plans, which had nothing to do with the Institute's, have fallen apart. Whatever is, has already been, and whatever will be, already is, as Solomon wrote.

I'm sorry I can't stick around, but other wheels need me to turn them. I'm sending Miss Phillips and my girls somewhere safe. You'll be welcome to join them. Sophia is a very old friend of mine, if you take my meaning. She can be trusted, at least as far as you can throw her. Certainly more than you ever could trust Octavian.

Speaking of, I know what he was holding over you. You probably think it's lost.

It isn't. He's not the only one who knows things.

When you're ready, go see her. If I can offer some advice, take your time. Some truths are hard, my dear. This one will be one of the hardest.

Be seeing you,
Ravenna

She signed the letter with a flourish, then left an address in a postscript. It was a town in Maine that I didn't recognize. I read the letter twice, then folded and handed it to Gloria.

"Here," I said. "You can read it, if you want. Burn it after."

"What? Why?" Irene exclaimed.

"What if you forget it?" Polly added.

I smiled. "I've never forgotten a thing in my life. I don't want this lying around, though. People will be looking for me. I don't want them knowing where to find me."

Gloria's eyebrows shot up. "Planning a trip?"

I nodded. "Eventually. You're welcome to come with me, if you like. All of you. When we're ready. First, though, I want to see my girlfriend."

27

❖

Nine days ago …

The myrmidon hive and *Amn-Zuhad* fought a fearsome battle in psychic space, while Vernon and eleven other technicians huddled in the cafeteria and Mark Pressler fought for his life in his lab. Meanwhile, the man who had inadvertently gotten me dragged into this mess lay naked and insensate in a hospital bed in the first sub-basement. Ralph Connor was still frozen between moments, forgotten in the chaos.

Forgotten by everyone except one man. A wall panel slid aside on the upper end of his split-level prison cell. Jeffrey West emerged with a head in a jar tucked under his arm and Frank Abbot in tow. Frank struggled with a metal dolly while carrying the heavy tank of biofluid in a sling on his back and a first aid kit on a strap over his shoulder.

"Here we are! Last stop!" West said cheerily.

Frank hesitated, staring down the steps at the corrupted body on the hospital bed. "What is *that*, doctor?"

"Someone else's experiment gone horribly wrong." West practically skipped down the steps. "Also, a tremendous resource for me. It's an ill wind and so on."

He paused on the steps, giving Frank a sharp look. "I have absolutely no use for squeamishness, Abbott. Get ahold of your stomach or get left behind. I still have time to collect my previous assistant, assuming he's still alive."

Frank swallowed hard and shook his head quickly.

"Good man. Get down here with that dolly. This is why we brought it."

"Sir?" Frank said, hurrying down the steps with the dolly.

West gestured at Ralph. "Unless you plan on carrying him in your arms? It's entirely up to you. I encourage initiative, to a degree."

He didn't wait for Frank to respond. West set the head in a jar down carefully, giving its lid a protective pat. Then he double-checked his pockets, presumably for foreign material. Finding the syringe, he nodded with satisfaction and entered the seal.

Frank cringed behind the dolly, as if it would provide any sort of protection. He didn't know much about Prospero's Keys, not even their name, but he'd been in the Institute long enough to see a few seals. He knew what they were capable of. When nothing horrible happened to West, he let out a palpable sigh of relief.

The doctor chuckled at Frank's fears, shaking his head at the young man's ignorance. It wasn't fair—one can't know what they were never taught—but I can't credit Jeffrey West with a sense of fairness. He withdrew the syringe from his breast pocket and uncapped it. He tapped the needle twice and gave the plunger an experimental squeeze. Then he disconnected one of the electrical cables powering the seal.

The energy vortex collapsed. Ralph, face already twisted mid-scream, let out a blood-curdling cry. His back bent up in an impossible arc as the infection of Watcher matter resurged. He bled black-green ichor from a dozen lacerations and burst blisters, and two dozen more fresh incisions. The bed shook as he began to hover, lifting an inch off the mattress.

Frank screamed back at him. West threw an arm across Ralph's chest and pushed him down, whispering soothing nothings into his ear. Then he jabbed the syringe into Ralph's neck and slammed the plunger home. A seizure ripped through Ralph's body. He nearly bucked West off of him. Then, as abruptly as he started shaking, he fell limp. Limbs and Watcher growths flopped nerveless, and his face went slack. He stared blankly at a spot on the wall, eyes dilated and unfocused.

West favored Frank with a sardonic glance. "Such tremendous help you are."

"What is this? What did you do?" Frank asked, seconds from panic.

"I administered a little cocktail of my own formulation. To be honest, I wasn't certain it was going to work." West felt Ralph's neck for a pulse. It was weak but steady. He nodded in satisfaction. "Yet it has. How splendid. Come along. Bring the gauze."

Frank fumbled for the kit at his hip. "Gauze?"

"We don't want him bleeding out, do we? Nor getting an infection. I shudder to think what staph would do to all of this."

Frank stumbled down the steel stairs, pulling a bottle of rubbing alcohol and thick rolls of gauze from the kit. They doused most of Ralph's body with the alcohol, wrapping his arms and torso as fully as possible. Ichor was already soaking through the wrappings, and Frank expressed doubt that it would do much good. West waved him off. They could clean him up better once they got to their next stop.

West's car was parked some miles away, inside of a barn where one set of escape tunnels let out. They were known only to the Director and the savants. West had one of the only sets of keys.

Yes, it certainly *would* have been helpful if Ravenna had told anyone else about them.

Eight days ago …

The Nova Anima Institute owned a fleet of five vans. Two were marked with the Institute's name and logo. Two claimed to belong to a florist's shop that appeared in no yellow pages in the country. The last was solid black and was used only for the most sensitive operations. Thanks to a seal painted on its ceiling, it emitted an unsettling aura, a sense of ill-defined creeping dread that struck unprotected viewers in their brains' most basic structures. That's why the survivors had left it. They couldn't even bear to look at it.

Mark Pressler was beyond caring.

Maybe his advanced training as a noetic specialist gave him some degree of psychic defense. Maybe his experience in the Watcher Below's lair had left him too numb and traumatized to register the seal's effect. Maybe the Watcher's infection subtly altered the structures of his brain.

He'd come to in a broken hallway in the third sub-basement. Myrmidons—if they could even be called that anymore—filed past him, dropping bodies into the pit. Mark tried not to think about that. About the many-armed thing lurking in the bowels of the Institute, the half-face and the dozen blue eyes that stared into his core. He tried to ignore the wet noises drifting up through the gaping hole in the floor, like a wide mouth eagerly slurping chunky fluid, like wet rubber stretching, like a chorus of whispers gurgling out of a hundred tumor-choked throats. He tried to pretend that last wasn't itching at the back of his mind.

He lurched to his feet, ignored by the monster's corrupted minions, and stumbled through the basement to the stairs. The creatures passed him in twos and threes, carrying or dragging corpses that he tried not to recognize. In some cases that was easy, although he drew no comfort from that—the myrmidons' brutality had left many of their victims with no identifiable features. The ruin of blood and brain could have been anyone. One of them could even have been Doctor West.

Mark didn't know which he would have preferred.

The hallways on the way to West's lab were clear of bodies. The creatures had already cleared all the easily accessible corpses. They hadn't removed the splashes of gore across the walls and floor. It would be a waste of perfectly good biomass if they didn't—nutrients and proteins and simple water. He imagined warped creatures crawling along the floor, swollen tongues lolling from distended mouths as they lapped up the gore, swallowing every drop to bring back to the monster in the basement. Perhaps they would vomit the offering up, watering the monster's roots. Perhaps they would simply surrender themselves to it.

Mark had crawled to the edge of the pit before he left. He watched a root wrap around Rob's corpse. Watched as a hundred small tendrils poked into the flesh that had once been his friend, sucking the meat into the monster.

"No," he said to no one at all. His words echoed through the empty halls. "No."

Mark wasn't surprised to see the lab door torn from its hinges, or to find the generation tanks smashed and empty. Ripped tubes dangled from the ceiling, dripping the remnants of their fluid reservoirs into the shattered tanks. The new batch of myrmidons had probably already been taken to feed the monster. What other use would it have for unfinished stock?

Bradley's body was gone, too. That was a small mercy.

The cultivation tanks along the far wall had been smashed open. The monster had reclaimed its flesh. He supposed that was to be expected. Only a single intact tank remained. Waiting for Mark. He had a task ahead of him.

The door to West's private lab had been torn off its hinges. Mark hesitated at the threshold before entering. He'd never been allowed in this space, and that old prohibition still held firm. West had condescended to him, overlooked him, and left him to die without a second thought. Yet, he was still Mark's mentor. Wasn't he?

A murky whisper in his mind said otherwise.

Mark had built the private lab up in his mind: a gleaming space outfitted with cutting-edge equipment, shining chrome walls hung with diagrams and formulae. He realized as he examined the actual space that it was the only one he hadn't cleaned himself. It was disgusting, even ignoring the effects of the creatures' rampage. There had been no bodies here for them to recover, just a handful of cultivation tanks, shattered and their contents recovered. This filth was all West's. Surfaces were covered in dust and mold, unsanitary equipment scattered over tables or left in corners. Mark allowed himself a moment to let his image of Jeffrey West the genius finally die. Then he set to work.

West kept his files in a black cabinet in a corner of the room, next to a table overgrown with exotic plants. The cabinet was untouched; it seemed neither monster had a need for West's notes. There were hundreds of documents in cardboard folders, sorted by West's idiosyncratic filing system. Mark idly considered taking the whole cabinet and sorting through it later, but he didn't think he could get the heavy thing down the stairs. Instead, he shoved debris off a rolling cart and piled it with whatever files seemed relevant. He focused on anything with a formula or a blueprint—in particular, that of the generation tanks, which he was happy to find in the third drawer. It took hours to sort through everything, but he had time.

When he rolled the cart out into the main lab, his heart almost stopped. A creature stood in the doorway to the hall. It carried a ten-liter tank of biofluid in its arms, metal and glass stained with various other fluids. Mark stumbled backwards, searching desperately for anything he could use as a weapon, but the creature didn't attack. It simply set the tank of goo on the cart. Then it returned to its macabre tasks.

Mark laughed, more out of reflex than any genuine emotion. He had his own macabre task to carry out.

He retrieved the last cultivation tank and wheeled everything out of the lab. It took some doing, getting it all down the stairs, but he managed it. The black van waited for him in the garage, the rear doors already open. He loaded it with the cart's contents, then climbed inside. He was unsurprised to see the key already in the ignition, a drop of black-green ichor clinging to the head.

Mark tried to ignore his reflection in the rearview mirror as he drove away. A twisting tracery of blue-green infection ran across his forehead, through his left eye, and down his cheek. It was unimportant. He told himself that over and over again. He couldn't care about that, about the way the back of his head bulged and pulsed with new growth. He had to focus on his task. Amid the clamor of voices in his mind, a single alien word repeated over and over.

Utsoggthua.

Five days ago...

The manor had been quiet for days. The myrmidons had finished collecting the bodies scattered throughout the building. The last drone had retreated into the shattered depths, sealing the hidden entrance behind it. The above-ground floors sat silent, but not empty.

Norman Rogers, or his body, still lay quietly in the infirmary. Two of the Watcher's servitors had gone through this space days ago. They dragged Tucker and Nancy's corpses away, but they hadn't bothered Norman. He hadn't wanted them to see him, so they didn't. He was nothing, a gap in their perception, a tiny hole in the middle of all things.

The IV drip that fed him was long empty. With no one to change his linens or bedpan, he lay in his own dried filth, though with nothing to feed it, his body had at last stopped producing more. It was consuming itself now. In a small way, this pleased him. A small smile played across his cracked lips. Everything was consumed, eventually.

The holy stillness was broken by distant shouting. The noise of shoe leather slapping against tile echoed through the empty corridors. Men in charcoal suits strode purposefully through the ruined manor, guns drawn, shouting orders at one another.

When Agent Poole shouldered his way through the infirmary doors, it pleased Norman to allow the other man to see him. He gasped pitifully and held out a skeletal hand in supplication. Poole swore and ran to his side.

He shouted over his shoulder, "Jesus, we got a live one!"

Norman grabbed the agent's lapel and pulled him close, stronger than his trembling arm should have allowed. Poole blanched to be so close to the other man's sunken face. He tried and failed to hide his disgust out of a rudimentary sense of empathy. Norman took no notice. He simply stared into Poole's eyes, his own pupils so wide that he had only the barest sliver of irises. Poole had limited psychic talent, but it was no matter. Norman had enough for them both. A brief connection, that's all it took.

Two more agents came in, answering Poole's call for help—Agent Fitzgerald, of the field investigation branch, and Agent Stark of the Specials.

Fitzgerald ran to the bedside, while Stark hung back warily. Poole shook his head as Fitzgerald joined him.

"Never mind. Guy just kicked it."

Norman's body fell against the hospital bed, arm going limp. His empty eyes stared at nothing as the thing animating him finally, mercilessly let go. Fitzgerald grimaced with disgust.

"Shame. Looks like the poor guy had been barely hanging on," he said.

"How very tragic," Stark said, unmistakably bored. "Leave the corpse and continue clearing. There has to be something worth finding in here."

The other agents obeyed, falling into step behind the Special as he went deeper into the compound. All the while, a little piece of the void gnawed at the center of Poole's mind.

Three days ago …

Vernon sat in a diner staring at his hamburger. He'd taken two bites. The burger had smelled delicious coming off the grill, but it hadn't tasted like anything. He'd chewed mechanically and swallowed, feeling the texture on his tongue but savoring nothing as he chewed it to mush.

He'd tried squeezing ketchup onto his fries, but the sight of the thick red sauce made him want to throw up. He'd wrapped the tainted potato sticks in a napkin and shoved it to the side of the booth, trying to pretend they weren't there. Trying to pretend he was okay.

He'd said goodbye to the other survivors days ago. Most of them had taken their share of the handful of bills Dr. Adler had left them and bought a ticket for the first bus out of town. A handful, the ones who had lives in Regina before the Institute, tried to return to them. Vernon hadn't heard from them since. He hadn't expected to.

He wasn't one of them. His old life was in Kentucky, but he didn't think he could return to it. He didn't think he could go back to anything. He'd seen too much, far too much. He'd kept one of the vans and the rest of the money. He parked the van in a different spot each night to sleep. Most of the money was gone now. It had been used for food and a couple of changes of clothes. He probably shouldn't have splurged on a diner meal, especially considering how unsatisfying it was.

He stared at the bottle of Coke quietly sweating on the table and wished it was something stronger.

A stranger slipped into the booth, sitting across from him. Vernon sucked in a sharp breath and almost shouted at him when he realized the stranger wasn't a *him*. She was a curvy redhead, her pale face dotted with freckles. Her cheeks dimpled prettily when she smiled, and she was smiling brightly at him. His mouth hung open, words drying up in his throat.

"Hi there." Her voice was low and husky. "Mind if I join you?"

Vernon stammered something incoherent. She smiled wider, taking that as a yes, and plucked a fry from his plate. She winked at him as she took a delicate bite.

"Sorry if I'm being *forward*." She leaned close. "I don't like seeing a nice guy on his own, all lost and lonely."

"I'm not lost." Vernon kicked himself for not thinking of a smoother reply. "Or, or, or lonely!"

"Oh, I *love* your accent!" The pretty girl brushed her fingers across his hand. "It's so earthy. Like a *real man*."

Vernon went fire-engine red. "I was born on a farm," he said, conveniently leaving out that he'd run to Regina to escape it.

"I knew it!" She took his hand. "You've got the arms of a *working man*."

He grinned sheepishly. "I'm Vernon Calloway."

"Pleased to meet you," Dorothy Weathersby said. "Call me Dottie."

Today …

Classes at Del Sombra had been over for two weeks now. The campus was quiet. Most of the students had gone home for the holidays, where the food was home-cooked and the laundry machines free to use. Lucille Sweeney's mother had expected her to be one of them, but she'd refused. Luci wasn't leaving her dorm room. I didn't know where her mother lived. When I came back, she knew I would come find her *here*. She wasn't going to risk being gone.

Luci sat cross-legged on her bed, in theory going over her research into the conspiracy. Her three-ring binder, stuffed with notes on everything we'd encountered, sat open in her lap. She wasn't looking at it. Instead, she was staring at her watch. It was two minutes to eleven. She had promised herself she wouldn't call before eleven a.m. today. That was reasonable behavior. She wasn't obsessed. Just concerned.

The moment the hour hand pointed to eleven, she leapt from the bed and bolted through her door. She slowed when she approached the phone in the middle of the hall. Luci tucked a stray strand of hair behind her ear, trying to appear to a nonexistent hypothetical observer as calm and collected. She was making a simple phone call. No need to panic.

She dialed the number to the Lane Diner and stared at the ceiling while it rang, bouncing on the balls of her feet. Her face fell momentarily when Andre Lane answered.

"Hey, Andre! It's Luci again. I was… uh huh. Uh huh. Okay. Could you call me when she gets back? Yes, I *know* I asked that yesterday. Okay. Thanks so much."

She hung up the phone and took a deep breath. If Gloria was missing too, she was going to scream.

She walked to her dorm room with her head down. She was so wrapped up in her thoughts that she didn't hear the sudden rush of air behind the door. She went inside and stared at her corkboard, the one charting her current obsession. She'd have to take it down soon. The university was almost certainly going to assign her a roommate when the spring semester started.

Behind her, I coughed politely.

She spun around and saw me sitting quietly on the pushed-together beds. I tilted my head and smiled, batting my eyes in what I hoped was a flirtatious manner. The look on her face was like watching the sun come up.

"And where the foul word have you been?" she said.

Before I could answer, she threw herself into my arms. She bowled me over, pushing me against the mattress. Our lips pressed together as she ran her fingers through my dark hair. I squeezed her tightly, entwining my legs with hers.

It was the first moment we'd spent together in two months, but I knew we'd have many more. I was free of the Bureau, and I wouldn't let anything keep us apart again.

ANOTHER TIME

The hour was late, and the second floor was almost entirely empty. Most agents had clocked out for the evening, heading home to their families in the suburbs. Only a handful of cubicles were still occupied—personnel still working hard cases, catching up on paperwork, or otherwise burning their candles at both ends. It was a common enough experience for Special Agent Erin Patricia Vance that it simply felt normal. Earning a dual major in metaphysical biology and multidimensional geometry had taken years of late nights spent studying and revising. Such an academic path was superfluous for most people seeking to enter government service, but Vance had set a specific career goal as a young girl and hadn't wavered from it. Other, less charitable voices might have called it an obsession. In fact, they often had, even here, but they'd learned to do it from a distance.

She didn't care, really. She had better things to do than tolerate schoolyard insults as an adult. She'd endured enough of them when she'd been of age for the schoolyard. But she was only human and couldn't entirely suppress the satisfaction when a "colleague" dropped his eyes from her glare or stuck to muttering under his breath the disparaging remark he'd intended to say aloud. It made her few friends at work, but as more than one intentionally abrasive person has said, Erin didn't come here to make friends. She came to fulfill her obsession. Which meant she felt a surge of satisfaction when her superior appeared at the entrance of her cubicle. After fifteen years, her obsession was finally going to pay off.

Still, she had appearances to keep up. Vance slowly turned her head away from her monitor, fixing her supervisor with a blank expression bordering on annoyance. Her pale gray eyes, nearly completely colorless, made her gaze even more unsettling. Special Agent Rich Barlow, a man who had seen his share of unsettling phenomenon, had to resist the urge to take a step back.

"Good news, Vance," he said, struggling to regain his composure. "The deputy AD has approved your request."

"I've put in a number of requests, Agent Barlow." Vance's voice was cool, but her heart drummed in her chest. "I'm going to need you to be more specific."

Barlow propped his elbow on the top of her cubicle and leaned in. He risked a grin. "Come on, Vance. Don't play coy. You think I'm here about your request for a more ergonomic office chair?"

"I have to sit in this chair for a minimum of six hours nearly every day. The least you could do is provide a chair that keeps my spine from collapsing."

"Buy a pillow. I'm talking about your request to access The Subject."

By this point, the archives recorded hundreds of subjects, but within the office only one merited the definitive article. Despite herself, Vance's palms began to sweat. She permitted herself a slight smile.

"Finally."

"Yeah. Come on, grab your coat."

Vance blinked twice when Barlow turned around and started to walk away. "What, *now*?"

"Yes, now," Barlow said over his shoulder. "Look, Eerie, you know you have a reputation. Do you know what it takes to get a reputation *here*? You're lucky you get results. That's why the deputy AD was willing to give you a window to access the subject. But it closes…" Barlow glanced at his watch. "Well, I'd walk fast."

Vance jumped to her feet and pulled her coat off the hook hanging behind her. Adrenaline flooded her system. She was so keyed up, she let the irritating office nickname slide. Although, who were any of these people to call *her* "Eerie"? She grabbed a notebook and a pair of pens from her drawer. Her hand hovered over her microcassette recorder.

"Are there any restrictions on what I can bring with me?"

"Just one. You'll have to lock up your service pistol."

Vance rolled her eyes. "Seriously?"

"With your reputation and your family history? Yes, Vance, seriously."

She scowled. Then she grabbed the recorder, a pack of blank microcassettes, and a small box of batteries. Shrugging on her coat, she shoved the supplies into her pockets.

"Let's go."

A wide corridor of steel and specially treated glass let from the main building's west entrance to the evidence chambers. From the outside looking in, the glass was opaque. From the inside, one could see drifts of autumn leaves piling up against the windows. Vance paid no attention to the outside; her eyes were focused on the end of the corridor. Electricity hummed through thin wires set into the glass. That, and the nearly subaudible hum they carried, set her teeth on edge, but she was resolved to ignore it. It was a weakness, and she learned long ago not to show any weaknesses to her colleagues. Not fellow students, not fellow agents. Not now, not when she was so close to getting answers.

A white-helmeted guard stood at the end of the corridor, in front of a bullet-proof glass barricade. A keypad suspended from a long metal bar hung beside him. The agents flashed their badges, and he pressed the button that opened the sliding glass doors on their side. A second set of doors waited three meters beyond. A slick black plastic barcode reader sat in the hallway between the two sets of doors. The guard didn't remove his hand from his rifle grip as the agents swiped their badges across the scanner. A green light flashed twice, once for each of them. The guard nodded to the closed-circuit camera hanging above his head. Another guard, sitting in a monitoring station deep within the campus, flicked a switch, and the second set of doors slid open. The evidence chambers lay beyond.

Past the guard post, the wide glass corridor split into a half-dozen narrow passages, each one leading to the topside structure of a buried chamber. The agents took the third corridor from the right. A pair of heavy steel doors stood at the far end, marked with a large numeral "2". They stepped in front of the doors and held up their badges to the ceiling-mounted camera. After a moment, the doors unlocked with a loud metal click.

Another guard post waited beyond the doors. This one was a small room walled off from the passageway, with a small steel door and a bullet-proof glass window providing access. A large elevator sat at the far end. The technician behind the glass squinted at the agents.

"What's your purpose here?"

Barlow held up his badge again. "Special Agents Rick Barlow and Erin Vance. Here to see Chamber 2-4-8."

The technician in charge pursed his limbs and pushed a clipboard holding a paper access log through a drawer beneath the window.

"Print name and sign. Observation access only without the deputy AD's approval."

"We have approval," Barlow said. He withdrew the memo and dropped it into the drawer.

The technician frowned. He pulled the drawer shut and picked up the memo between two fingers. Holding it at arm's length, he scanned it, eyes darting back and forth. When he was done, he let out a disbelieving snort and dropped the paper into the drawer.

"This is highly irregular." He scowled. "Not to mention inadvisable. But the paperwork seems to be in order."

He yanked the drawer back out, making Barlow jump to the side to avoid a severely bruised abdomen.

"Service pistol in the drawer. Fill out the log and the weapon receipt. You have forty-six minutes. Make 'em count."

Barlow filled in his information, then passed the clipboard to Vance. She withdrew her pistol and unloaded it, dropping weapon and clip into the drawer along with the paperwork. Once they'd returned it to the technician, he flicked the switch that unlocked the elevator. It was a long, shuddering ride down to the fourth sub-basement. They passed it in silence, comfortably for Vance and awkwardly for Barlow. He'd learned early on that Vance had little interest in small talk.

The elevator finally shuddered to a halt. Another armed guard waited beyond the doors. Barlow stepped forward and held out his badge and the memo for approval.

"Here to see The Subject in Chamber 2-4-8."

The guard took the memo with his free hand and scanned it. His scrutiny was much more thorough than that of the technician in charge. He was less likely to escape if something went wrong down here.

He passed it to Barlow but turned to address Vance. "Fourth chamber on the right. No touching the glass. Door's locked and access to the inner chamber is only allowed with two authorized observers. Do I need to describe the anti-contamination procedures?"

The two agents shook their heads. They were well familiar with the evidence chambers' anti-contamination procedures. There had been an annual brief for decades.

"Good. You're on a time limit. You leave at 1930 *on the dot* or I drag you out."

"Fair enough." Barlow took a step forward, right into the guard's outstretched palm.

"Access is authorized for Special Agent Vance only." The guard's voice brooked no disagreement. "You wait upstairs."

Agent Barlow stared at the guard, then at Vance. He clutched the memo, creasing it as he reread it. His name wasn't mentioned at all, only his subordinate's. She shrugged and pushed past him, ignoring his sputtered objections.

The sub-basement was a single brightly lit hallway, four meters wide, adjoined by ten concrete chambers. They were large rectangular concrete shells fitted with heavy steel doors and bullet-proof plate glass windows. Half of the chambers were divided into a large inner space and a smaller observation room. Chamber 2-4-8 was one of those.

Vance entered the small room. Four steel folding chairs stood against the far wall. She grabbed one and sat facing the large interior plate window. Like the other occupied chambers, the room was lit with bright light. It reflected off the white interior walls, so that the chamber's sole occupant cast no shadow. The Subject sat in a folding chair of her own, staring out the window—what appeared to be a tall, dark-hired woman in a sensible yet unremarkable black dress. She looked to be in her early thirties, although Vance knew she was nearly fifty. That was assuming her real age wasn't closer to several hundred orders of magnitude more. No one was certain, Vance perhaps least of all.

She leaned forward, certain The Subject could hear her through the glass. "Hello, Subject 19," she said. "Welcome back to the Bureau of Extranormal Investigations."

Acknowledgements

After so many years of struggling to finish writing a book, it's incredible to be sitting here putting the finishing touches on my *third* novel, and only a year after finishing up the last! The past year has been an amazing one for my creativity. I feel like I'm rushing to make up for lost time. Sometimes I look back and wonder how much more I could have written if I'd figured myself out sooner. Most times, instead, I try to be grateful for what I've written already.

My greatest supporter has always been Frankie Valentine, my beloved wife and the world's best cover artist. This story and all the others I've written exist because she has loved me, encouraged me, and pushed me to keep going. I'm tremendously grateful for her.

My found family, Kelsey, Ryan, and Johanna continue to be my very dear friends and most enthusiastic fans. I hope they enjoy this book as much as I enjoy their friendship. Love to you all!

I wrote the second draft of *Along Torturous Paths* while recovering from gender affirming surgery. I was afraid I would be too loopy to write, but fortunately for us all my surgical team declined to give me The Good Stuff. They did take great care of me, and I'm tremendously grateful to them and the nursing staff at Walter Reed for their support.

I'm eternally grateful to my incredible publisher, Narielle Living of Blue Fortune, who continues to take chances on my weird little books. I'm pretty certain she was just looking for a cozy little LGBTQIA+ imprint for her small press. Instead she has me. You won't believe what we have in store for you!

No writer is an island unto herself. In the past year, I've been welcomed into the small community of queer indie writers. Where others treat publishing as a zero-sum game in which they knife-fight for sales and readership, these amazing weirdos are dedicated to building one another up. There are few things better than seeing that cool indie writer whose books you think are cool yelling about how cool your book is. Jessica, Kait, LA, Mel, Shimaira, Mae, Matt, Megan, Kara, also Kara, Sara, and so many others—you are awesome and you deserve all the good things.

Seriously, now that you're done with this, go grab one of their books.

As always, thank you, you beautiful disaster, for reading along with me.

Until next time!

Vivian Valentine is a rad trans lady who loves monsters. When she was a child, she found the Crestwood House Monster Series at her local library and it's all been downhill from there. Now everything she likes is horrible. When not writing, Vivi enjoys card and board games and plotting out more tabletop RPG campaigns than she will ever have time to run. Vivi lives in Virginia Beach with her amazing wife Frankie and their son, as well as an ever-growing collection of action figures. *Along Torturous Paths* is her third novel in the Amelia Temple series, and she has also written short stories in the horror genre.